COWBOY NOBILITY
The Duke's Cowboy • The Viscount's Rancher
The Earl's Wrangler

DREAMSPUN DESIRES
The Lone Rancher
Poppy's Secret
The Best Worst Honeymoon Ever

EYES OF LOVE
Eyes Only for Me • Eyes Only for You

FOREVER YOURS
Can't Live Without You • Never Let You Go

GOOD FIGHT
The Good Fight • The Fight Within
The Fight for Identity • Takoda and Horse

HEARTS ENTWINED
Heart Unseen • Heart Unheard
Heart Untouched • Heart Unbroken

HEARTWARD
Heartward • Homeward

HOLIDAY STORIES
Copping a Sweetest Day Feel • Cruise for Christmas
A Lion in Tails • Mariah the Christmas Moose
A Present in Swaddling Clothes
Simple Gifts • Snowbound in Nowhere
Stardust • Sweet Anticipation
With Amy Lane: Holiday Cheer Anthology

LAS VEGAS ESCORTS
The Price • The Gift

LOVE MEANS…
Love Means… No Shame • Love Means… Courage
Love Means… No Boundaries • Love Means… Freedom
Love Means … No Fear • Love Means… Healing
Love Means… Family • Love Means… Renewal
Love Means… No Limits • Love Means… Patience
Love Means… Endurance

Readers love the Must Love Dogs series by Andrew Grey

Rescue Me

"This was a beautiful story of overcoming abuse, of two men who each want to be in a loving relationship and have to put the past in the past."

—Paranormal Romance Guild

Rescue Us

"I thoroughly enjoyed every moment…. It's well written, well thought through and has a wealth of detail that bring both the people and the animals alive."

—Love Bytes Reviews

Rudolph the Rescue Jack Russell

"This was just a sweet, fun, short little Christmas read. I really enjoyed… this story that's all about finding love in the most unexpected place."

—TTC Books and More

Secret Guncle

"The only thing I wish? That this had been a longer story…. The romance was sweet, and gave you a feel-good ending that satisfied."

—Sparkling Book Reviews

Frosty the Schnauzer

"This was a fun and sweet read and just the thing to start off the holiday season!"

—The Geekery Book Review

By Andrew Grey

BY ANDREW GREY (CONT)

TASTE OF LOVE
A Taste of Love • A Serving of Love
A Helping of Love • A Slice of Love

WITHOUT BORDERS
A Heart Without Borders • A Spirit Without Borders

WORK OUT
Spot Me • Pump Me Up • Core Training
Crunch Time • Positive Resistance
Personal Training • Cardio Conditioning

Published by DREAMSPINNER PRESS
www.dreamspinnerpress.com

MAY YOUR DAYS BE

Furry and Bright

MUST L♥VE D🐾GS HOLIDAY STORIES

ANDREW GREY

Published by
DREAMSPINNER PRESS

8219 Woodville Hwy #1245
Woodville, FL 32362 USA
www.dreamspinnerpress.com

May Your Days Be Furry and Bright
© 2025 Andrew Grey

Rudolph the Rescue Jack Russell originally published by Dreamspinner Press, December 2022
Secret Guncle originally published by Dreamspinner Press, November 2023
Frosty the Schnauzer originally published by Dreamspinner Press, November 2024
The Gift of the Maltipoo originally published by Dreamspinner Press, November 2025

Cover Art
© 2025 L.C. Chase
http://www.lcchase.com
Cover content is for illustrative purposes only and any person depicted on the cover is a model.

ISBN: 9781641088862
Trade Paperback published November 2025
v. 1.0

Table of Contents

ANDREW GREY

Rudolph
THE RESCUE
JACK RUSSELL

A MUST L♥VE D🐾GS COMPANION STORY

To Dominic, who loves me unconditionally, and to Zack, the Jack Russell mix who inspired the story.

Prologue

I STILL miss Mom Claire. She got me when I was just a puppy, and I remember her looking me in the eyes and smiling. I licked her face and peed on her because I was so excited to meet her. Mom Claire always smelled better than dog biscuits and even ham, though she didn't smell better than chicken, because nothing smells better than chicken. The breeder lady called me bad, but Mom Claire smiled and said it was okay. I licked her face again, and she held me close. That was when I knew she loved me.

Mom Claire took me home and fed me good stuff. She gave me a nice place to sleep right at the foot of her bed on a small pad of my own. I always thought of Mom Claire as special… and she was.

People came and went. Some were nice, and some, like her son Weasel—or Wesley, I'm not sure—were not nice and smelled bad. I knew I had to protect Mom Claire from him, even if she didn't know it.

I always thought Mom Claire and I would be together forever, but then one night, I was asleep and the angels came and took Mom Claire away. They didn't take the people part of her, just the love part. I missed her and stayed with Mom Claire because I didn't want her to be alone.

Then Weasel came and put me in a crate. I barked and snapped at him because I wanted to stay with Mom Claire, but she was gone, and now so was my home and everything. He drove and drove. I liked the car with Mom Claire. She used to stop at McDonald's, and she always gave me a bite of her hamburger. But Weasel didn't do anything like that, so I lay down in the crate, my head on my paws, watching the back of the seat. I didn't know what was going to happen, and I was scared. The car smelled funny, like old cheese and stinky feet. I love cheese, but this smelled yucky and gross.

Finally the car stopped, and Weasel lifted the crate out of the stinky car. I was happy for the fresh air and stood, looking out the crate door, wagging my tail in excitement. Was this my home? No, not home. *Shelter*. I heard that word a lot.

There were lots of other dogs. Some of them watched like me, wanting to play. Others were old and tired. Some were even sick, but Mitchell, the good man at the shelter, tried to make them feel better. Mitchell was nice and gave me treats. He also gave me a shot, which wasn't nice, but then he gave me a treat, so that was okay, and the shot didn't hurt *that* much.

Still, the shelter was loud, with barking dogs and stuff, and I missed Mom Claire a *lot*. I missed sleeping with her and the walks we took, and I missed looking out the front window to watch out for things. Mom Claire didn't have dog eyes, not like me. Mostly I missed the love.

People came and went, and a lot of them took dogs with them. For everyone, I put my paws on the door of the enclosure and wagged my tail, excited to see if they would like me and take me to a forever home. That was all I wanted—a forever home, like what I thought I had with Mom Claire. But I wasn't a quitter. Mom Claire had loved me with her whole heart, and I wanted that again, so I didn't give up, no matter what.

Chapter 1

"YOU KNOW you don't have to do this," Palmer said with his usual gentle expression. He had been Alex's therapist for the last few years, and Alex knew he was right. There was no real need for him to go to the shelter, except that he was determined to conquer one of his fears. The list of things he avoided was long: birds (they carried disease); heights (because he just knew he was going to fall); clowns (the damned things were scary); even rabbits (he just knew those beady eyes were judging him). And dogs. Every other kid he'd known growing up had a dog, and they had to shut them away every time Alex came over, which he didn't do very often because they didn't want to play with the weird kid who didn't like Fido.

So here he was standing outside a shelter near Carlisle, Pennsylvania, where he could hear the barks, yips, and howls of what sounded like a million dogs. His instinct was to get back in his car, close the door, start the engine, and peel the hell out of there, except that would involve another of Alex's issues—wasting his tires by spinning them. Instead he stood still, breathing in through his nose and out his mouth the way Palmer had taught hm.

"Are you Alexander?" a "stop the clocks and hold time still so Alex could take in the epitome of gorgeousness" man asked as he strode across the gravel path from the converted barn that held the shelter. Alex willed himself not to do something stupid as the man's lips parted and his mouth drew upward and deep blue eyes took on a sparkle. "I'm Luther. We talked on the phone a little while ago." Luther wore jeans that hugged his thighs just the right away. His coat was unzipped, so Alex got a peek at his lime green shirt, open at the collar to reveal the barest hint of golden skin before it disappeared behind the fabric.

He refused to draw into himself the way he usually did when he met people he knew were so far out of his league that he might as well not even try. The barks and yips drifted out of the building and into the cold early winter morning. Alex's fear threatened to rise, but Luther simply smiled more brightly. "That's me," he finally answered, proud his voice didn't crack.

"You said on the phone that you have an issue with dogs and that you were hoping to have a chance to face it," Luther said. "That's pretty brave."

"How many dogs are there?"

"We currently have fifteen. There are some larger dogs as well as smaller ones. We are working with a few to correct some behavioral issues. Those are not ones we're going to put with you. Since you said that you were trying to get over a fear of dogs, I thought of five that are really well behaved. Can I ask what it is that you're actually afraid is going to happen?" Luther asked gently.

Alex liked that Luther didn't make a move toward the shelter or try to push him forward. Talking was good. That was what Palmer had told him. "I don't know. Maybe it's going to attack me or… eat my face or something." He could tell Luther was trying not to grin.

"Okay. First thing, we don't have any face-eaters here. All of the dogs I think I can introduce you to are sweet animals. They might try to lick you, and a few of them will bound around because they're so excited to see you. These are dogs who love attention and people."

Alex felt himself tense. "Are you sure?"

"Very much so," Luther said. "Why don't you come inside? All of the dogs are in enclosures. I thought you could just look around and see them. They can't get out, and you can take your time." He led the way to the door and opened it, then held it while Alex decided if this was truly a good idea or the worst thing he'd tried since those watermelon smoothies with vodka last summer. Yuck.

Making up his mind, he took a step inside. Enclosures lined both sides of the concrete aisle floor, some larger than others. The scent of dog was prevalent but not unpleasant. "There's a lot of them."

"Yes, there are, and we got a call an hour ago about a couple more that Mitchell is going to pick up when he finishes at the clinic. I volunteer here a couple days a month just to help out after work and on weekends."

Alex swept his gaze over all the dogs. Some of them looked like the embodiment of him: closed off, way back in their enclosures. One even shook a little. "So these are all alone?"

"Yes. We are trying to find each dog their forever home. Don't feel like you have to hurry. I know this is a big step for you, and the dogs are always a little energetic when someone comes in, but they'll settle down."

Alex nodded, his heart racing as he took a step toward one of the enclosures. "Is something wrong with him?"

"Her," Luther corrected gently, those big eyes going even softer. "Yeah. When we found her, she had three puppies and was giving them everything she had. Elsa here was so thin and malnourished that a lot of her hair had fallen out. The pups are weaned now, and we've been feeding her well, so her hair is growing back." Luther knelt by the cage, and Elsa came over to him. She was reddish brown, wide in her shoulders, but not too big. Luther opened the enclosure, and Elsa went right to him and rested against his leg.

"She looks strong."

"Under normal circumstances, she would be. But now she's a little weak. You can pet her if you want. She's a real sweetheart." The way Luther said the words almost broke Alex's heart. He could hear the hurt for her in his voice, but more than that, Alex saw the pain in those big brown doggie eyes, like she understood a hurt that went so deep, you didn't know how to climb out. "You don't have to."

"What will happen to her?" Alex asked, not ready to try touching… yet.

"Hopefully we can find her a home. Mitchell spayed her, and she's growing stronger. I've been thinking about adopting her myself," Luther said. "But I want to do that with each of the dogs, and Mitchell says I need to be sure." He lifted his gaze to meet Alex's. "I'm a big softie."

"It doesn't look like it at all to me," Alex said before clamping his lips closed.

Before Alex could die of embarrassment, Luther chuckled warmly, his gaze darkening for just a second. "I really am. If I could, I swear I'd take half the dogs home with me."

"You don't have one?" Alex asked. He found his attention drawn to Luther, his worry about the dogs around him abating somewhat.

"No. I've moved a couple times in the last few years, and I haven't been settled enough for a dog. I just got a job in the psychology department at Dickinson College, so hopefully I'm going to be here for a while. I just have to make sure I get the right companion." For a second Alex wondered what kind of company Luther wanted, but then he was probably being foolish. Of course he meant one of the dogs. He wasn't talking about Alex, even though Luther made Alex's temperature rise. He gave Elsa a gentle pat, and she licked his hand. Then Luther guided her back in the enclosure and closed the door.

Alex followed him through the shelter, watching each dog as they passed. A few whined, and one barked, making Alex jump.

"That's Janie. She's just loud," Luther said as he approached the enclosure. The dog stopped barking and stretched, her backside in the air, tail wagging. "She's just getting my attention." He petted her gently, and Janie settled down. "Sometimes it's just a matter of seeing what they want." They moved on, and Luther opened another enclosure and took out a small dog that couldn't have weighed more than five pounds. "This is Dolly. She loves people." Luther held her gently. "Come on over. She's just a sweetheart."

"Okay." Damn it all, Alex felt like a kid. Hell, most kids did this all the damned time, and here he was ready to piss himself over a tiny dog. He reached out and lightly stroked behind her ears, half closing his eyes, ready to pull away at any second.

"She likes you."

Alex continued gently stroking between her ears, and Dolly looked up at him with beautiful eyes. "She's so nice."

"Yes, she is. Most dogs are. I know that some can be really energetic, like Rex over there. He has so much energy he doesn't know what to do about it, so he comes off as aggressive, but he just wants attention." Luther continued holding Dolly for him, and Alex kept petting her. Before he knew it, Luther had transferred Dolly to his arms, and Alex just petted her while she lay there.

Alex blinked when he truly realized he was holding a dog. "How did you do that?" he asked. "You just gave her to me and…." He could feel his tension rising.

"You were comfortable, and she's happy with you." Luther gently stroked his shoulder. "You aren't going to hurt her, and she likes you."

"She does?" All the dogs he'd met growing up had tried to jump on him to push him down. They barked and raced at him like they wanted to chase him away. Dolly was sweet, and she slowly turned her head, then rested it against his chest.

"She'll stay right there for as long as you want to pet her," Luther said quietly before taking Dolly and gently setting her back in the enclosure. "You realize you held a dog? And I think you liked it."

No one ever teased Alex, but Luther seemed to be. For a second, he wondered if Luther was picking on him, but that smile had returned.

"Okay. I guess I did." Alex smiled to himself. He and Palmer had been dealing with his anxiety issues for a while, and they had agreed that Alex should try working on just one of them to start. Alex had chosen dogs because he passed by the veterinary office and the shelter every day on his way to work at a grocery store corporate office, where he was in charge of store payouts.

"How about another?" Luther asked. "This is Rudolph. He's mostly Jack Russell terrier. He was brought in because his owner passed away. Her son brought him here to get rid of him."

Alex found himself almost unable to talk. "You mean he just threw away this little guy?"

"He did. From what Mitchell said—Mitchell runs the shelter and is the vet up the street—Rudolph here hated the son with a passion, barking at him and snarling all the time. So if we know nothing else, Rudolph has good people instincts, because the guy was a real jerk." Luther let Rudolph out, and he pranced right up to Alex and wound through his legs, happy and maybe a little jumpy, tail going a million miles an hour. Rudolph put his front paws on Alex's legs and looked up at him with what had to be a doggie smile.

"What do I do?" Alex asked.

"Just pet him. Rudolph is so wonderful. We've had some interest in him, but everyone seems to pick a different dog. He's really special, though."

Alex took a deep breath, and sweat broke out on the back of his neck. But he had just held a dog, so he could do this. Before he could change his mind, he leaned down and petted Rudolph, whose tail just wagged faster, if that was possible. Rudolph licked his hand, and Alex pulled back. "Is he tasting me?"

"Sort of," Luther said. "He isn't going to bite you. Dogs use their nose and tongue to explore the world the way we use our hands and eyes. So it's okay. He's just getting to know you." Alex tried again, petting Rudolph. He wasn't sure how much more of this he was going to be able to take. The dogs had been good and the experience was positive, but Alex wondered how long it would be before something went wrong— because something always did.

"He's really sweet," Alex said to try to reassure himself. Palmer had said that saying positive things out loud so he could hear them when he was stressed might help him.

"Do you want to sit with him?" Luther asked. Then he led Alex to a chair. He sat, and Rudolph jumped onto his lap and balanced on his legs, tongue out, tail going, watching him with that doggie smile.

Luther said nothing, and Alex petted Rudolph, who sat down. "I think I like him."

"He sure likes you."

Alex kept petting Rudolph. "Do you get a lot of dogs at this time of year?"

"Christmas is a hard time for a lot of people. Mitchell says that the holidays are a time when lots of people get dogs. Some get them as gifts for others, but Mitchell discourages that. A dog is a personal choice. Last year he had someone bring a dog back the day after Christmas for a refund." Luther rolled his eyes, and Rudolph licked Alex's chin. Under normal circumstances, something like that would send his anxiety through the roof, but Alex didn't seem to mind with Rudolph.

"I really like him. You're a good boy," Alex told Rudolph, who leaned against his chest. "You seem to like me too." Alex took a deep breath, and to his surprise, some of his general anxiety began to abate. The world tended to be a source of worry for him. He and Palmer had talked through this a number of times. He was on medication and had tried yoga, breathing, meditation, and God knows what else. But this little dog soothed him in a way he never would have thought possible.

"Hello," someone called from the door.

"Should we put him back?" Alex asked as a man and a woman came inside. "You need to help them."

Luther smiled at him once more. "Just sit there with Rudolph and relax. I'm going to help these people. You can take all the time you want." He leaned closer, his breath warming Alex's cheek. "Maybe what you both need is a little attention and care, and there is nothing like a little puppy love." He went over to greet the couple and show them through the shelter while Alex sat with Rudolph.

He watched and petted the energetically sweet dog. Alex kept half an eye on the couple as Luther talked to them about various dogs. They took a few out, including Elsa and a dog named Tally, as well as Rex and Tipper, but they couldn't seem to make up their minds.

"I think I want a smaller dog," the woman said. She looked at Dolly and one other before turning her attention to where Alex sat. As soon as she looked at him, Alex's anxiety went wild. He had no idea why, but he didn't like the woman at all. Something got his back up, and he put an arm around Rudolph to shield him from her.

"Is that dog available?" she asked, pointing a manicured finger in their direction.

"That's Rudolph. He's been here in the shelter a few weeks," Luther said. He gave her Rudolph's backstory as the dog pressed closer to Alex, pulling his tail close. The wagging came to a halt. "He's—"

"Not available," Alex found himself saying in a rush. "He's being adopted. But I'm sure you'll find the perfect dog for you." *Preferably someplace else*, he added in his mind. "Isn't that right, Rudolph? You're coming home with me." That tail started going fast, like he understood Alex. Rudolph licked his chin again, prancing on Alex's legs even as Alex wondered if he'd made a huge mistake.

Chapter 2

ALEX CONTINUED petting Rudolph, looking halfway down toward his feet while Luther led the couple away. What had he done? Alex slowly realized that he had committed to a dog. He had to be out of his mind, and yet Rudolph sat on his lap, soaking up attention—and what was even more shocking, Alex *liked* having him there.

"Do you really think you're up to this?" Luther asked once the couple had left with Dolly cradled in the woman's arms. They seemed happy, and Alex hoped they were, but they weren't going to be taking his dog. Alex registered the thought and stifled a gasp.

"I really wish I knew. They looked at Rudolph here, and I just knew they weren't going to be taking him. Not that *I* have the first clue how to take care of him." Still, he petted Rudolph and realized he had done the right thing. Alex had no illusions that a few hours in the shelter had cured him of his issue with dogs—or his anxiety—but this dog seemed to soothe something inside him, and that was way too valuable to walk away from.

"Well, I can give you a list of things you'll need to get for him, and there are some forms you'll need to fill out."

"They didn't do that," Alex said, referring the earlier couple.

"This wasn't their first visit. They have been looking for a dog for a few weeks and stopped in before and registered. They actually saw Rudolph last week but passed him by." That explained why they were so methodical and kind of aloof.

"Well, they can't have my dog." Alex still didn't know how he was going to live with Rudolph, but the little guy seemed so happy, and that was catching. There hadn't been a lot of joy in Alex's life lately, and this dog seemed to have brought some light into it. That was precious.

"Luther," a man interrupted. "I'm sorry."

"Hey, Mitchell. This is Alex, and he's been sitting with Rudolph here. The Dobsons just left with Dolly, and she's happy. Alex here is interested in adopting Rudolph."

Mitchell narrowed his gaze. "Aren't you the man who called because he was trying to get over a fear of dogs?"

Alex nodded. "I have a lot of anxiety issues, and dogs are part of it. But Rudolph makes me feel better and less jittery and stuff. Nothing else seems to, and…." Alex stroked Rudolph as Mitchell smiled.

"You two seem to fit together," Mitchell said before turning to Luther. "I'm about to close up for the night. There's some snow expected in an hour or so."

"Then let me get these forms filled out." Alex didn't want to get up, but he had to get this done and home before the snow hit. Though he didn't have anything for Rudolph—Luther had said there was a list of things and…. The anxiety returned big-time. Alex liked to do things a certain way.

"Luther will help you with the forms, and I'll check over Rudolph one more time. There's a pet mart in town. They close in a couple hours."

"Okay."

"I'm finished here for the night," Luther said. "I can follow you to the store and help you get everything you need to make Rudolph feel right at home." His smile had Alex's belly doing little flips, and Alex nodded slowly.

"Are you sure?"

"Of course," Luther said as Mitchell lifted Rudolph off Alex's lap and carried him through to the back. Luther helped Alex with the forms. Then he went over how to care for Rudolph, how much to feed him, and how often he needed to be walked.

"Where does he sleep?"

Luther's eyes widened. "He spent four years with a retired lady before she died, so I expect he slept with her. You should get him a dog bed of his own anyway so he has a place that's his."

"Is him sleeping with me safe? What if I roll over and hurt him?" Alex was horrified at the thought.

"Rudolph will most likely sleep curled up near your feet. I don't think you have anything to worry about. Are you used to sleeping alone?" Alex narrowed his gaze, and Luther's cheeks colored and he cleared his throat. "Sorry. I wasn't coming on to you or anything."

Alex wasn't sure how he felt about that. Part of him wished Luther *had* been. It would be nice to know that all his anxiety issues hadn't driven away the entire male population of Pennsylvania. "I didn't think that exactly." It had been a while since anyone had bothered to try to chase him, with his bundles of anxiety and almost obsessive ways of doing things.

"This guy is in real good health," Mitchell said as he brought out Rudolph, complete with a little red bow on his collar. He looked so cute, and Alex pulled out his phone and snapped a picture. He still couldn't believe he was adopting a dog, and yet when Mitchell handed Rudolph to him, he snuggled right up against his chest and Alex calmed once more. "I have a leash for you, as well as a small seat belt for him." Mitchell walked Alex out to his Prius, and once Rudolph was settled in the back, Alex said thank you and waited for Luther to get into his car so he could follow him into town.

THE PET supply store was big and bright, and filled with fish, reptiles, and turtles. The animals in tanks didn't bother Alex at all, though he had no intention of actually touching any of them. He had Rudolph on a leash, and they stood inside by one of the windows, waiting for Luther. In traffic they had gotten separated. Rudolph's tail wagged harder when he saw Luther.

"This place has so much stuff," Alex said once Luther joined him. "How am I going to find what I need?" The anxiety rose once more, and he went through all the things he needed again in his head just so he wouldn't forget anything.

"Don't worry, I have the list of what I went over with you." Luther got a cart, and they started through the store. That is, until Alex nearly tripped over Rudolph's leash. At first Alex thought it was because he had been paying more attention to Luther than to where he was going, but as soon as he untangled the leash, Rudolph ran around his legs and got him tangled once more.

"What's wrong?" Alex asked Rudolph, who looked up at him, wagging his tail as though there was nothing amiss and Alex hadn't nearly fallen on his face.

"Dogs will do what comes natural to them. That's always their go-to. You need to remember that when Rudolph misbehaves, most of the time it's your fault. But you have good instincts. You didn't get mad at Rudolph just now, you tried to figure out what was wrong. That will do you well." When Alex turned to Luther, he got one of those gentle smiles, and Alex wondered what it would be like if maybe it was possible that Luther could sort of like him. God, that had to be the most roundabout jittery thought in history.

"I don't know about that. I spent my life afraid of them, and now I have one," Alex said after he transferred the leash to his left hand. Now Rudolph happily walked between them, occasionally looking at Alex and then at Luther.

They went up the various aisles, with Luther helping him pick out food and bowls, as well as a mat. Alex squeaked various dog toys and got a number of them that Rudolph seemed to like. Flea treatments and a bed, along with a few other items, completed the list. "Who knew a small dog needed so much," Alex said as Luther pushed the full cart to the checkout.

By the time Alex had paid for his purchases and they were ready to leave the store, snow was falling heavily. "Thank you for all your help," Alex said as they went out to the car. He got Rudolph in the back first to get him out of the snow. Then Luther helped him get his purchases stowed and closed the trunk lid. Alex stood across from Luther as snow caught in his dark hair. Neither of them moved right away, and Alex knew he was going to say something stupid at any moment just to break the tension he didn't seem to understand.

"I was wondering if you'd like to have dinner sometime?" Luther asked. "Or maybe we could meet in the park when you take Rudolph for a walk?"

Alex knew he was dense at times. "Are you asking me out on a date?" His social skills weren't the best, so he wanted to be sure. Except now maybe he was coming off as kind of dumb. He wished he had kept quiet.

"Yes," Luther answered.

"Oh, okay, then," Alex said before going around to the driver's side of the car.

"Alex…," Luther said as he opened the car door. "Was that a yes?"

Alex paused. "It was. I'm sorry. It's been a while since I've been asked out, and yes, I'd like to have dinner with you."

"Good. Give me your number."

Alex did, and Luther typed the number into his phone. Then Alex's rang. "Now you have mine. I'll call you." He waved and hurried through the falling snow to his car, and Alex got inside his, closed the door, and started the engine to give both him and Rudolph some heat.

"THIS IS your new home," Alex said after he brought Rudolph inside. The drive had been rough. The wind had come up, blowing around the increasing snow, making visibility worse by the second. He let Rudolph off the leash before returning to the car. Then he brought in all his dog purchases, set up Rudolph's feeding station, and put his dog bed on the floor in his bedroom. He fed Rudolph and gave him some toys before setting about making himself some dinner—but he only got halfway through before the power went out, plunging the house into darkness.

Since he cooked with natural gas, he finished making dinner and ate using a flashlight. Once he put his dishes in the sink, he got a blanket and pillow, then got comfortable on the sofa with a battery lantern on the table. Rudolph jumped up and settled on Alex's lap.

"There isn't much to do except wait for the power to come back." He petted Rudolph. A night like this would usually leave him feeling very alone, but Rudolph filled the room with life and energy. Rudolph eventually curled into a ball, and Alex reached for the book he was reading, but he had to give up because there wasn't enough light. Instead, he simply curled under the blanket to wait it out until the power came on.

A ding pulled Alex out of his doze a while later. *How is Rudolph?* It was a message from Luther. *The power is out here.*

Us too. Rudolph is keeping me company as we wait it out. He sent the message as Rudolph thumped his leg with his tail. *I think I need to take him outside.*

Bundle up, it's really cold, Luther messaged. *Are you free tomorrow for dinner?* the next message asked. *We could go to Café Belgie.*

"That would be nice." He had to work, but hopefully the power would be back on and he could work from home. Otherwise he'd have to go into the office because they had generator power. But then he'd have to leave Rudolph, and he didn't want him to be alone all day. Other people sometimes brought their dogs to work, which had always bothered Alex because he was afraid of them, but he had never said anything. Instead, he had avoided the dogs when they were there. Well, now he had his own, and they could work around Rudolph. Sometimes his mind went in too many directions.

Text me your address and I'll pick you up at six. Luther sent a grinning smiley face, and Alex sent his address and added his own excited face. Maybe it was too much, but it had been a while since he'd had an actual date. Setting his phone on the coffee table, Alex pulled the blanket up higher, petting Rudolph and letting his mind wander over thoughts of Luther.

"WHY?" ALEX asked the following morning when he found toilet paper all over the bathroom floor.

Rudolph stood in the middle of the floor, tail wagging, looking as proud as punch. "Did you want to protect me from the evil toilet paper monster, or were you just playing?" He began cleaning up the mess and got his answer. Rudolph chased after each piece that fluttered to the floor. Finally Alex finished disposing of the shredded paper and closed the bathroom door. Rudolph followed him through the house, and Alex wondered if he should take Rudolph into his home office, but decided to give him a few treats and see if he could settle down in his bed, which Alex had moved to the living room.

Instead, Rudolph followed him everywhere, a bundle of energy that never seemed to wane. When it was time to start work, Alex took Rudolph outside to brave the snow and potty. Once he had finished, Alex dried him off and brought Rudolph's bed into his office and tried to get to work. But Rudoph decided that his lap was where he wanted to be, making it impossible for Alex to get anything accomplished.

"You and I need to come to an agreement. If I can't work, then I can't afford dog treats for you." Alex's frustration level rose higher as his routine-driven existence seemed tossed out the window by his new four-legged friend. After setting Rudolph down on the floor for the third time, he carried him out of the office, along with the bed, and set Rudoph on it before closing the door. Then he sighed and got to work reviewing line drawings for various product assortments. That was when the barking began, following by a mournful howl that ran up Alex's spine. Then, as if that weren't enough, Rudolph scratched at the door.

He didn't want Rudolph to hurt himself, so he opened the door. His dog bounded inside and up onto his chair, tail wagging and tongue out like he had just won the doggie lottery. Sighing and at a loss, with his anxiety growing, he snatched up his phone, took a picture of Rudolph, and sent a description of his problem to Luther.

He expected a text, but his phone rang instead.

"I take it he's got a mind of his own," Luther said, his smooth, mellow voice wrapping around Alex, taking his worry down in a few seconds.

"What do I do? I gotta work, and…."

"It's cool. He probably has a little separation anxiety," Luther said, instantly speaking Alex's language. "His previous owner died and he was brought to the shelter, so he's probably worried you'll leave him too."

"Oh."

"Can you work in another room of the house? Maybe in a place where Rudolph can sit next to you?" It went counter to Alex's grain. He worked in his office and lived in the rest of his house, without mixing the two. Still, he had things he had to get done, and this might be a simple solution.

"I'll try." Alex unhooked his laptop from its larger monitor and regular keyboard.

Luther chuckled gently. "I can wait here to make sure it works. I have a few minutes."

Just knowing Luther was on the other end of the line helped. Alex brought his laptop to the sofa and sat down with it on his lap. Rudolph sat next to him, then lay down, pressed close to him.

Alex picked up his phone from where he had placed it on the coffee table. "He seems happy."

"Good. But the important thing is, are you happy?" Luther asked.

Alex looked down at the white and light brown face, smiling. "I am. Thank you for everything." He felt kind of dumb now that the solution was so obvious.

"Good. I have to go. But I'll see you tonight." The simple thought made Alex smile again, and his belly fluttered a little in anticipation before he ended the call and got to work.

"I THINK we're done for the day," Alex told Rudolph hours later, once he completed his last task and closed his computer. Rudolph had been really good all day, but as soon as the laptop closed, he jumped down off the sofa and raced around the room like he couldn't contain his happiness and had to burn off all the pent-up energy. Alex got a ball he'd bought and rolled it toward the kitchen. Rudolph chased after it, then raced around the room again in a game of puppy keep-away. Once he slowed, he set the ball at Alex's feet so he could do it again.

Alex played with Rudolph, fed him, refilled his water, and then took him outside. Then he went to change clothes, unsure what to wear on his date but refusing to get too wound up. He decided on a light gray pair of pants, a blue button-down, and a sweater in navy with a touch of white and red in it. He checked himself in the mirror as the doorbell rang. Alex answered it, and Rudolph greeted Luther like a long-lost friend, bounding around his legs until he petted him.

"Would you like something to drink?" Alex asked, trying to think what he had in the house.

"Just some water would be great. I called ahead to make sure we'd have a table," Luther said, taking the offered seat on the sofa. Rudolph followed Alex into the kitchen and watched as he filled two glasses from the filter pitcher in the refrigerator. When Alex returned, he sat down next to Luther, and Rudolph jumped up next to him, then walked over Alex's lap before scooching between them until Alex moved to give him room.

"He's goofy sometimes," Alex said, gently stroking Rudolph anyway.

"How do you like being a dog parent so far?" Luther asked, his gaze meeting Alex's in a way that gave his words more meaning and seeming important enough that Alex's temperature rose. He knew he was being dumb. This was one date, and yet the idea that Luther—with his beautiful eyes, full lips, high cheekbones, and dark hair that flowed to his shoulders—seemed to like him left Alex's heart racing.

"I think I do. Rudolph slept with me." He couldn't help smiling. "And I was calmer. It's been a while since I wasn't alone at night." Alex purposely left it like that.

"He sure seems to love you," Luther said as he stroked Rudolph. "Dogs are great judges of character. This guy loves people, and yet when he was dropped off by his previous owner's son, Mitchell told me that Rudolph hated the guy, nipping and growling at him nonstop. Mitchell said he didn't like the little turd either." Luther smiled. "I've come to trust the instincts of dogs better than my own."

Alex sipped from his glass. "You seem like a real people person to me."

"I am generally, but it's my instinct when it comes to guys that seems to be total crap." He tensed a little and continued petting Rudolph.

"We have that in common," Alex said. He hadn't wanted to discuss his past dating disasters, but Luther had brought it up. "The last man I dated lasted three weeks, and then he said that I was just too much work and effort to deal with. I wasn't any fun, and everything had to be done my way or else I'd ruin everything." He knew his anxiety got in the way, and maybe Dewey had had a point.

"How long ago was the breakup?"

"Two years. It was the impetus for me seeing my therapist. After that I decided that I really wanted to work on my issues. Palmer has been really good for me." He smiled down at Rudolph. "Heck, because of him I have a dog now." He was still going to be nervous around other dogs, he knew that, but Rudolph was quickly weaving his way into his heart. "I'm honestly trying to work on my other issues, and maybe I can be less… weird." He knew people saw him that way.

Luther brushed his hand over Alex's as they both petted Rudolph. Alex stopped moving, and Luther's hand rested right on top of his, warm and gentle. "You don't need to be anyone other than who you are. It's admirable that you're working on what you think you need to better yourself, but worry less about pleasing others and just be you."

Alex held Luther's gaze and smiled. No one had ever said something like that to him. Alex had never fit in. He was too jittery, worried too much, looked too geeky, skipped when the other boys didn't—you name it. He never seemed to do anything right. He'd worked hard in school but wasn't a gifted student. So he always felt like he was on the outside looking in… and he worried about it all the time. Hell, he obsessed about *everything*—but looking into Luther's deep, incredible eyes, all the other anxieties faded away as he wondered if something with Luther could be possible. Maybe he wouldn't mess this one up.

"My ex was just a world-class jerk. He drove trucks for a living, and I found out that he was very well acquainted with every truck stop from coast to coast and that the cab of his truck where he slept was very rarely empty."

"I see." Alex's anxiety rose again, only this time it was for Luther. Alex took his hand. Rudolph shimmied around to see what was happening and why he wasn't getting attention, but then settled down once more, resting his head on Alex's knee. "How long were you together?"

"That's just it," Luther said, confusion in his voice. "He and I had talked about getting a house and a dog. We were going to start building a life. Ken was starting to expand his business and was looking into starting his own company so he could stay home more and have others drive for him. We were making all these plans, and then…." He sighed, and Alex took a chance, leaning against him slightly, their shoulders touching.

"I'm sorry." He knew how much that had to hurt. "Maybe I'm lucky that none of the guys I dated ever stuck around for too long. I guess my quirks and weirdness scared them off before anything ever got to that point."

Luther straightened up. "Don't put yourself down like that. You're pretty brave. Most folks don't stand up to their fears. They let them rule their life. You decided to conquer yours, and look… you have a dog now."

"But he's Rudolph, the best dog ever," Alex said with a smile. Luther grinned and squeezed Alex's fingers. "Is it time for us to go?"

"We'll miss our reservation otherwise," Luther said, and they got up to a huff from Rudolph, who jumped down and hurried to the door like he was going to get to go too.

Alex made sure he had water and, since he had already fed him, a few pieces of kibble as a treat. He also brought out his dog bed and toys. Lastly, he got his coat on and then gave Rudoph a dog bone before he and Luther left the house, with Alex less nervous than he had been on his last date with his ex, and damned grateful for it too.

Chapter 3

"Is it strange that I miss Rudolph? Not that I'm not having a good time, because I am, but…." Alex could feel himself rambling and tried to rein it in. If he let himself fixate on things, he would blow it, so he concentrated on keeping everything breezy, not rearranging the silverware because the server put the knife in the wrong place, or worrying about how he moved Alex's water glass when he refilled it.

"He's new in your life." Luther sipped from his beer glass. "Besides, you're probably wondering if he's getting into mischief." He winked like he was kidding.

Alex smiled. "I wasn't until you mentioned it." He paused, widening his eyes. "Now I can't stop wondering if Rudolph is tearing through the house or using the coffee table for a chew toy." He gasped and then grinned.

"Damn, you really had me there." Luther chuckled, flashing Alex a bright smile. "Can I ask you something?" The server brought their dinners. Luther took the first bite of his chicken and hummed softly. "This is good. How is yours?"

"Wonderful." Alex had decided to be adventurous and ordered the duck. Usually he stuck to what he knew, but he decided to go for it. He took another bite and swallowed. "You wanted to ask something."

"Yeah. I noticed you don't have a tree," Luther said.

"I usually get a smaller one closer to Christmas."

Luther shrugged in response.

"What?"

"I guess I pictured you as an artificial tree kind of guy."

Alex shook his head. "Nope. Mom and Dad always had a real tree growing up. It always made the house smell like pine. I was going to get one this weekend, but with Rudolph I'm wondering if that's such a good idea. What if he gets confused and tries to pee on it or knocks it over?"

Luther shrugged again. "He's a dog, and he'll make mistakes just as the rest of us do. But that's not a reason to stop living your life or worry about it. If he does pee on it, then you clean it up and tell him no. As for knocking it over, he's a small dog. Rudolph is more likely to pick off ornaments to play with, so put them out of his reach. The likely scenario is that he's just going to ignore it altogether as long as no one wraps food to put under it." Luther laughed.

"I take it there's a story there." Alex took another bite of his amazing duck with raspberry sauce and leaned forward.

"We had a poodle mix growing up. Toni was a really good dog. I took her to obedience class, and she was always good. One Christmas morning when I was fourteen, we came out to the living room, all excited, to find a real mess. Wrapping paper littered the floor, as did packaging and bits of plastic. The packages from under the tree were all over the place. Dad was mad, and Mom was upset. I started cleaning up the paper and found a tag. It was a present from Aunt Vicky that she'd apparently put under the tree when they'd visited Christmas Eve. She later told us it was meant to be a surprise."

"What was it?"

"A Hickory Farms summer sausage gift box," Luther answered.

"Oh my God," Alex said. "So Toni was just being a dog and going for the food."

"Yeah. None of the other packages were damaged, just moved and pushed aside in her quest to get to the cheese and meat. Dad was mad at the dog, but it wasn't her fault. It was Aunt Vicky's for sneaking the food under the tree without telling us. At all times it's good to remember that Rudolph is just being a dog and that we are the ones who can think and adjust our behavior. Still, they were mad. Toni felt bad, you could tell, but she was just being a dog." Luther made a face, and Alex smiled. "And I didn't have to eat any of that summer sausage. Aunt Vicky always thought it was something special, but I never liked it."

It felt like he was sharing a secret, and Alex smiled. "So you're an only child?"

Luther nodded. "I was actually my parents' third child. The older two didn't make it, and that was hard on my mom. Do you have brothers and sisters?"

"I have a younger sister, Melody, who is a bit of a terror. She's six years younger than me and the spoiled baby of the family if there ever was one. I had to look after her a lot when we were younger." He didn't need to go into their dysfunctional family dynamics, at least not on a first date. Melody could do no wrong, so every time he'd had to babysit, she was out of control and Alex would get in trouble for what she'd done.

"Do you get along?"

Alex shrugged. "I'm on my own. I see my family once a month or so for dinner or something. But otherwise I try to keep myself busy. They aren't very conducive to my mental health, as Palmer has helped me see. Every time I visit, I'm anxious for days afterwards."

"Will you be seeing them for Christmas?"

Alex shook his head. "Mom and Dad have decided that they are going on a cruise for the holidays and taking Melody. They hinted that I could go along but never really asked me, and if I wanted to go, then I'd have to pay my own way and share a cabin with my eighteen-year-old sister, who would spend all her time trying to sneak out to get some time to herself. So if I went, I'd end up as the babysitter again, and that isn't a lot of fun." So he was spending Christmas on his own for the first time. At least he had Rudolph to keep him company. His parents had said that they would send him a Christmas box with his gifts.

"So you'll be alone?"

"With Rudolph. Maybe he and I will watch the other Rudolph together. I'll get us each treats, and we can sit on the sofa and eat until we both fall into a food coma."

Luther set down his fork. "Or you and Rudolph can come spend Christmas with me and my family. Mom loves to cook, and we usually have Aunt Vicky and a few other friends and family with us. Mom always invites people she knows will be alone for the holiday."

"I don't want to impose." While his words were polite, Alex wasn't sure he would be up to spending the day smiling with strangers. What if Luther's family didn't like him, or what if his mother didn't want more people for the holiday?

"It's not imposing. My mom will be happy to have you there, and so would I." That smile came again, and Alex was tempted to say yes. "I'll pick you and Rudolph up on Christmas morning."

That made Alex pause. He was inviting him *and* his dog for the holiday. Alex had already been wondering what he was going to do with Rudolph if he did come to Christmas dinner, and here Luther had not only answered the question, but extended an invitation to him too. "Are you sure about this?"

Luther leaned forward. "Of course." He said it as though it truly wasn't a big deal, but for Alex, it definitely was.

"Thank you." At least he wasn't going to be eating a frozen dinner or Chinese takeout on the holiday, and he was going to be spending it with Luther. Though he didn't want to read too much into that. Luther was probably just being nice. As much as Alex would welcome the idea that Luther might like him, he didn't dare let himself hope too much. Alex knew that his issues were more than most other people could take, and he didn't blame them.

"So you'll come?" Luther asked with a touch of excitement, and Alex nodded, trying not to get his hopes up but feeling truly happy for the first time in a while.

"THAT WAS a great dinner," Alex said as he and Luther went out to the car. The cold night air had stilled, and flakes of snow drifted through the air before settling in the wreaths that decorated the downtown lampposts. "Thank you." He had reached for the check, but Luther had gotten to it first and paid for their dinner.

Luther unlocked the car, and Alex settled into the passenger seat and closed the door. Snow had obscured the windshield, but the wipers brushed it away as soon as Luther started the engine to take him home.

At the house, Luther parked, and as they headed up the walk, Rudolph peered out of the window, his tail wagging. Once they got close, he jumped down, and Alex wasn't surprised when he opened the door to Rudolph bouncing with excitement.

"What did you do?" Luther asked.

Alex lifted his gaze to the stuffing strewn over the floor. He gasped and started checking over the sofa cushions and then the chairs. Then he bent down and picked up a bit of orange fabric.

"It looks like the carrot toy we got him." Relieved, he began picking up the bits of fluff. Rudolph jumped on the couch cushion, watching the proceedings with pride.

"Did you protect the house from the evil carrot monster?" Luther asked, giving Rudolph attention.

"I thought at first he had gone after one of the cushions or something."

"Nope," Luther said. "You have yourself a good boy here. He tore into one of his toys." He sat down, and Alex tossed away the remaining bits of dog toy before sitting next to him, Rudolph bounding onto his lap.

"I find myself tensing sometimes when he does that," Alex confessed. "Like I'm scared of him, and then I remember that I'm not." He petted Rudolph, who wagged his tail, mouth open in puppy happiness, before settling between them for a few minutes. But as soon as Alex began to relax, Rudolph jumped down and ran off, tearing around the room in circles. "I should let him out." Alex hurried out back, got the leash, and took Rudolph out in the backyard.

"You should fence this area come spring. Then he could run in back without you worrying about him getting out." Luther was close enough that Alex could feel his heat in the cold air. Alex inhaled and got a nose full of Luther's head-spinning scent.

"There are lots of things I need to do. Usually I try to do them myself, but building fences is probably beyond my skill set." This was his first house, and Alex was trying to put as much sweat equity into it as he could. "Still, that's what the internet is for."

"And friends," Luther added softly, sending a ripple of heat through him.

Rudolph did his business on one of the boxwoods and pranced away like he was proud of himself. Then he hurried over and raced around Alex's legs, tying him up in the leash.

"He has too much energy," Alex said.

"It's a trait of the breed. Just learn to go with it and take him on walks to let him work it off." Luther shivered, and Alex got Rudolph inside and the back door closed. Then he took off Rudolph's leash, and the dog raced onto the sofa and watched him over the back. Alex and Luther sat down again, with Rudolph taking his place between them, settling in for pets.

"We could watch a movie," Alex offered, not sure what he should do. This type of thing was hard for him. Did he offer drinks, a movie, snacks? What did he talk about? Was just being quiet okay? A million things raced through his head, and each time he had to admit he didn't know only increased his worry that he was being an idiot.

"That would be great," Luther answered. "I like comedies or action flicks. I can look to see what's available if you like." And just like that, Luther took away the worry.

"Cool. I have beer if you like, or some juice. There might be a soda or something too." Not that Alex drank beer, but his dad did, and he had left a few the last time his parents visited. At least he hoped so.

Luther smiled. "Whatever you're having is great." There was a smile, and Alex was so grateful Luther hadn't told him to just relax. His parents had tried to help him get over his anxiety more times than he could count, but their efforts more often than not involved them telling him to just relax or to chill—words that always had the opposite effect.

Alex went to get drinks, and by the time he had returned, Luther had *Lethal Weapon 2* up on the screen.

"Is this okay?"

Alex grinned. "I love this one." His parents had hated it when he watched this type of movie. His mom told him once that she thought movies caused his anxiety. Alex had rolled his eyes at the idea.

Luther started the movie, and Alex placed the sodas on the table before settling in to watch. Rudolph climbed onto his lap after a few minutes, and Alex stroked his back, tension slowly easing from him until the action on screen got his heart racing once more. About the time that Danny Glover was found sitting on the toilet bomb, Luther leaned closer until their shoulders touched.

Suddenly the sound from the television receded under the pounding of his heart. He turned to Luther, who leaned closer. Under normal circumstances, Alex would have worried about whether Luther was going to kiss him and if he was ready for it, but Luther just drew nearer, and Alex found himself responding. Without thinking, he deepened the kiss, sliding his eyes closed and just letting himself enjoy the way Luther tasted, the feel of his lips. It was wonderful… and over before Alex could wonder or worry.

"Was that okay?" Luther asked.

"Uh-huh," Alex said as Rudolph licked his chin. "I think he's jealous."

Luther chuckled before lifting Rudolph to the floor, where he went after another of his toys, and Luther leaned in again. This time Alex was ready, and he slipped his arms around Luther's neck and held him through a second kiss. Part of him wondered if this meant that Luther wanted to take things further, but Luther backed away and sat up straight as the movie continued. He did take Alex's hand, and they sat together as the house on the hill came crashing down. Not that Alex's attention was on the TV—instead, it was centered on his hand in Luther's.

By the time the credits rolled, Rudolph was on Alex's lap and Alex was leaning against Luther's shoulder. He was comfortable and kind of blinky. "I think I should go," Luther said softly.

"Oh, okay," Alex whispered, and then Luther's heat was gone as he stood. Alex saw him to the door, with Rudolph prancing to get Luther's attention for a goodbye pet. Then he hurried off to tear apart another of his toys, and Alex stood at the door. "I'll call you tomorrow. Maybe we can go tree shopping?"

"That would be fun," Alex answered, unsure what came next, but Luther kissed him gently and then left the house.

Alex stood in the doorway watching as Luther got to his car. Alex's heart was still racing, his lips curled upward, and the smile lasted well after he'd closed the door and started cleaning up the glasses. He refused to let his mind wander to what the evening meant and what was to come. Instead, he tried to let himself be happy—at least for a while.

Chapter 4

"WHAT ABOUT this one?" Luther asked as he pointed out a tree on the lot of the Weis supermarket.

"Isn't it a little tall?" Alex asked.

"We could move the table in front of the window and put it there. The lights would shine through, and it would be festive." And just like that, Alex could picture the tree in that spot.

"It's perfect," he said quietly. He stroked the tree's soft needles and paid the attendant before he and Luther loaded the tree on top of Alex's car.

He drove home slowly, and once they were there, Luther hefted the tree off the car, and Alex hurried ahead to get the stand ready. Alex put the table in the spare room, and then they brought the tree inside and got it in place. Rudolph hurried over to check out the new addition, sniffing and poking around under it before prancing away and jumping onto the sofa, where he stood with his front paws on the arm to watch the proceedings like the prince he seemed to think he was.

"We need music," Luther said, getting out his phone. Instantly, "Sleigh Ride" began to play, and the room seemed to fill with cheer.

Alex already had the boxes of decorations and lights in the corner. He got out the first string of multicolored lights, which he had made sure still worked, and Luther bravely began winding them onto the tree branches. Alex's first instinct was to point out imperfections, but he held himself back. Once he had the lights strung, Luther stepped back and used the final string to fill in any holes. "That's better than I usually manage," Alex told him. "Thank you."

"Is there any pattern to the ornaments that you like?" Luther asked, interrupting his singalong rendition of "Jingle Bell Rock." Alex hadn't had this much fun in a long time.

"Not really. There aren't a lot of them." He was afraid his tree was going to look bare, but Luther seemed to have a way, and they placed the ornaments with enough space that by the time they were through, his tree didn't look completely pathetic.

Then the song changed to "Mele Kalikimaka," and Luther tugged Alex over and slowly danced him around the room.

"You're a nut."

"But a fun one."

Alex couldn't argue with that and put his head on Luther's shoulder. The two of them swayed through the rest of the song. Then Rudolph wanted to get in on the action, running in circles in his own happy dance.

The song came to an end and Luther kissed Alex, this time harder than before, with passion that rose between them quickly. Alex's head swam in it, and he sighed softly in Luther's tight embrace, holding him in return.

Alex cupped Luther's cheeks in his hands, returning the kiss with one of his own just as the doorbell rang. A knock followed, sending Rudolph into a barking frenzy.

"What is that? Are you expecting someone?"

"No. But I know who it is." The knock came again, more insistent this time. "It's my mother."

It was Luther's turn to tense. The way he held Alex shifted, and then he pulled away. What was it about his mom? "You'd better answer the door before she decides to break it down." His humor seemed gone, and in an instant, the holiday cheer that had filled the room evaporated like fog in the wind. Luther lifted Rudolph, calming him as Alex opened the door and let the whirlwind that was his mother into the house.

"I knew you were home. I could hear the music," she declared as she stepped inside. "Did you get one of those dog alarm doorbells?" Her question died as she saw Rudolph. "When did you get a dog? You were always afraid of them." She set her purse on the nearest chair and took off her coat. She usually draped it over the back of the chair, but now she held it like she didn't quite know what to do.

Rudolph growled, and Luther did his best to soothe him. Clearly he didn't like her.

"Can you hang this up for me? I don't want to get dog hair on it." She handed over the coat without even looking in Alex's direction, knowing he would do as she asked. "Who are you?"

"This is Luther. He's a friend, and he volunteers at the shelter where I got Rudolph. He helped me get the things I'd need for him, and the two of us have been seeing each other." God, why did he always feel like a teenager again when his mother looked at him that way?

"But you hate dogs," she said softly, as though she were dissecting everything Alex did. It was unnerving. "You always have. Remember the time the neighbor had that brown boxer and he snapped at you for no reason? And the time your cousin's chihuahua snapped at you when you went to pet it? Nasty little thing." She turned up her lip, and Alex's mind clicked on those instances and a chill went up his spine.

"Rudolph is a wonderful dog, and Alex has been courageous enough to face his fears." Luther came over and passed Rudolph to him. Alex cuddled Rudolph close, and he stopped growling, though he never stopped watching Alex's mom.

"What did you need?" Alex asked. "You don't usually just drop by." His mother was more the kind of person who called in advance like she was making an appointment to have her hair done.

"Yes. You made me forget. Your father and I were talking, and we can arrange for another cabin. There are a few left on the ship. We thought you should come with us for the holidays. I always thought it a shame that you wouldn't be with us. This way we can all be together as a family. You and Melody would have your own cabins next to each other." She said it as though it was the greatest idea ever and like she was doing him a big favor.

"Maybe I should get ready to go," Luther said softly. "You and your mom have things to talk about." He turned away.

"You don't need to go," Alex said gently.

"I think I should," Luther said, and Alex nodded. He couldn't make Luther stay, but he didn't want him to go. Hell, he wanted to beg him to stay. His anxiety was already going through the roof. His hands shook, and the tension in the room seemed to pull out all the oxygen.

"Don't," he managed to say, touching Luther's arm. He took a deep breath and closed his eyes, using a technique he had since he was a kid, trying to shut himself off from everything. Rudolph licked his chin and up his neck, making Alex smile a little, and some of the chill slipped away. "Mom isn't going to be staying very long."

"We need to talk about this cruise. If you're coming with us, there are a lot of things that I'm going to need so we can get everything filled out properly. I thought I could book the cabin using your computer, and then we can fill out all the passenger information. They're going to need it right away."

Luther gently squeezed Alex's arm gently. "I'll call you tomorrow." Alex nodded, and Luther leaned close. "I promise. You talk over what you need to with your mom." He got his coat, and Alex still held Rudolph as Luther reached for the door. Alex was well aware that Luther couldn't get out of the house fast enough, and he felt like if he didn't stop Luther somehow, he was never going to see him again. His nerves jangled, and he didn't know what to do. Luther opened the door and then paused. He returned to where Alex stood, leaned down, and kissed him gently. He also gave Rudolph a few pats and then left the house, closing the door behind him.

"Good. He's gone." She brushed off the seat of one of the high-backed chairs before perching on the edge of it. "Now you and I can talk about the plans for the holidays. Your father and I thought we'd make the cruise your Christmas present...."

As she went on with her plans, he stood there, barely listening as his mind clicked in a million different directions. For as long as he could remember, he'd always been nervous and anxious. "Mom," he said gently. "It's great that you, Dad, and Melody are going on a cruise for the holidays, but I don't want to." He really wasn't interested. "It's nice that you want me to go along now, but it's not what I want." Besides, she hadn't considered the fact that he had already told them that the vacation schedules in the office were set. "I can't get the time off at this late date anyway."

"Please. Like what you do won't wait until after the holidays." She rolled her eyes.

"Mom," he said more firmly. "If I go, then Jane will have to cancel her plans, and I won't do that to her. Someone from my department needs to be in the office, and I let the people who work for me have the time this year." God, he felt better standing up to her a little. She always steamrolled over what he wanted or thought.

"Still, your father and I think—" she began, the way she always did. Like what the two of them thought should hold sway over everything and everyone.

"No, Mom," he said more forcefully. "I can't do that. I appreciate the offer to join you, but I can't." He sat on the sofa, and Rudolph stood on his lap, his tail still, watching Mom without moving, which was rare for his energetic dog. "Was there something else that you came over to see me about?" She could have just called—that would have been easier. But it was harder for him to tell his mother no in person, and she knew that.

"Can't I come to see you?" she asked.

"You can, but you don't usually." She kept watching Rudolph. "Do you want to hold him?" Alex asked. "Rudolph is really nice, and I'm finding that he's good company. Luther is helping me learn how to take care of him properly."

She shook her head. "I don't care for dogs. Never have. Melody kept asking for a dog all the time, but you were so terrified of them, so we told her no."

Alex leaned forward. "Except it was you who didn't like dogs. You never wanted Melody to have one either, so you used my anxiety as an excuse to tell her no when it was possible that if I got used to a dog, I'd get over my issues and come to love them." He'd certainly come to adore Rudolph easily enough.

"How was I to know?" she snapped, eyeing Rudolph like he was the devil himself. "It was best that you didn't get one. We were always traveling, and it would have been hard on any animal that we got, being left in a kennel or with a pet sitter."

Alex stood and brought Rudolph closer. His mom's eyes widened, and she sat back to try to get away.

"And you're scared of dogs. All those years you told Melody that it was me when it was really you." He sat back down. "So what else have you projected onto me?" After years in therapy, he had learned the lingo pretty well.

"You *were* afraid of dogs," she said. "I didn't do that." She sat up straighter, and Alex knew that expression. She would deny doing anything wrong to her last breath.

"No, but you used it." His entire childhood, he'd heard his mother tell Melody or her friends that they couldn't get a dog or that they couldn't go hiking because Alex was anxious around animals or that Alex didn't like the outdoors because there could be bears. And yeah, he had been worried about stuff like that, but his parents hadn't soothed him or tried to talk him away from the fear. Mom had just told Melody that they couldn't go camping or to Yellowstone because of him. "I like dogs. At least I like Rudolph, and I know now that they aren't going to bite or attack me. I met a number of dogs at the shelter the other day, and I'm going to go back until I get over this fear. I'm tired of being worried all the time and anxious about everything."

"Well, that's good," she said gently and then sighed. "So you aren't coming with us." She never seemed to let anything go.

"No. I can't get off work, and I have Rudolph to look after. Even if I could take the time off, I wouldn't put him with a pet sitter or in a kennel. He and I are just figuring things out." He gently stroked Rudolph's wiry head. "You and Dad have fun with Melody. I already have plans for Christmas Day. Luther invited me to spend the day with his family, so none of you have to worry that I'll be alone." He glanced at the tree near his mom and smiled at what Luther had helped him do. "Is there anything else?"

She stood, and Alex got her coat. "I'll see you before you leave next week," he offered.

"Don't feel like you have to. I'm sure you're going to be very busy," she told him. He knew it was because she wasn't getting her way. The invitation to join the cruise was nice, and Alex appreciated it, even if they had waited until the last minute. But he wasn't going to let her make him feel guilty or anxious about not going. It just wasn't possible, and that was all there was to it. Maybe if they had asked him months ago, when they'd initially decided to go, he could have. But right now Alex had a good excuse to stay home, and that was the right thing for him.

Alex saw his mother to the door and kissed her cheek before closing the door behind her, then set Rudolph down.

His family was going away for the holidays, and he was staying home. A few years ago, the thought would have sent him into worries about loneliness and being left out. But now all he could feel was relief. It was best that he made his own way, and he was looking forward to spending the day with Luther… and even meeting his family. Now *that* was a surprise.

Chapter 5

WORK THE following day was long and boring. Alex kept watching the clock. A good share of the people in the office were either on vacation or getting ready to leave, which meant the place was growing quieter. A few times during the day, music drifted into his office, and Alex found himself humming along to various Christmas carols.

"You okay?" Wendy asked after rapping lightly on his door frame. She was the senior of the people who worked for him and probably had more experience than the rest of his team together. "You seem extra happy and un-jumpy. What's going on?"

"Nothing," he answered out of habit. "Well, I got a dog."

"Is that why you didn't jump down Renee's throat when she messed up everything for the fourth time? Maybe we should have gotten you a dog a year ago." She sat down. "Whatever it is, keep it up. It's nice to see you happy."

"Thanks. It's kind of nice not to be jumpy and wondering when things are going to go to hell all the time."

"Where is this dog of yours right now?" Wendy asked.

"At home. I went to let him out and check on him at lunch. Rudolph was tickled to see me. You know, it's great to have someone at home thrilled to see me when I walk in the door."

Wendy scoffed lightly. "What you need is a man to do that for you."

He swallowed hard and glanced down at the top of his desk.

"I see. There's one of those too. Did they come as a set?"

Alex rolled his eyes.

"They did." She grinned. "Now tell me how a man who practically jumped up on his desk when I brought Henri into the office last month ends up with a dog and a guy in his life at the same time. 'Cause, honey, I may need to go out and get me another dog if they're giving away cute guys as a gift with purchase. Maybe then I could trade in Herb for a newer model." Alex knew she was kidding. She and Herb had been married for thirty years, and he sent her flowers at work every once in a while.

"Luther is nice, and I met him at the shelter. He started off helping me get the things I'd need for Rudolph, but since then we've been on a few dates, and I really like him."

Wendy relaxed in her seat. "So what's the problem?"

"He met my mother yesterday. She wants me to go on the family cruise and offered to get me the passage as a Christmas present. I turned her down, but I think she might have scared Luther off." He hadn't called or texted yet today, and Alex was a little worried, but he was trying not to get wound up about it.

"Wow." Her expression clearly showed she thought he was kidding.

"I'm serious. He couldn't get out of the house fast enough. We had gotten a tree and just finished decorating it when she showed up."

Wendy tilted her head forward and looked at him over her glasses. "If that's all it took to scare him off, then he wasn't worth bothering with in the first place. Besides, he could have been busy. What does he do?"

"Teaches psychology at Dickinson."

"Then it's finals time, and he's probably really busy during the day. Give him a break and don't worry about it." She leaned forward. "Besides, I saw Joe walking down the hallway in this direction, so it's possible you may have something real to worry about." She stood and stepped out of the office as Alex's vice president peered in.

"Do you have a minute?" he asked and then sat right down. "I just got a request for a complete relay of store 340. Apparently they need to rework the assortment in the store. They have the new assortment, and they want to make the changes to the store layout in January." He sat back, and Alex could already see the writing on the wall. "They need this done right away so they can get it approved and start work." Which meant they would expect Alex to work through the holidays in order to be on time. "I told them that they were being too aggressive and optimistic on their timelines for this time of the year."

"And they don't care." Alex knew the drill as well as Joe. "I have the current layout for the store in the system. I can finish a proposed layout before the holidays, but then it's going to need approval, and shepherding that through takes time. You know that."

"I'm scheduling a meeting for between the holidays with all the parties. They can review what they need to, and we'll get their approval at the meeting. Then we can input the details and have the final layouts after the first of the year."

Alex already felt the pressure building. They did this to him every time. Alex was amazing at his job, and yet he was expected to do the impossible time and time again. "You know none of this will happen, right?"

Joe smiled. "Of course I do. But I put out the plan and stipulated that any deviation will push back their timeline. And I stipulated that all approvals had to be done at the meeting, no exceptions. So if you can get your layouts done before Christmas, we'll send everything out, and the departments have to be ready or they don't get what they want." He made it sound simple. "I know you can do this. I'll shepherd it through the approvals. I got your back."

Alex thanked him. He was a little relieved, but in the end he had been handed days of work to complete on his own. It would keep him busy, but he could do much of it at home, so he could work there the week before Christmas without anyone disturbing him. He already had permission to work from home. "Then I'll get it done." He just needed to make sure he had all the information he needed.

"Thank you," Joe said and stood. "Have a good holiday." He smiled and left, with Alex shaking his head. Joe was always careful to say the right things, but sometimes Alex swore he was the Grinch in disguise. He checked the time and made a list of things he would need to redesign the store layout. Then he finished his outstanding tasks and left. He still hadn't heard anything from Luther and was beginning to get a little worried.

ALEX HURRIED into the house and was greeted by a jumping Rudolph. He got the leash and took him out to potty right away. Then he turned on the tree, its multicolored lights livening up the room and adding some festive cheer. Alex settled on the sofa with a drink and turned on the television, trying to occupy his sometimes too-active mind. He thought about messaging Luther to see if he was all right, and he picked up his phone and stared at the screen. What the hell was he afraid of?

He sent off a quick message to see how Luther was and then leaned back on the sofa, Rudolph jumping into his lap. Alex ended up watching one of the myriad romantic holiday movies that seemed to be on, and he got caught up in it pretty quickly. This one was about a prince and a girl from New York somewhere. He swore he'd already seen this movie plot a dozen times, but he got into the story nonetheless.

His phone buzzing on the coffee table pulled Alex out of the story. He picked it up, smiling. *Sorry. Got really busy with exams and closing out the term.*

Do you want to come by? Alex sent and received a smiley face in response.

Be there in half an hour. It was followed by a bunch of Christmas emojis that made Alex smile.

"Luther is coming over," Alex said before jumping up. There were things he needed to do, and he quickly picked up the house and ran the vacuum. He also changed the sheets on the bed in a fit of wishful thinking. They had kissed, but Luther seemed intent on taking things slowly, which Alex liked. Luther seemed to understand that Alex needed a chance to process things.

The last thing he did was put on some Christmas music before answering the door. Rudolph bounded around Luther's legs like he hadn't seen him in days. Luther gave the little jumping bean pets and then stood straight.

"I'm sorry about my mom yesterday. She gets a little intense."

Luther tugged Alex closer. "No need. I thought maybe the two of you needed to talk, and well…." He paused. "I figured you needed to work out the details of your cruise, and you didn't need me to be here." The disappointment in Luther's eyes was unmistakable.

"I'm not going. I can't take off work at this late date, and besides, I was invited to Christmas dinner with my boyfriend." They had never talked about what the two of them were, and maybe Alex was jumping to conclusions and the ten minutes he'd just spent changing the sheets were wishful thinking.

"You're not going with your family?" Luther asked.

Alex shook his head. "My mother always thinks that everyone should just drop what they're doing because she wants them to. My job isn't important—only what she happens to want." He sighed. "And what she really needed was someone to watch Melody so she and Dad could go out and do their thing. I don't want that kind of trip." He drew closer. "I'd rather spend the holiday with you."

"With me, as your boyfriend?" Luther asked, and Alex nodded. "I like that." He kissed Alex hard, and Alex held him in return, energy building between them.

"I do too," Alex whispered as he pulled back. "But… how long before you get tired of me?" He had to ask. "How long before my anxieties become too much for you? My last boyfriend couldn't get away fast enough. He seemed to think that everything would just go away and…."

Luther smoothed his hand down Alex's arm. "And the more he pressured you to change, the more your anxiety intensified." It was like Luther had been there. "You are who you are, and caring for someone means that you love them for the person they are, not what you think they'll become or how you can change them. Besides, you have courage and strength. Rudolph is proof of that." Luther smiled as he leaned closer.

"But will you get tired of me?" Alex asked.

Luther shook his head. "Somehow I very much doubt it. You have this way of keeping me on my toes. You surprise me, and not many people do that." He kissed Alex once more.

"Still." Alex felt his hand shaking and tried to cover it up. Luther took it and gently stroked the back of it. "I worry about things."

"You don't need to. I'm not going to walk away because you get anxious or need change to happen slowly in your life. There are things that none of us can change, and there are things we can control. But the best parts of ourselves come out when we trust someone enough to place the things we get to have a say in in the hands of the people we care about."

Rudolph barked from where he stood on the sofa. Clearly he felt a little left out.

"Maybe we can test this theory of your upstairs?" Alex asked quietly, still uncertain what Luther wanted, but he got his answer with a heated smile and a gentle tug toward the stairs.

"This isn't the time for you to be up here," Alex told Rudolph as he barreled up onto the bed just as Luther worked his shirt off.

Rudolph perched on the edge of the bed, tail wagging, mouth open in that knowing doggie smile he had.

"Off the bed and go downstairs."

Of course Rudolph ignored him. Thankfully Luther lifted him off the bed and left the room.

Alex took the opportunity to remove the rest of his clothes while Luther clomped down the stairs and then returned a few minutes later, closing the bedroom door. "I gave him a bone." Luther stalked closer. "Damn, you're stunning." He kicked off his shoes and stripped off his pants, baring his built and honed body to Alex's gaze. Alex had imagined what might be under Luther's clothes since they met, but reality beat his imagination by a mile. Luther grinned as he climbed onto the bed, his gaze as hot as a summer day. He drew closer, his hands gliding up Alex's chest to his neck and cheeks.

"You're the one who looks great naked. I'm just a skinny guy who needs to gain a few pounds." Alex had no illusions about how he looked. Thankfully, body image wasn't one of the things he was anxious about.

"Nope. I'm not buying it." Luther caressed his sides before kissing Alex hard, probably so he couldn't argue. And who was he to tell Luther he was wrong? Hell, talking became unnecessary over the next hour as Luther took him to heights Alex had only dreamed about. Outside the house, the night air was cold and the wind whistled around the house, but in this room, there was heat, passion, and everything Alex could ever want, building up to a breathless pinnacle that left him satiated and panting.

He and Luther lay side by side, Luther's fingers entwined with Alex's. "Jesus," Alex whispered, not daring to move.

There was a scratch, scratch, scratch, followed by a sharp bark, then more scratching.

"I think your dog is done with his bone," Luther said and then laughed. Alex got a few tissues, and they cleaned up quickly, then opened the door before Rudolph could dig a hole through it.

"You know, we never did have dinner," Alex said.

"We had more important things to do," Luther breathed and patted the bed. Rudolph scurried between them and settled right down.

"You really are a naughty thing," Alex scolded lightly. "Do you mind that he's here? I can put him in his bed."

"It's nice." Luther stroked Rudolph gently and got a doggie kiss on the chin. "I really like the little ball of energy." Luther leaned closer, and he and Alex shared a kiss that threatened to reignite the fire they'd lit earlier.

This time Rudolph took the hint and got out of the room.

Chapter 6

ALEX SAVED his work and closed his laptop. He had gotten the store layout done and sent to Joe for his review. He had been determined to have it done before Christmas, and it was four o'clock Christmas Eve and it was done.

"Are you ready to start the celebrating?" Luther asked, slinking his arms over Alex's shoulders and down his chest.

"I had to finish this," he said. "I'm sorry I've been so busy this past week." He sighed and let some of the tension wash away. He was starting to get better at doing things like that. His main task was done, and Joe was largely going to take things from here.

"You know it's okay." Luther kissed the top of his head. "If you're done, why don't you put your work things away?" The tree was already lit, and at some point Luther had added cut greens with white lights threaded through them to the top of his fireplace. Those were on as well. Alex was happy to be able to leave work behind for a while, and it seemed Rudolph was too.

"Where did you get that?" Alex asked when he saw the red bow attached to Rudolph's collar. He practically jumped up into Alex's lap as soon as he pushed his chair away from the dining room table, where he'd been working the past few days. "Did Uncle Luther get that for you?" he asked and got frantic doggie kisses on the chin. He held Rudolph close, turning to watch happily as Luther dimmed the lights. Christmas music began to play, and Alex sighed, holding Rudolph and finally letting go of all the tension. It had been a long time since he'd been this content and, dare he say it… in love. It had only been a few weeks, and yet Alex was sure of how he felt. It seemed fast, but he was beginning to understand that when good things happened to him, he needed to embrace them rather than worrying them to death.

Luther bounded over as soon as he had the room the way he wanted. "Do you want to open our presents tonight or take them with us to my parents'?"

Alex shrugged, biting his lower lip and then releasing it. He wasn't going to worry about meeting Luther's family. After all, they raised Luther and he was pretty amazing, so chances were that they would be too. He had received an email from Luther's mom to say hello and how excited she was that he and Rudolph were going to come. Alex thought it pretty amazing that she included an invitation for his dog too.

"What do you want to do?" Alex teased, but the excited way Luther's eyes goggled every time he looked at the tree told Alex everything he wanted to know. "Let me guess, you shook every present when you were a kid, trying to figure out what it was." God, he loved Luther's playfulness. It made Alex want to play as well.

"Of course. Didn't you?" Luther asked.

Alex rolled his eyes. "You met my mother, remember? She knew where everything was. There were no 'Christmas shenanigans,' as she put it, in her house."

"Trying to figure out what your presents are is part of the fun." Luther sat on the sofa, his long legs stretching out in front of him.

"Would you mind if we waited until tomorrow? That way I won't be sitting at your folks' watching everyone else open gifts with nothing to do."

"Sure. Have you opened the stuff from your family?"

Alex shook his head. "I'll do it in the morning." There wasn't much—two presents and a card—which was fine. They were out having fun, and honestly, he was happy for them. Heck, he was happy right here.

He lifted Rudolph, and the two of them sat down next to Luther. Rudolph pranced over both their laps before jumping down to sniff the packages. "I put the things for him up in the front closet." Luther got up and returned with a chew bone squeaky toy that sent Rudolph into a fit of doggie rapture. He raced through the house with it in his mouth before settling under the table to try to rip it apart. "You got presents for my dog?"

"Of course I did. It's his first Christmas with his new daddy, and I figured that if he was busy, then maybe we could be too." Luther turned to Alex and kissed him as he pressed him down onto the cushions. "Are you sure you don't want to open your present?"

Alex chuckled and drew Luther closer. "You are the best Christmas present I've ever gotten. How could anything else compare?"

Rudolph raced over and jumped onto the sofa near Alex's head.

"Yeah, okay. You're the best present too." Alex smiled and got a doggie kiss across the lips.

"We can't both be the best present," Luther groused playfully.

"Sure you can. I got you both at the same time, so you're both the best Christmas present I've ever had." Alex paused, his belly clenching a little, but then he let it go. "Because love is the best gift of all."

For a second he wondered if he might have rushed in too soon, but Luther kissed him hard, showing Alex that he truly had both given and received the best present possible.

Epilogue

I WOKE at the foot of the big bed, listening for any sounds in the house. I heard nothing other than Daddy Alex and Luther breathing under the covers. I was a little cold, so I got up and quietly drew closer to Daddy Alex, then settled down right between the two of them where it was toasty warm.

Daddy Alex petted me gently and then went back to sleep. I closed my eyes again. It was what Daddy Alex called Christmas morning. I didn't really know what Christmas was, but there were packages under the tree and some that smelled like bacon and sausage in the closet. The ones under the tree in the house didn't smell like anything, so I left them alone. But I really wanted the ones in the closet. I saw them when Daddy Luther opened the door yesterday, and I'd dreamed about them all night. Daddy Alex had called him Uncle Luther, but I knew he was really Daddy Luther. I could tell that they loved each other, even if they didn't know it yet. Dogs can always tell. I wasn't sure if the treats in the closet or my daddies made me happier. I supposed it didn't matter what made my tail thump on the bed.

I didn't think about Mom Claire as much as I used to, but I missed her and hoped she would be happy that I found a forever home. She always loved me, and I would always love her in the depths of my doggie heart, but now Daddy Alex was there too, and I wasn't going to be alone. I would be loved, and Daddy Alex and Daddy Luther would always be there for me; I just knew it.

I closed my eyes, my doggie mind filling with the things I loved: bacon treats, my new squeaky bone, and my two daddies who petted me in their sleep. The best doggie Christmas ever.

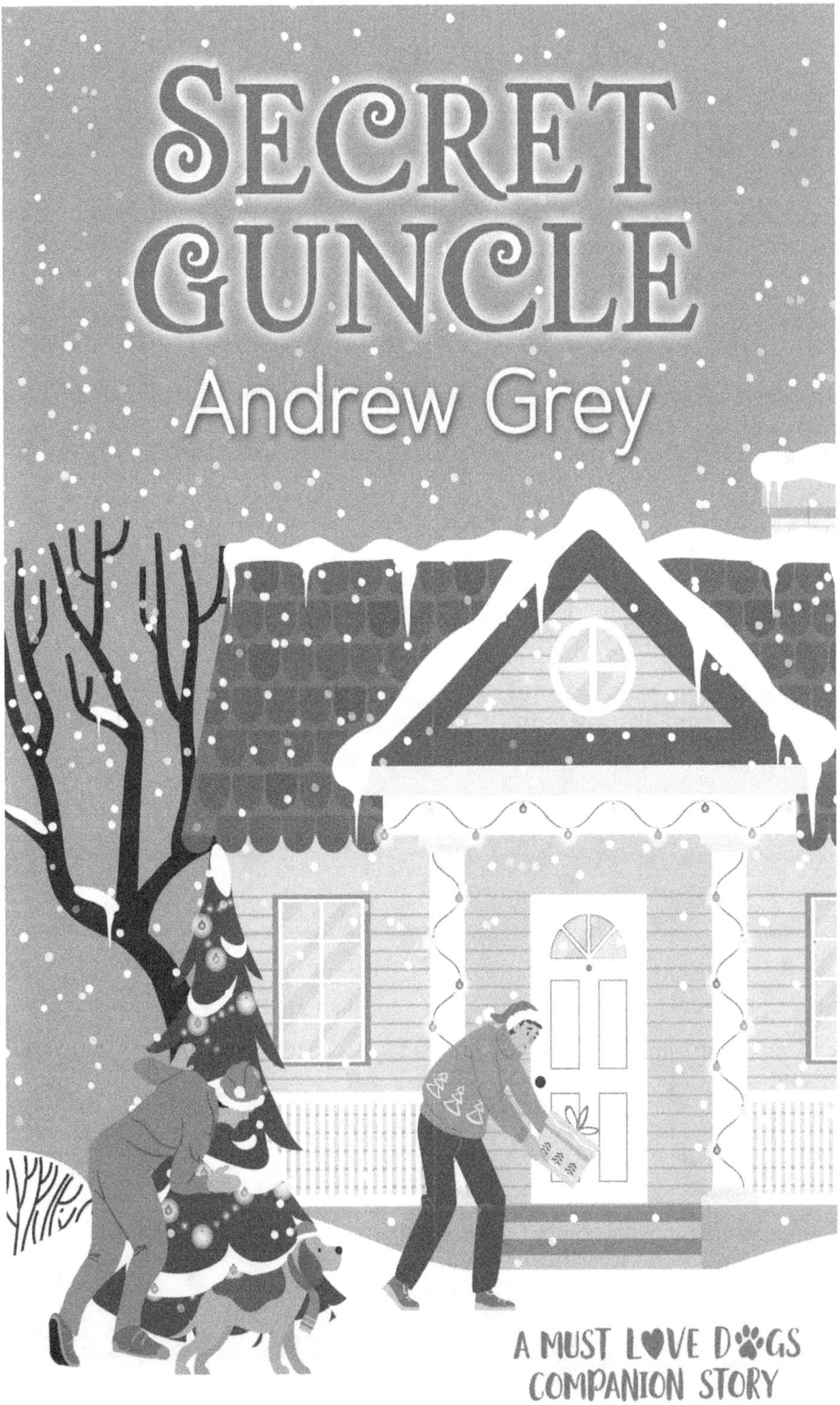

SECRET GUNCLE

Andrew Grey

A MUST L♥VE D🐾GS
COMPANION STORY

To Karen, my sister from another mother. Your help has been invaluable, but your friendship is priceless.

Chapter 1

DUTTON SET down the food bowl and stepped back as Roysten barreled over with too much energy. Fortunately, the boxer skidded to a halt in time before attacking his food. He always got so excited at feeding time. He was never aggressive otherwise, but nothing came between him and his food as soon as he saw the dish.

"I don't know what to get them this year." Dutton sighed because he knew he looked stupid talking to the dog, but there were no other humans in the shelter right now. Roysten, Picky—a cute poodle mix in the next enclosure who always seemed to watch Dutton as though she understood what he was saying—and the thirteen or so other dogs in the rescue center were better company than most of the people he knew. "Okay, okay, you'll all get fed," he said to calm the general restless anticipation of feeding time.

He picked up speed, getting dishes for more of the dogs, who settled right in to eat. A tuxedo terrier whose cage tag read Fonzie watched him intensely as he put the food inside his enclosure. The dog remained sitting until Dutton closed the cage door, and then he gently began eating, like he was savoring his kibble. "I know, you think you're cool." He rolled his eyes at his own joke because there was no one else to hear it. "And last but not least, Sweetie Pie." He placed the bowl in the huge Rottweiler's enclosure and backed away. All the dogs in the shelter were good dogs, Dutton felt that to his bones, but some of them had had hard lives that hadn't been filled with love, and he was determined to help try to change that. "I know," he said gently to the huge dog. "You went without food for a long time, and now you're trying to make up for it." He watched as Sweetie Pie gulped his food.

"Excuse me," a man said from behind him.

Dutton jumped slightly, but at least he didn't squeak the way he had a tendency to do when he got startled.

"I was told at the veterinary clinic that this was where I could adopt a dog." It took Dutton a second before his eyes widened in recognition. "Dutton…?"

He smiled. "Randy," he said gently, hoping the name didn't come out too breathily. "How are you doing?" Dutton had had such a crush on him in high school. Dutton had been the stereotypical gay kid: shy, quiet, just trying to stay out of everyone's way, too tall and skinny for anyone to be interested in. Randy Grant, on the other hand—even now, just saying the name in his head made him want to sigh dramatically. He still had the same piercing blue eyes and perfect smile, and damned if he hadn't continued working out. In five years, Randy had definitely gone from teenager to man, all over. Back in high school, Randy had been a baseball star, and when he'd come out of the closet junior year, anyone who said an unkind word found themselves on the outside looking in, fast. Dutton hadn't followed the same path back then, but he had admired Randy for his courage.

"I'm fine. Graduated from Penn State and returned to Carlisle for law school. Mom is thrilled that I'm back here." He smiled that same smile with perfect teeth, but what surprised Dutton was how genuine it seemed. Hell, Dutton hadn't even realized that Randy Grant knew who he was back in high school. "What about you?"

"I got a scholarship to Shippensburg, and I'm working here at the shelter and at the vet clinic part-time. I want to go to vet school, and I've been accepted to the veterinary program at Penn State starting in the fall." He couldn't help smiling. He had worked hard to get accepted there and on a scholarship.

"That's really great," Randy said. "You always worked really hard."

Dutton almost took a step back in surprise. Guys like Randy weren't supposed to know stuff about wallflowers like him. "You said you were looking to adopt a dog?"

"Yeah. Mom has been spending a lot of time alone, and since her last dog crossed the rainbow bridge about six months ago, she's been making sounds like it's time to get another one. So I thought I'd see what you have, and maybe I could get her one for Christmas. She likes smaller dogs. I'll check with her before actually taking the dog."

"Let me show you what we have." Dutton couldn't help being a little excited as he showed Randy around. "Usually we keep the larger and smaller dogs in their own areas, but we have more small dogs at the moment, so they've spilled over." He showed Randy around, letting him look at each one.

The dogs put on quite a show, with most of them looking for attention, wagging their tails. A few of them even let out some yips. "This is Gabby. She's a chihuahua mix. Really sweet little girl."

Randy smiled. "Who is this?"

Dutton chuckled. "That's Picky. She's a real sweetheart." He opened the cage and gently lifted her out. Picky went right into his arms like she belonged there. Dutton had been thinking about adopting her himself, and she felt so at home right in his arms. But he passed her to Randy anyway. Mitchell, the veterinarian and owner of the shelter, had told him when he started that the hardest thing about this job was the fact that you couldn't take home every dog—you had to be able to let them go.

Randy smiled as Picky licked his hand and relaxed against him. "She's so sweet."

"Yeah, she is. We think Picky is a little over two years old. All our dogs have had their shots, and she was spayed when we found her. Poor little thing was found hiding in an old shed. She had no tags or collar. We think someone just dropped her somewhere." The thought made Dutton angry. "She and your mom are going to love each other."

Randy held her up to look into her eyes, and Picky licked his nose. He smiled and brought her back into his arms. "I think she'd be the perfect companion for Mom." He set her back in the enclosure and pulled out his phone. "Would you mind taking her picture with me?" He handed Dutton the phone and lifted Picky once more. Dutton snapped a few pictures and handed the phone back. Randy shifted Picky slightly and then sent the picture with a soft phone swoosh noise. After a few seconds, Randy's phone dinged, and he smiled. "What paperwork do I need to fill out?"

"Come with me." Dutton led Randy to the business area. He got a leash and clipped it onto Picky's collar. Randy then set her down and started filling out the form.

"Wow, you ask a lot of questions," Randy said.

"We want to make sure that your dog will be well cared for and that you understand what's involved with pet parenting. We've had a lot of animals come through the shelter. Mitchell does a dog rescue, but we've had snakes, a few cats, a tortoise, and even a tiger last summer. Mitchell was able to get Raj into a breeding program with one of the prominent zoos, and he's doing well. All the animals we have here are rescues, even the tiger." He was so proud of the work they did.

Randy continued filling out the form and signed it at the bottom. He also wrote out a check for a little more than the adoption fee and handed it to Dutton. "The additional amount is a donation." There went that smile again. "I'm working at Foster's Toys in town, helping out my uncle for the season. You should stop in to say hello. Maybe we could have coffee."

Dutton nodded, but he had to turn away for a second.

"Hey, I didn't mean to upset you," Randy said.

Dutton plastered on a smile. "You didn't. I'm fine. Sorry."

Randy drew a little closer. "You don't look fine. What happened? Did you stop in and my uncle spent an hour rhapsodizing on the beauty of model trains?"

Dutton shook his head. "You just reminded me that I have to buy something for my niece and nephew for Christmas, and I have no idea what to get them."

"What do they like?" Randy asked as he lifted Picky into his arms. She curled right into his warmth and settled there.

Dutton sighed. "I don't know." He swallowed hard. "I haven't seen them in two years. My sister doesn't agree that being gay isn't something that I chose. She thinks that I should just find a girl and get married. We had a fight about it a couple of years ago, and she ended it with 'I'm not going to let you see the kids if you can't even make an effort to change your deviant lifestyle.'" The words had stung something awful.

"Oh my God," Randy said softly, but his eyes blazed with anger on Dutton's behalf.

"Well, there's nothing I can do about it." He had come to grips with it, mostly. "She won't budge, even for Christmas, because Mary is as stubborn as they come. You can't tell her anything—never could."

"And you need gifts for the kids?" Randy asked, a little confused. Dutton nodded. "I know this is going to sound harsh, but why?"

"The kids can't help that their mother is a little nuts. Mary has issues." To put it mildly. "So I get them some gifts and things on the holidays and I leave them in a basket on the porch. My friend Ashley writes the cards for me. He works nights driving truck, so he puts the baskets on the porch when he's in that part of town." He couldn't believe he was telling Randy this, because up until now, only Ashley knew his secret. "But the kids are just old enough that I don't know what to get them."

Randy's expression softened, and he smiled. "For helping me with a major piece of my Christmas shopping, come to the store tomorrow and I'll help you pick some things out. Uncle Foster has a lot of things that I'm sure they'll like, and we can get you all fixed up."

"Thank you," Dutton said softly. "I wasn't sure what I was going to do. My niece is seven, and my nephew is five. Like I said, I haven't seen them in two years. Easter and the other holidays are easy because they are about the candy and a few small things. But I want to get them something special for Christmas. After all, it isn't their fault about Mary, and…." The truth was, he wanted some kind of connection with them. It was probably stupid, because they were never going to know, but Dutton always figured that he would know that he'd done what he could, even if he had to do it without Mary knowing.

"We'll definitely find something." Randy smiled, and his gaze locked with Dutton's for a few seconds. Dutton's pulse picked up, and he licked his lips. Picky began squirming, and the moment passed quickly enough that Dutton wondered if he had imagined the whole thing. "I should get this little girl home."

"Of course. I'll stop into the store a little before noon. I have to work at the clinic tomorrow afternoon and early evening. If that works?"

Randy nodded. "It's perfect. I'll see you then." When he left the shelter, the December air slipped in along with a few flakes of snow. Then Randy closed the door, and Dutton kept watching him for a few seconds and then returned his attention to making sure the dogs were all settled in for the night. He also cleaned out Picky's enclosure to get it ready for the next dog. He checked his phone for the time and got ready to leave, still finding it hard to believe that Randy Grant remembered him and that he was going to see him again tomorrow. Dutton told himself not to get his hopes up. Randy was probably just being nice, and everything else was only in Dutton's head.

He drove downtown and parked behind his building, then walked up the stairs to his tiny apartment above a pub. The real shame of it was that he was only three blocks from his sister and her kids, but they might as well be half a world away.

Chapter 2

"WHAT HAS you so excited?" Uncle Foster asked as Randy looked toward the door… again. "Whatever it is, can we get some work done?"

He was good-natured, and Randy did have a ton of stocking to do. The past few weeks had been amazing. He went to the back, grabbed a stack of boxes, and hauled them out front, where he priced and filled the display of games. It was the holidays, and they'd had a steady stream of customers all morning. Uncle Foster had been promoting the store as a source for back-to-basics toys, and it had been working.

Randy took the empty boxes to the back, broke them down, and brought out some more, this time filling a display of wooden puzzles that everyone seemed to want.

"Can I help you?" Uncle Foster sounded run off his feet, and it was not yet noon. Not that any of them were going to complain. This was the time of year when the store did a lot of its annual business.

"I was going to meet Randy," Dutton said.

Randy paused what he was doing and glanced up. Dutton looked the same in some ways, but in others, he had really changed since high school. His hair was short now. Gone was the black hair that had flopped in his eyes, which were stunning now that they could be seen. He had filled out and was less gangly. He also seemed to stand taller and straighter, like he wasn't waiting for the next verbal volley or to be shoved in a locker.

"Hey," Randy called. "I need to finish this up, but I'll be right back out in a few minutes." He straightened the display and took the boxes back before finding Dutton at the display of dolls. "Looking at one for your niece?"

"I was thinking about it, but I know Cassie has a doll that she was given years ago, and the last I knew, she was still sleeping with it." Dutton seemed hesitant.

Randy nodded. "Dolls and stuffies tend to be comfort toys, and kids don't give them up easily. You said she was seven, right?" Maybe a doll was not the best idea, especially if Cassie already had a number of them. If they put their heads together, they could probably come up with something a little more memorable.

"Yeah. And Todd is five. I think he's easier. He always loved blocks and things like that. I bet he'd like a building set. But I don't want to get him one of those where you build something specific. I thought about giving him the bag of Legos that I had as a kid, but Mary would probably recognize it."

"Give me a minute," Randy said and found his uncle behind the register. He waited until he was done with the customer. "Where is that case of building sets that we got in that was damaged?"

"It's in the back on the top self near the back door. They said it wasn't worth shipping them back, so I was going to toss them out. I got the replacement shipment the other day. Why?"

"I have an idea, and it will get the case out of the room and help someone at the same time." He got Dutton and led him into the back, where he pulled down the case. He set it on the receiving table and pulled out the various boxes inside. They had gotten some bad water damage, and some of the packaging was falling apart. "Can you get that blue cloth bag over there?"

Dutton got it and set it on the table. "What are we doing?"

"These sets are dead, but the blocks inside are still good. So let's make up a bag of them that you can give Todd." He pulled over the trash can and started throwing away the cardboard. They tore apart all the packaging and piled the blocks on the table.

"He's five…."

"Yeah, so these really little ones probably aren't a good idea. But there are plenty of larger blocks in a lot of colors." Randy began filling the bag with the blocks as Dutton worked through the last of the packaging. By the time they were done, the trash can was nearly full and they had a decent-size bag of plain building blocks, wheels, and windows. "That should be pretty cool." He handed the bag to Dutton. "It cost Uncle Foster twenty-five bucks in shipping for the replacement shipment, so does that seem fair for the blocks?"

Dutton's eyes widened, and he nodded. "That doesn't seem like enough."

"They were going to be thrown away because the packaging wasn't saleable, so this way Uncle Foster comes out even and you get a gift for your nephew." The way Dutton reacted made Randy wonder how long it had been since someone had done something nice for him. He seemed almost surprised and maybe even shocked. "Now, how about you get a building set to go with them and he'll be really happy?"

"Cool. That's one down, but Cassie is another thing."

"It's not that difficult," Randy said, bringing the bag out front. He set it behind the register, and once Dutton had picked out the building set to go with the blocks, Randy led him to the section of the store with toys geared toward little girls. "I know you said no dolls, but Barbie is always popular, and with the movie, especially so this year."

"I know. But she'll go to Christmas parties and stuff and get them."

Randy had to agree. It was the present everyone gave little girls. "Do you remember what else she liked?"

"I don't know," Dutton said, growing agitated. "I haven't seen either one of them in two years. About once a month or so when Mary gets worked up, she sends me text rants in the middle of the night. If I answer her, then I get a nasty comment in return."

"Why don't you block her?"

Dutton shrugged. "I don't even read the messages any longer. But I keep the lines of communication open as best I can in case something happens to the kids. My sister made her own bed and she can deal with the consequences, but I won't turn my back on Cassie and Todd, even if she doesn't want to see me." He sounded so strong, and Randy wondered if that was an act. Dutton was most definitely hurting, and Randy wished he could do something about it. "Back to a gift for Cassie."

"I know." He went to the craft corner. "How about this? It's an easel. We have rolls of paper to go with it. There are also paints and brushes and things. But instead of that, which can get really messy, maybe some other art supplies to go with it?"

Dutton looked it over. "It seems kind of big. I'm going to have to have this delivered to the house after dark and everything."

Randy chuckled. "That's one of the beauties of it. The easel comes in this size box and will need to be put together. It isn't hard to do, but…."

"Mary will have to do it." He chuckled. "That seems really petty… and perfect. Let's go with that and the roll of paper. I know that Cassie has art supplies because I got her some for Easter, and I put some things in her Halloween pumpkin." He seemed happier. "Okay. Let's get all that for the kids."

"Let me ring you up. I'll leave the purchases behind the counter and maybe we can get some coffee or something. I don't know about you, but I'm starved." He brought everything to his uncle, who rang up Dutton and took his credit card. Randy told his uncle he was going to lunch.

"That's fine. Your aunt will be here in a few minutes." Uncle Foster was one of those people who took everything in stride and rarely got flustered. Fortunately the activity had died down—for a little while, anyway. Randy grabbed his coat from the back and met Dutton near the front door.

"You don't have to do this. I'm sure you're busy, and you've already been nice enough to help with the gifts."

"Come on," Randy said. "Let's get something to eat before we keel over. Picking out the right gifts is hard work." He opened the door, and they stepped out into the wintry afternoon.

"WHAT CAN I get for you?" Tammy asked from behind the counter of Courthouse Perks, just off the square in Carlisle, Pennsylvania. "I was wondering if you were going to come in today or if your uncle was keeping you too busy." She smiled and her gaze shifted. "I know you," she said. "Dutton, right? We were in Spanish class together, and you helped me with verb conjugation and stuff. Man, I never would have passed that class without you." There was another one of her smiles. "Pick your poison."

"I'll have a Brazilian blend with cream," Dutton said.

"Same, and bring us a couple of your special sandwiches," Randy added before paying for the order and finding a table near the front windows. "Tammy owns this place. Her grandmother bought the building years ago and it sat empty for a while, so Tammy pitched the idea of the coffee house and boulangerie. Apparently her grandmother loves coffee, so they went into business together."

Tammy came over with their coffee and sandwiches. "So what have you been doing?" She asked Dutton. She was never shy about anything.

"I'm working part-time at a veterinary practice as well as at the dog rescue. I'll start veterinary school in the fall." Dutton sipped the coffee, and Randy could almost see him trying to sink into the woodwork.

Randy had noticed Dutton in school, and he'd approached him a few times, but Dutton always seemed to slink away, like he'd been expecting Randy to give him a hard time. At the time he didn't have the tools to know what to do or how to approach Dutton. And the truth was that then, his life had been so full with sports and stuff… and to top it off, he was a stupid teenager who didn't look much farther than the end of his nose. Randy liked to think he was smarter than that now.

"A vet? How cool. Gran has two cats, and they're okay. I'm more of a dog person myself." She settled in to talk a little while longer before Randy gave her the stink-eye, and she rolled her eyes back at him.

"You seem to know a lot of people," Dutton said. "I've lived here all my life and I feel like a stranger in town most of the time. I'm, like, the guy no one pays much attention to."

That wasn't totally true. Randy had paid plenty of attention to him. But Randy had also known that coming out of the closet was one thing—having a boyfriend and flaunting it in people's faces was quite another, especially in small-town central Pennsylvania. It had been his mom's suggestion that he concentrate on baseball and his grades and that the rest would come in time. As he looked back on it, she may have been right. He had a much easier time of it than Dutton had, but still, Randy wished he'd had the courage to be more forceful back then. "That's not true. Tammy remembered you, and so did I. You were just kind of shy, and high school tends to run at a faster pace and I guess you sort of got…."

"Overlooked? Not that it's anyone else's fault. I spent most of that time trying not to be noticed, and I think it worked really well. Maybe too well."

"Actually, it is our fault," Randy said, looking at Tammy, who nodded. "We should have made more of an effort back then." He swallowed hard. He hadn't been one of the guys who picked on Dutton, but he hadn't put a stop to it either, and now he wished he had.

Dutton took a bite of the sandwich. "This is really good." It was clearly an effort to change the subject, which Randy was grateful for. The past was just that, and all he could control was the present and, if he was lucky, maybe some of the future.

"Tammy's grandmother bakes the bread every day, so it's really fresh. I get one of those all the time."

Tammy smirked slightly. "I swear you keep me in business."

"I tell everyone about your food," Randy told her.

"I know. We've started baking more bread because we were selling out." She gave them both a smile as a gust of cold air blew in through the open door, and a group of college-age students made their way right to the counter. Tammy waved as she hurried back to work, and Randy and Dutton shared a smile across the table.

Dutton finished his sandwich and sat back to drink his coffee, jumping slightly when his phone rang. He answered it, speaking softly. "Okay. I'll be right there." He hung up. "I'm sorry, but that was Mitchell. He's overloaded at the clinic and needs my help." He looked around as though he weren't sure what to do. "I need to get the gifts and…."

"It's okay," Randy said. "What's your number?" He entered it in his phone and then dialed Dutton. "Now you have mine. Text me your address, and I can bring the presents over when you get home."

"Are you sure?" Dutton drank the last of his coffee and was already shrugging on his coat.

"Of course. Send me your address when you get a chance, and I'll bring the stuff over once I'm done working. It's no problem." He watched as Dutton headed for the door.

"Thank you… again." Dutton paused, those huge eyes wide in surprise that someone would do something nice for him. "I'll see you later." He hurried out, and Randy turned back to his coffee. He was sad that their time had been cut short before they had a chance to talk much, but on the plus side, he was going to see Dutton again.

Chapter 3

HE SMELLED like kennel and God knows what else. The clinic had been a madhouse. Mitchell was going from room to room with scheduled appointments, along with looking over five dogs that the sheriff's department had brought in from a hoarder house outside town. The poor things had been frightened and were way too thin. Dutton had taken charge of them, feeding them slowly and making sure they got fluids. Mostly he sat quietly with them to try to keep them calm. Change was hard on people, and it was equally difficult on dogs, especially when they were taken away from everything they knew.

"It's okay." They all ate like they were afraid this was their last meal.

"How are they doing?" Mitchell asked as he popped his head into the small room they used for quarantine when necessary. "I really appreciate you coming in."

"They're calming down, and four of them are eating. This little one is only nibbling, but she's drinking water."

Mitchell handed him a small bag. "Try those treats. If she eats and keeps them down, then we can find a food that she will eat long-term."

Dutton nodded, and Mitchell left. He offered a treat to the little terrier mix, who gobbled it down. He gave her another and a third. Then he gave her a piece of kibble, and she ate that as well. "You're just Miss Fussy Pants and want to be treated like you're special." He kept giving her small amounts, and finally he set the bowl in front of her with a small amount of food. She ate and then drank a ton of water before settling down on the mat in the small crate, closing her eyes.

The others had started to settle down as well, and Dutton moved slowly, lowering the light in the room. Sure enough, all of them had had enough excitement. He continued sitting with them for a while and then went to the front desk to see if he could help out.

"Anything I can do?"

Daniel sighed. "That would be great. I finally have everyone in a room, and Mitchell is making it through the last appointments. Please watch the desk and answer the phones and stuff. I'm going to go see if I can help him." Daniel hurried back, and Dutton settled into the chair as the phone rang with an emergency. He sent both Mitchell and Daniel a message and received an almost immediate response. He returned to the frantic lady and told her to bring her cat in right away.

He stayed late, and just about the time when Mitchell and Daniel had caught up, a lady came in with a carrier that contained a cat who was barely moving. Dutton got her right into a room and alerted Mitchell, who hurried in after him. He very much wanted to be a veterinarian like Mitchell. In fact, Mitchell was his professional hero.

"Is there anything else?" Daniel asked with sadness in his eyes.

"No. That was the last," Dutton told him. "I need to check on the new arrivals." He left the desk and returned to the quarantine room, where all five dogs looked up when he came in. Tails thumped, and Dutton gave each of them some attention, filled water bowls, and offered a little more food, which all of them seemed to be tolerating.

"We should take them over to the rescue and get them settled there," Mitchell said. "We can then let them each out for a while to get a little exercise."

Dutton was already tired, but he nodded and helped get the dogs loaded into Mitchell's truck and then followed him down the road to where Mitchell lived with his partner and their daughter.

He unloaded each dog and took them around the yard to stretch their legs before going inside and getting them settled away from the others.

"How is the cat that came in doing?" Dutton asked.

Mitchell grew quiet and shook his head. "She was too far gone." He turned away and left the shelter, returning with one of the larger dogs.

Once they had them all in enclosures, Dutton picked up the little terrier from earlier. "I'm going to call you Muffy," he said.

Mitchell laughed. "You know, it kind of fits. But her new owners will probably rename her."

He shook his head. "Nope. Once she's through her quarantine and you've looked her over, I'm going to take her home with me. She'll be a really good companion, and since I have a small space, she'll be the perfect size." Dutton was tired of being alone. "And I figure I can bring her here with me once she's had all her shots." He cradled the little pup with huge ears. "Would you like that?" Muffy licked his nose. "I'll take that as a yes."

"Excellent," Mitchell said. "Now let's get things closed up so we can all go home." They finished up, and as he was getting ready to leave, Dutton messaged Randy with his address and that he was on his way and should be home in ten or fifteen minutes. He didn't expect Randy to rush over or anything, so he was surprised when Randy was waiting at the base of the stairs with a box of toys and a smile.

"You didn't need to get here that fast."

"I was done at the store, and it's only a block away." Randy followed him inside and then up the tall, narrow stairs to the second floor. Dutton's one-bedroom apartment was in the back. He unlocked the door and stepped aside so Randy could come in.

"Just set the box on the table." He had to get wrap, bows, and ribbon so he could finish getting the gifts ready. Randy unpacked the presents and pulled out all the supplies he could need, as well as tape and scissors. Then he took off his coat, and Dutton stood speechless.

"I figured we could wrap everything."

Randy was going to wrap presents with him. "Okay." He hadn't figured on this. "I have some things left over from last year somewhere." He went to the bedroom to check the top of the closet. Then he checked under the bed, where he found the flat plastic tub with the few things he had inside. He carried it back out to where Randy waited in the living room.

"Is there a reason you don't have any decorations?"

Dutton shrugged. "I don't have a lot of room, and since the kids don't come over, I don't have much reason to put something up. Last year I got a tree at the craft sale. The garden club makes them out of boxwood, and I got a really pretty one. I missed the sale this year, and I figured...." He didn't have anyone to put decorations up for except himself, and there was no reason to bother when it was just him and he'd have to take them down again anyway. "I've been so busy."

"You know, you're worth putting a tree up for yourself. And that way, once you have the gifts wrapped, you'd have a place to put them."

"Okay. I guess I'll see what I can find." Maybe he could get a small artificial one that he could put in the corner on a table." He sat at the table, and Randy joined him. To help him get into a festive mood, he found some Christmas music on Spotify and played it on his phone.

"How do you want to pack the gifts?" Randy asked.

"I don't know. I hadn't thought that far ahead. Maybe I'll get a box or something that I can put them in. I don't want it to be anything that Mary will recognize as coming from me, otherwise who knows how she'll react." The truth was that she might simply take the presents and make sure the kids never saw them. She could be cold and vindictive when she got on her high horse about something. And all Dutton really wanted was to make sure the kids had a nice holiday.

"Okay. How about a large Santa bag? Uncle Foster has some at the store. I'll see about begging one, and then we can deliver the presents in that. The kids will see it and think Santa brought the gifts."

"I like that." He unrolled some wrap and started working on one of Cassie's gifts. He kept his mind on how happy the kids would be rather than on how much he wished he could be there to see their faces. That simply wasn't possible.

Randy worked on Todd's gifts using paper that featured Santa in an airplane. He put the last piece of tape on the first gift and set it aside. "I have to ask. Is there any chance you and your sister will—?"

Dutton was already shaking his head. "I wish, but no... I don't think so. She's bitter, and the things she's said to me...." He figured there was no need to show Randy the texts. No one needed to see that garbage. "Let's just say that she's made her feelings very clear."

"Okay. I just thought...."

Dutton nodded. "I used to think that she'd change her mind or realize what she'd done, but that hasn't happened." And there was only so much vitriol that someone could take before they had to protect themselves. He really felt sorry for his niece and nephew living in that environment, but there was nothing he could do other than try to see to it that they had a Christmas of some sort, even if they didn't know where it came from.

Randy set down his tape and scissors before coming around to his side the table. Dutton wasn't sure what was happening until Randy hugged him. It was a little awkward, but Dutton didn't care. He closed his eyes, instantly surrounded by Randy's deep, rich scent. Damn, that was hot, and he wished he could bottle the stuff. "You know this has nothing to do with you—that it's all in her mind—right?"

He nodded slowly. "That's true, I know that. But sometimes it's hard to believe. I keep wondering what I did to make her hate me so."

"People are the only beings on the planet who hate for no reason. Other animals react the way they do out of fear, instinct, or to eat. We will hate someone on sight. I know that isn't the case here, but I do believe that whatever is going on, she's probably blown it all out of proportion."

Dutton couldn't help chuckling. "You hit that one on the head. Sometimes I think that Mary never grew out of her teenage years. She's nearly thirty but often acts like she's still in high school." There was nothing he could do about it, but he had to admit that he liked the way Randy held him. He was strong, and yet gentle and caring. Still, he couldn't help wondering why Randy seemed interested in him. As far as Dutton could see, he was pretty boring. Randy could have his pick of guys. Heck, tons of them would probably follow him around waiting for him to crook his little finger. So why was Randy here, and what could he possibly see in Dutton?

"Come on. We should finish this up," Randy said gently, his arms slipping away. Dutton missed them almost immediately, and he forced himself to return to the wrapping. "What do you like to do for fun?" Randy asked once he sat back down. The change of subject was very welcome.

"I love animals, as you can probably guess." He leaned over the table. "We got in five dogs from a pretty bad situation today. They hadn't had enough to eat, and one of them is so sweet. I named her Muffy, and once Mitchell looks her over, I'm going to bring her to live with me. She's a small terrier with these huge ears and eyes that seem to take in everything. I've wanted to get a dog for a while, but I have a tendency to fall in love easily. Say... how did your mom and Picky get along?"

Randy's eyes went soft. "Like they had been waiting for each other. Picky took one look at my mother, bounded into her lap as soon as she sat down, and made herself at home. Someone had house-trained her, and she went outside right away. She is eating well, and apparently Mom got her a dog bed for when they're downstairs, but she sleeps at the foot of Mom's bed."

"Any weird behavior?"

"Maybe a little. Apparently Mom said that she can be food defensive, but I suppose that's common when a dog hasn't had enough to eat."

"That can happen. Also be sure she keeps her on a lead. She was a little wild when we first brought her in. Picky is a sweet dog, but she might forget that she has a home and could try to fend for herself if given the chance." Dutton finished up the last of Cassie's gifts and set them in a pile on one of the side tables. Then he sat back down, watching Randy as he finished up.

"You look like a man with a question."

Dutton cleared his throat. "I guess I keep wondering why you're here. Don't get me wrong—it's very nice and I'm glad you are—but you're really smart and funny and, well, geez, you've looked in a mirror... and...." God, he was rambling and sounding like an idiot.

"I'm here because you were kind and I sort of liked you in high school, but I didn't act on it. And then when I came to find a dog for my mom, there you were again."

Dutton swallowed hard. "You liked me? I didn't even realize you knew who I was back then. High school was such a cluster for me."

"I know. Me too." He lowered his gaze to the table.

"Really? I always thought you kind of had it all. Popular, smart, good at sports, and people didn't seem to care if you were gay." It seemed to him like Randy had everything.

"Not everyone was good about it. Yeah, there were supportive people, and I'm grateful for them, but a lot of the guys didn't want to change in front of me. Eventually I would change in one of the bathroom stalls because they were afraid that a gay guy was going to take one look at them and go wild with desire or something." He rolled his eyes, and Dutton laughed. He was well aware of that particular phenomenon. "I didn't date, and I went to the prom with a friend. I didn't make waves and I didn't stand up for myself or other gay people the way I probably should have. Instead, I did what you did, kept my head down and tried to make it through." Randy put the presents he'd wrapped with the others. "I should probably go. It's getting late."

"Yeah... okay." Maybe Randy was just being nice with the gifts and stuff. Dutton stood and saw Randy to the door. "Thank you for all your help."

Randy shrugged on his coat and paused at the door. Dutton blinked a few times, and his breath hitched as Randy drew closer. "You're more than welcome." He drew even nearer. Dutton's pulse sped up and his eyes slid closed as he wondered if this was really happening. Randy kissed him gently and then pulled back. "Maybe this weekend we can get you a Christmas tree."

"Sure." He found himself agreeing without thinking.

Randy turned and left. Dutton closed the door, smiling to himself because Randy Grant had kissed him.

Chapter 4

"YOU GOT a date or something?" Uncle Foster asked.

Randy smirked. "I do. You remember the guy I got the blocks for last weekend? I helped him get his gifts wrapped, and tonight we're going to get him a tree." He was a little bouncy at the thought.

"Dutton... something."

"Glenroth, yeah. He and I went to school together."

Uncle Foster nodded. "There's a Mary Glenroth renting a house near your cousin Rachel's place. The kids play with Rachel's."

"That would be his sister," Randy said. "Apparently they don't talk. But Dutton still gets gifts for the kids and has them delivered so his sister doesn't know where they came from." Randy thought that was about the sweetest thing he ever heard. "He's afraid if she did, she wouldn't let the kids have the presents."

Uncle Foster shook his head as Randy broke down the last empty boxes. It was getting close enough to Christmas that the stock room was nearly empty, and almost everything they had was on the sales floor. "Sometimes family is just too weird."

Dutton grinned, and Uncle Foster snickered. "Cousin Wendel," they said together, sharing a laugh as a couple came in. Randy left his uncle to help them and carried the boxes into the back, where he put them in the recycling. He went through what else was there. All they had was a few items left over from the summer, but with a section on the side wall empty, he carried them out and set them up. People went on winter vacations to warm places, and it was better than having empty space.

They got busy for a while, with Randy helping customers and his uncle ringing people up, but once the pace slowed, he began cleaning up and putting toys back on the shelves.

"You can go and get together with your friend. It's less than an hour till closing, and it will likely be slow. But I'll need you to help tomorrow. I know it's Sunday, but the weather is supposed to be nice, and I expect people will be out and about."

"No problem." He pulled out his phone. "Dutton was going to meet me here." Randy had no issue helping his uncle. He paid him well, and it meant he'd have more money for school. He texted Dutton to let him know he was free and got a response right away that he was on his way there.

"I take it he's heading over," Uncle Foster said. "You must really like this guy."

Randy nodded. "I guess I do. Dutton is nice, and…." He paused.

Uncle Foster had never been one to mince words. "And he isn't like Anson. Your aunt and I hated that man on sight."

Randy stepped back. Part of the reason getting rid of Anson had been so hard was because he thought his family really liked the guy, and he didn't want to disappoint them. "Why didn't you tell me?"

"Because you seemed happy, and we knew if we were right, he'd show himself soon enough, which he did." Uncle Foster's gaze grew hard. "And if we were wrong, then our opinion didn't matter. But we were happy when you kicked the gold-digger to the curb. He was only interested in dating a future lawyer and seeing what he could get from you. I take it Dutton is nothing like that."

Randy checked the front door and then began straightening the supplies behind the register. "He's nothing like Anson. But I keep thinking that I might have blown it. We knew each other in high school, and I didn't treat him very well back then."

"Did you bully him or pick on him?" His tone was sharp as nails.

"No. Of course not. But I didn't stop others from doing it. I always felt like a coward, and I should have done more." He finished putting away the stray bags that had fallen to the floor.

"Everyone is a coward in high school. It's part of the gig. As long as you're good to him now, that's what counts. And make sure he's good to you too."

"Oh, Dutton's good, all right," Randy said as the door opened and Dutton entered the store. His serious expression slipped into a smile as soon as he saw him, and Randy returned it. "Uncle Foster, this is Dutton. He and I are going to get a Christmas tree."

"It's good to meet you, and thank you for the blocks and stuff. I'm sure my nephew is going to love them." They shook hands.

"You two kids have fun, and I'll see you tomorrow, Randy." He got busy, and Randy went in back, grabbed his coat, and left with Dutton before his uncle could change his mind.

"Where did you plan to go?" Dutton asked as they walked down the street, light snow drifting down around them. "I saw a lot over near the YMCA, and there's one out near the grocery store on High Street.

"There's one out by Dickinson just a few blocks from here. We can look there, and if we don't see anything, we'll try one of the lots farther away." They headed in that direction, passing through the main square with lighted angels on the lamppost and the huge town tree with large multicolored lights next to the old courthouse.

High Street was decorated with lighted bows and garlands on the lamppost. Everywhere they looked, it seemed festive, and Dutton walked close to him, his hand brushing Randy's every now and then.

"You kissed me," Dutton said, sort of out of the blue, but Randy figured he must have been mulling over what to say for a while.

"I did, and I'd like to do it again."

Dutton's steps faltered. "Why?"

"Is that your favorite question? Do you always have to know why something happens? Can't you just enjoy it?" He gently moved them into the shadows, pressing Dutton against the brick before kissing him again. Dutton moaned softly, and that sound went all the way to his soul. Randy kissed him again just to get him to make that noise, and damned if he didn't. "Does that answer your question?"

Dutton thought a second and then shook his head. "Maybe you need to try again to get your message across." A slight smirk formed on his lips, and Randy kissed him again... for the sake of communication.

Others approached, and Randy backed away because every cell in his body urged him forward, and there was no way he was going to take things further out where they could be seen. The feelings bubbling up inside him were for Dutton alone, and he wasn't about to share them with the rest of the damned town. "Come on." He took Dutton's hand, leading the way to the Christmas tree lot.

A corner home had been taken down that year after a fire, and the lot was being used to sell Christmas trees. To Randy, it seemed like a good way to add some cheer and positivity after a loss.

"They have quite a bit. But I need a smaller one. I don't have a lot of room."

"Then go ahead and look over there," Randy offered. "I want to check out one for Mom." He figured if he found one, he could buy one and tag it for pickup later. Randy wandered through the lot, but he didn't see what he wanted, so he made his way back to where he'd seen Dutton, and found him hiding behind a Douglas fir. "What's going on?" He followed Dutton's gaze to a woman with a little boy and girl.

"That's my sister," Dutton said softly.

Randy tapped him on the shoulder, straightened his back, and marched up to her. "Can I help you?" he asked as though he were a salesman. "There are great trees here."

"Yes," she said and began a rambling story with eight detours from everything about trees in general to the origins of the Christmas tree, eventually talking about the kind of tree she wanted. Randy's mind went in circles at her rambles, and he glanced over at Dutton, who was talking with his niece and nephew. They seemed to be picking out a tree, so Randy let Mary ramble on, telling stories and imparting information, most of which Dutton knew was wrong.

"Mom, we found the perfect tree," Cassie said. "It's right over here."

Randy pretended to follow, but instead he melted away into the other trees, meeting Dutton near the checkout. "Did you get to talk to them?" Randy asked.

"It took me a second to figure out that was your plan. Next time warn me." He smiled. "But yeah, I did. They helped me pick out my tree." He pointed to a five-foot one that seemed really nice. "I just need to pay and we can get out of here, hopefully before Mary sees me and makes a scene." He paid for the tree. Randy hefted it, and they left the lot and walked back toward Dutton's building.

"What did the kids say? Did they know you?"

Dutton shook his head. "Nope. I think Cassie might remember me as someone familiar, but that's all. We talked about Christmas and the trees. Todd and Cassie were so excited to be getting a tree. Cassie said they usually put lights on one of Mary's indoor plants or something. I helped them pick out a tree that wasn't too expensive." He wiped his eyes, and Randy leaned the tree against the brick of one of the buildings and hugged him tight. "They don't know me at all. I was there when Mary brought Cassie home, and I held her when she was a few days old. Mary couldn't breastfeed, so I got to bottle-feed Todd while Mary slept in the hospital. I've been there for those kids since they were born, and...." He buried his face in Randy's coat, and Randy just held him as snow fell all around.

"It's okay. Let it out." He stroked Dutton's short, soft hair and just stood there with him. It was impossible for him to understand what Dutton was going through, but his hurt just made Randy angry, and he wanted to do something about it, though this was way out of his control. Randy's instinct around problems was to try to fix them, and there was nothing he could do about this.

Dutton pulled away, sniffling a few times. "Sorry." He wiped his eyes once more and then straightened his stance. "Let's...."

Randy lifted the tree, and they walked the rest of the way back in silence. There was nothing to say at the moment, and Dutton probably needed time with his thoughts. Once they got there, Dutton unlocked the door, and Randy brought the tree inside.

A stand had already been set out, so Randy got the tree placed into it and set it in the cleared corner of the living room.

"I'm sorry. I should be grateful that I got to talk to Todd and Cassie." He sat on the sofa. "They are really sweet kids." He wiped his eyes, and Randy sat next to him.

"Did your sister see you?" Randy asked.

"No. And I didn't tell the kids who I was. I just talked to them a little bit and asked what kind of Christmas tree they wanted. I felt like I was stalking them and maybe I should have stayed away, but all I wanted was to see them a little. I'd never hurt them."

"Of course you wouldn't." Dutton was a kind person and wouldn't hurt anyone. "I spoke with your sister." He shivered. "I think that woman is nuts. I asked her what kind of tree she was looking for and got a dissertation on the history of Christmas trees, most of which was either wrong or filled with some sort of spiritualistic fantasy." He really felt sorry for the kids.

"I know." Dutton sighed and leaned against him. Randy slipped an arm around his shoulders and held him gently. "I wish I knew what to do."

"There's little you can do other than what you're doing already. If she isn't going to let you be part of her or the kids' lives...."

"They don't even remember me," he said softly. "But I suppose that's best. They won't know that they're missing out on family."

"What about your parents?"

"My mom and dad divorced when I was ten. Dad took a job in California, remarried, and has a new family out there. They're decent, and I've visited a few times. He's an okay guy, and he always paid his child support and stuff. And when Mom died a few years ago, he was there for the funeral. He also helped pay for college and has said he'll help with veterinary school as well."

"Sounds like a pretty decent guy," Randy said.

"He is. Dad reached out to Mary as well, but she won't have anything to do with him and got angry at me because I didn't cut him off like she did." Dutton sighed. "She blames Dad for the divorce, but Mom always told me that the two of them grew apart. Maybe that's why she acts like she does. Though you got a taste of her—I don't think she really needs a reason." Dutton shook his head and then stood. "I think that's enough of a trip down Depressing Lane." He brought over a few boxes from next to the sofa and set them on the scarred coffee table. "I've got lights and some ornaments. Let's decorate this sucker."

"Are you sure? We could wait until later if you want."

Dutton put on some holiday music, cranked it up, and began swinging that tight butt of his to the music. "It's time to banish what I can't do anything about and bring in some Christmas cheer." He opened the box and began pulling out strings of lights. They were a little tangled, but Randy got to work straightening them out and making sure they worked while Dutton strung them on his tree.

"What do you think?" he asked a few minutes later, stepping back.

"It looks nice." He opened the box of ornaments. Dutton took out a few and placed them gently on the tree.

"These are ones a friend of my grandmother made just after I was born." He seemed to have a story for each one. "Mom got us ornaments each Christmas, and years ago, she separated them out for us." There weren't that many, but Dutton spread them out so the tree looked covered. "I haven't seen some of these in a while since I haven't been putting up a tree." He turned out the overhead lights once he was done, and they sat together on the sofa, listening to the Christmas music.

Randy stood and held out his hand. "My mom taught me to dance to Christmas music when I was a kid." He waited for Dutton to stand before pulling him into his arms. "She always told me that dancing was at its best when you were happy, and nothing made her quite as happy as Christmas songs. And that's still true." He moved with the music, bringing Dutton along with him. "Every year she makes me dance with her."

"I'm not very good at this sort of thing," Dutton said with a stumble.

Randy paused and then began moving again. "Close your eyes, let the music take you, and don't worry about your feet. I'll guide you along." He slowly moved through the room, and Dutton went along with him. "See, that's it. Don't worry about the steps or anything else. Just have fun and follow me."

"Jingle Bell Rock" gave way to "White Christmas," and he took Dutton closer, holding him around the waist as they rocked together slowly. "I always loved this one. I used to watch the movie each year."

"Me too," Randy whispered, and they continued dancing as the songs changed again and again. "This is Christmas."

"Dancing?"

"Happiness, contentment, being with someone you care for. That's what the holidays are about. It isn't the presents or anything else." They picked up the pace as the music changed, but Randy didn't let Dutton go. This was amazing, and he loved having him in his arms. "There's something nice about just being like this."

"Me stepping on your toes?" Dutton teased.

"No. Dancing. It's as intimate as two people can get with their clothes on. There's nothing between you. I can feel your excitement and hear your breathing. Heck, I can even tell if you ate onions. You didn't. Dancing with someone tells a lot about them." He swung Dutton around and then held him close once more. "It takes trust and care… looking out for your partner and listening to them… communicating without saying a word." He grew quiet, gliding Dutton through the open space. Dutton's breathing picked up, and he grew tense. Randy held him tighter and slowed their movements, holding him close and just letting the music, familiar and gentle, wash over them and spread some quiet holiday cheer.

Chapter 5

DANCING. NO one had ever taken him dancing, and even though they never left his tiny apartment, it hardly mattered. As the last in a long line of Christmas songs came to an end, Randy pulled away.

Instantly, Dutton felt the loss of his warmth, and he was tempted to tug him back into his arms. He was also tempted to lead them to his bedroom, but it was too soon. The truth was that Randy was kind and thoughtful, but Dutton wasn't ready to believe it was real. Not yet. It just seemed too good to be true.

"I should go. It's getting late, and I need to help my uncle tomorrow. There's only one more weekend until Christmas, and if he is to have a chance to make the year a success, he's going to need all the help he can get."

Dutton nodded. "Tell your uncle that I can come in to help if he needs it. I'm off tomorrow, and I can stock shelves or clean things up. Stuff like that."

Randy smiled and hugged him. "That's really sweet of you. You need the day to rest because the animals will need you on Monday, though. But if you stop in, maybe I can get a few minutes and we can have some coffee together."

"I'll do that." Dutton was already looking forward to seeing Randy again as he shrugged on his coat and zipped it up. Then, to Dutton's delight, he hugged him tight and kissed him, this time with more heat and, dare he hope, a promise of more to come.

"I'll see you tomorrow." Randy backed away and left the apartment, closing the door quietly after himself.

Dutton waited a few seconds before locking the door and cleaning up the packing material, which he placed back into the ornament boxes before putting them away. Once everything was where it should be, he settled on the sofa, reaching for his phone as it vibrated with a text. He expected to it to be Randy, saying he had made it home, but it was from Mary. He read the first sentence and sighed.

Remember when I was twelve and wanted a new bike, but you got a scooter…?

Dutton scrolled down. The message went on and on—a rant of epic proportions spelling out all her grievances, real and imagined. He didn't bother reading it or responding because he had seen it all before. He skipped to the end, where she actually had the gall to ask for something. Shaking his head, he simply closed the app and set his phone on the coffee table. She was always about old grievances and rehashing slights that never seemed to end. And in her mind, that was the prelude to a request, because she was just crazy enough to think that others would feel guilty… or something.

Dutton remembered that the scooter had been his birthday present, and Mary had been upset because she didn't get presents too. Dutton wished more than anything that Mary would get the help she needed, but as far as he knew, she didn't think anything was wrong. It was always someone else. With a sigh, he put it out of his mind and turned out the lights, put on some Christmas music again, and pretended he was dancing with Randy in order to wash away the worries about his niece and nephew.

DUTTON SLEPT in as best he could, and in the morning, once he had gotten up and could think clearly, he made a small pot of coffee. He'd had a rough night, his mind going in circles about Mary and the kids. There was nothing he could do except try to help as best he could without Mary knowing. He turned to the pile of packages for the kids under the tree and smiled to himself. After finishing his coffee, he got dressed and hurried out of the house and down the street.

The toy store was open, so he went inside and greeted Randy's uncle. "Is Randy here already?"

"In the back." He tilted his head toward the door, and Dutton went through.

"Good morning," Randy said as he looked up from where he was assembling a scooter. Two more sat on the floor nearby. "What's up?"

"Are you the build-it department?" Dutton asked.

Randy shrugged. "We have these still in stock, and Uncle Foster thought they would sell better if they were fully assembled. There's not all that much to it, but parents like to have things ready to go, especially when it gets closer to the holiday and their time seems to get away from them." He set down the wrench. "How are you?"

"Okay." He sat next to Randy. "I thought I'd see about that bag you were talking about and maybe get something else for each of the kids."

Randy put an arm around his shoulders. "The bag I was talking about is behind the counter, and Uncle Foster and I came up with a few smaller things we can put in for them. They came out of the package, so they can't be sold, but we thought they could be added for a little extra fun. They're with the bag too." Randy drew him closer, kissing him gently at first, but the kiss and the feelings deepened quickly, and Dutton found himself pressed harder against Randy's strong chest.

For a minute he lost himself in the taste of Randy on his tongue, the firmness on his hold, and the Christmas carols in the background. All of it seemed surreal, and yet he couldn't help wondering if it was possible that he was going to get what he truly wanted this Christmas. He pulled away, and his head cleared. Dutton chuckled and buried his face against Randy's shoulder when the bell on the front door tinkled softly. "You know, we're making out in the back room of a toy store. And your uncle could come in here at any time."

"I did," Uncle Foster said from the doorway. "And I left again."

Dutton felt his cheeks heat, and he wanted to die of embarrassment.

"Uncle Foster," Randy half whined. "Really?"

"I promised your mother that I'd keep you out of trouble if she let you stay here for the holidays. You know she wanted you to go with them."

Randy rolled his eyes. "Mom has this thing about Disney. She loves to go for the holidays. I've been eight times, I swear. I thought I could stay here and help Uncle Foster with the store and make some money. Instead, I get a busybody uncle who's worse than my mother." He fake glared and then smiled.

"If your mother were here and she saw you making out, you know she'd have a fit." Uncle Foster sighed. "My sister accepts that Randy likes boys, but she's one of those people who doesn't want to see it."

Dutton gasped. "Your mom's a prude?"

Randy hugged his close. "I think every mother is a prude when their child's love life gets too close to home. Mom still thinks of me as a kid, and she probably always will."

"Anyway," Uncle Foster said, "it's getting busy out here. So, Randy, you need to finish up and help me with customers." He left, and Randy's arm slipped away.

"I have to get back to work." He returned his attention to the last scooter and tightened the handlebars. Dutton had never been particularly handy, so he passed him the tools when he asked for them, and once the scooters were ready, they took them out front. Randy placed one in the front window and put the others on top of the shelves to fill up some of the empty space in the store.

Before he knew it, customers started asking Dutton questions, and he found himself helping them without really thinking about it. "Your son is going to love the scooter," he told a lady after she picked out the blue and silver one from the window. He got it and replaced it with one of the red ones, then took the one she'd chosen to the register. When he turned around, he almost bumped into Mary.

She glared at him and backed away. "How are you and the kids?" It was all he could think of to say in that moment. Seeing her was such a surprise.

Mary shook her head, her eyes blazing. "Like you care," she spat and turned away, heading over to one of the shelves. "I have things I need to do." She waved like he was to get away.

Randy's uncle must have heard her and rushed to where Mary seemed to be fuming to herself. He spoke softly, and once Mary gaped at him in shock, she left the store in a huff.

"Wow," Randy said softly.

"Yeah," Dutton answered. For a second it felt like all the air had been sucked out of the room. "Maybe I could understand it if she was super religious or something, but she isn't. This attitude is all on her." He sighed and took a few seconds to get himself together. "I'll be fine. This isn't the first time I've seen her around town, and it probably isn't going to be the last." He blinked and did his best to pull himself out of the moment. "Is there anything we need to do?"

"Yeah," Randy said gently. "I need to help Uncle Foster with this group of customers, and then we can go get coffee." He smiled and hugged Dutton firmly.

Dutton hugged him back. "If anyone had told me in high school that this would happen between us, I would have thought they were crazy."

"This isn't high school any longer," Randy said. "We're out in the real world, and we have to make our own way." He released Dutton and returned to the sales floor.

Dutton sat down and tried to figure out what was going on with his sister, but he soon gave up, because logic just didn't play much of a part in her life at the moment. Dogs were so much easier to understand. They just wanted to be cared for and give love in return.

A soft chime pulled him out of his thoughts, and he pulled his phone from his pocket. Mitchell was scheduled to feed the dogs at the shelter but had been called away on an emergency. Dutton messaged back that he'd do it and then let Randy know before hurrying out of the store.

SOMETHING ABOUT the shelter always calmed him. Even when the dogs were agitated and a dozen of them were barking all at once, it was still a calming place for him, especially as he settled each dog one at a time with a dish of food and a little attention. Soon quiet reigned as the dogs ate. With that complete, Dutton put some of the larger dogs in the runs and got leashes for the smaller ones to take them for walks. They all needed exercise, and Dutton desperately wanted a chance to think.

The last dog he took was Muffy. He walked her around the yard, and once she did her business, he brought her back where it was warm and sat on a bench. Muffy jumped up next to him and pranced over to curl up on his lap.

"Is everything okay?" Mitchell asked as he closed the door.

"Yeah. Just taking a second. They're all fed and exercised. We had a few cage accidents that I cleaned up, but other than that, there are no issues." He held Muffy and closed his eyes.

"What's going on?" Mitchell asked.

"It's nothing. Just stupid family stuff."

"This is Christmas, and there are some things that are certain. There will be lights all over town, we'll eat cookies till we burst, there will be presents, and no matter what, there will be family drama. But don't let that stop you from enjoying everything else."

Maybe that was the issue. "I don't think I know how."

Mitchell chuckled lightly. "Sure you do. Just think back to when you were a kid and how magical the holiday was. Maybe Beau and I have it easy because all we have to do is watch Jessica and we see what Christmas is like for a kid."

Dutton nodded. "Oh, I do that, or at least I try. I haven't had family to celebrate with in a number of years, so the holiday became just another day. One year I went out for Chinese food." It seemed stereotypical, but it was true.

"But things have changed?" Mitchell said, and Dutton nodded. "And you're worried about…?"

"What if I'm just a dud?" He stroked Muffy's fur, and she sighed softly, soaking in the attention.

"At Christmas?" Mitchell seemed surprised.

"Maybe. I mean, if I can't do Christmas, then what about the rest of the year?"

Mitchell gently hugged him. "Dutton… I heard you telling Daniel what you're doing for your niece and nephew, and that is the most Christmassy thing I think I have ever heard of. You don't want them to go without, so you're being their secret Santa."

"Yeah, well…."

Mitchell shook his head. "You can't change the way your sister feels or the way she acts. It just isn't possible. What you can control is what you do for those kids and how you act yourself, and how you feel about a certain guy who was thoughtful enough to adopt a dog for his mom." He winked. "By the way, Muffy is ready to go, and she seems to have made herself at home with you." Mitchell stroked her head gently.

"I keep wondering what's wrong with me," he admitted. "My sister hates me."

"There's nothing wrong with you. Like I said, you can't control your sister, so don't let her control you. Be good to your niece and nephew, or at least as good as you can be, and from there, let yourself be happy." He patted Muffy gently and then stood. "I'll handle the evening feeding tonight."

"I was going to ask how the emergency call went."

"Very well. I had a cat who decided to eat part of a string of Christmas lights, and one of the lights got caught in his throat. I got it out and took an X-ray. I expect the other bits to pass naturally, but we're keeping an eye on him." Mitchell headed for the door. "Take Muffy home and go have yourself some fun." He left the old barn that had been converted into the shelter, and Dutton made sure all the dogs were settled before taking Muffy to the car with him. He messaged Randy to tell him that he was heading to the apartment. Dutton stopped at the pet store to make sure he had everything Muffy was going to need before taking her to her new home.

Chapter 6

"HOW DO you want to deliver the gifts?" Randy asked as he sat on Dutton's sofa. The tree was lit, and Muffy sprawled across their laps like she owned both of them, her tail swishing against Randy's chest. She was definitely one happy dog.

"I don't know. A friend usually did it for me, but this year his kids are old enough that Christmas is a huge deal, so he took the week off. I've been trying to find someone who could do it for me."

"Then we'll do it." Randy grinned. "Mary doesn't know me from Adam, so we'll go on over on the twenty-third to make the delivery. We'll take my car, and I'll be the one to leave the gifts, but you can be there."

Dutton but his lower lip. "Are you sure?"

"Definitely." He squeezed Dutton's hand. "I have to help out Uncle Foster on the twenty-fourth...."

"We can both help him. It's the least I can do after you've both been so good to me. Then you can spend the holiday with your family, and—"

Randy couldn't help kissing Dutton right then. He knew what he was going to say. Dutton would spend the day here, alone. "Uncle Foster usually collapses on the holiday after weeks of running and all the work at the store. And my parents are in Florida, so maybe you and I can spend the holiday together." He smiled, and Dutton leaned against him.

Dutton tensed for a second. "Are you sure?"

"Yeah." He got out his phone, put on some Christmas music, and shifted enough that Muffy climbed off their laps. Then he tugged Dutton to his feet and they danced slowly in the living room. "I mean it. No one should spend the holiday alone. My Aunt Alice, Uncle Foster's wife, invited me for dinner that evening, and she told me to bring a friend if I wanted. So we can have dinner there and come back here afterwards." He lightly kissed the back of Dutton's neck, and Dutton groaned softly, stretching to give him more access.

"That's good."

"The kissing or the plans?" Randy asked.

"Both," Dutton answered, and Randy smiled to himself as he ran his hand down Dutton's back. "It's been a while since I had anywhere to go for the holidays, and I really like the idea of eating something not frozen." "Greensleeves" ended, and "Rudolph" started to play. Dutton began to sing along, and soon Randy joined in. His singing voice was awful, but Dutton and Muffy didn't seem to mind, though the dog watched them both like they were crazy. "I think this is already the best holiday I've had in a long time."

"Good, because there's more where that came from." Randy felt on top of the world at the moment, and he spun Dutton around, loving the smile and the sparkle in his eyes. Once the song ended and "Frosty" began, they sang along to that as well. If happiness was catching, then it seemed like Dutton had finally gotten a good dose of it.

"I SHOULD go," Randy said a few hours later. The room had grown warmer as the evening progressed, or it could simply have been Dutton in his arms, the heat from his body and his rich scent, sending Randy into overdrive.

Dutton pulled him closer and kissed him hard. "You could stay," he whispered.

At first Randy wasn't sure he'd heard him over the music. When he realized what he'd said, he very nearly agreed, but he pulled back. "I don't think that's a good idea."

"Oh," Dutton said softly, pulling away. He reached for his phone and switched off the music, plunging the room into silence. Muffy raised her head from where she'd been sleeping on the side of the sofa. "I guess…." Dutton's cheeks pinked, and he turned away before picking up the glasses off the coffee table. "God, I feel so stupid." He strode away into the kitchen.

Randy followed him, catching up as Dutton placed the dishes in the sink. "I didn't mean it that way." He paused. "I know it may sound stupid, but I don't want to rush things. I did a lot of foolish things when I was an undergrad. I slept with just about everyone who was interested, and many times I woke up in the morning in strange beds, or in my own… alone. I figure that since I want something different this time, I should act differently." He had made plenty of mistakes, and the worst had been Anson Fields. "I don't want to mess this up."

Dutton slowly turned around.

"I had a college boyfriend. It started out as a one-night stand, and I suppose that's what it was… only it lasted four months, and I thought Anson loved me."

"I'm sorry," Dutton said softly.

"I was really just someone who looked good when we went out. He got bored fast, and while I thought we were dating, he thought we were just fuck buddies." Randy swallowed hard. "I don't want to make those same mistakes. I always jumped into bed first and then tried to get to know the guy, which doesn't really work. This time I want to do things right." He slipped his arms around Dutton's waist. "Which is why I need to go, because otherwise I'll slip back into old patterns." He kissed Dutton hard, leaving them both breathless and Randy's eyes rolling. His willpower was already weakening, and he backed away and left the kitchen. Dutton's eyes drew him in—and those damned kissable lips that he wanted another taste of. His heart raced, and he knew he had to leave now or he wasn't going to. "So I'll be a gentleman and leave right now before I change my mind." His breathing was already heavy, his resolve hanging by a thread.

"Oh. I thought…."

Randy smiled. "I know what you thought, and it couldn't be further from the truth. You just test my resolve, but you deserve to be treated better than hurrying off to bed."

"And I thought I was the only one being tested." Dutton's eyes seemed to boggle. "I've never asked anyone to stay overnight here. I haven't in a long time."

Randy lightly stroked Dutton's soft hair. "I never thought you did. I want to get to know you, take you out to dinner, date you properly. You deserve to be treated that way." He closed his eyes, pulling on his last reserves. Randy had always prided himself on his self-control, but Dutton seemed to get past it very easily. "I have to help Uncle Foster for the next few days, and I'm sure you'll be busy at the clinic and the rescue. The holidays are busy for everyone. But I'll call you, and we can arrange to play Santa for your niece and nephew, I promise." He kissed those plump lips once more before leaving the apartment and heading home, knowing he had done the right thing and hoping Dutton understood.

DECEMBER 23 was as busy at the store as Randy had ever seen it. Every last-minute shopper seemed to be frantically searching for that perfect gift. He and his uncle did their best for each of them, and Randy was never so happy as when Uncle Foster locked the front door and flipped the sign to Closed. They were only open until two the following day, and then the retail holiday season would be over for them. "Are you going to be visiting Dutton?"

"Yeah. He and I have a job we need to do tonight."

His uncle smiled. "Delivering the gifts?"

"Yeah. And I asked Dutton to Christmas dinner." He figured since Christmas was at his uncle's house this year, he probably already knew, but still….

"Of course you did. Now go on and get yourself a nice dinner. I'm going home to put my feet up and try to sleep a little. I'll see you tomorrow."

Randy left the store with the last things he had for Dutton and hurried over to his building. As he climbed the stairs, he heard Muffy bark a couple of times. When Randy opened the door, Dutton hugged him tight, with Muffy dancing around his legs. "I got everything ready to go."

"And I found out through a cousin that your sister and the kids don't have plans for tonight. They'll be at home, so we need to wait up until late to make sure they're all in bed. Then we can head over and leave the gifts." He kissed Dutton, who then stepped back. "I see you decided to decorate a little more."

"I found some decorations that Mom gave me a few years ago. I didn't think I had them any longer, but I found them in a box in the closet. Mom made the snowman in a ceramics class. She made one for Mary too." Dutton grinned at it, and Randy slipped his hand under his shirt. Dutton was warm and felt good on his skin.

Dutton turned slowly. "You know, we have a few hours before we can deliver the gifts."

Randy let his hand set where it was. "Yes. You and I need to get something to eat, and then I have a surprise for you: a whole set of

Christmas movies guaranteed to make even the biggest Scrooge combust with the holiday spirit."

DINNER AT Café Belgie was wonderful, and when they got back, Dutton turned off the lights, except for the tree, and made some popcorn. Once they settled on the sofa with Muffy, Randy put on the first movie.

"I think I'm seeing the theme of the night," Dutton said when the opening credits for The Santa Clause began to play. They settled in for a quiet evening, with Dutton nodding off next to Randy once the credits rolled for the second movie in the series.

"It's getting late. We should get everything ready and load my car."

Dutton nodded. "I'm nervous. Ashley always did this in the middle of the night, and there was no way Mary was going to recognize him. But…."

Randy nestled closer. "I can do it. Just give me the address, and I'll take the gifts and come back here."

"No. I should go and see this through." He paused, biting his lower lip. "At least I know they'll have a nice Christmas." Dutton got up, and Randy did as well, and Dutton turned off the television. Randy made sure that each package was property tagged in his handwriting. Then he carefully put them into the large red cloth bag before following Dutton out of the apartment and down the stairs.

Chapter 7

DUTTON FELT a little like Santa, especially after watching those movies. Randy carefully put the bag into the back seat of his car, and they drove to where Dutton's sister lived. It was a small house out in the alphabet avenues. The snow that had started earlier had picked up and was now coming down heavily. As Randy drove, Dutton sat quietly, the car blazing a trail down the snow-covered street.

Randy put on holiday music, and it soothed Dutton somewhat, but he was still nervous. "Which house is it?" He continued slowly forward.

"That one right there." He pointed to a small white house with a crooked snowman half melted in the front yard.

Randy pulled into an empty parking space and turned out the lights. Dutton lowered the windows to listen. The neighborhood was quiet, and the house had no light in the windows. Many of the others on the street had Christmas lights reflecting in the snow, but not Mary's.

"I'm going to get out and take the gifts up to the porch. You stay here." Randy got out and opened the back car door before lifting out the bag. He crossed the street and made his way up the front walk, nearly slipping as he went.

"Dutton?" a woman asked as she approached the car. For a second Dutton thought it was Mary, but then she came closer.

"Do I know you?" He swallowed hard.

"I'm Rachel, Randy's cousin. My kids play with your niece and nephew. And don't worry, I understand all about Mary and her issues. Most of us on the block do what we can for those kids." Her knowing, gentle gaze told him that she truly got it. "Uncle Foster told me that you guys would be making the Santa delivery." She smiled and handed him a thermal cup. "I figured you could use something warm."

"Thank you." He turned as Randy placed the bag up against the house, next to the door. Then he made a return trip down the walk and across the street. "Are Todd and Cassie okay?"

Rachel patted his arm. "They are adorable kids. The neighborhood tends to look out for them, and we do what we can. Mary always thought that the gifts and packages were from one of us or some community agency. None of us have fessed up, but we haven't denied it either."

Randy got back in the car and started the engine.

"Didn't think you'd be playing Santa, did you?" Rachel asked Randy.

"Nope." He reached over and squeezed Dutton's leg, heat racing from the touch to the rest of him. "I think this is the most Christmassy thing I've done in years."

Rachel nodded. "And don't worry. None of us are going to give it away." She handed Randy a cup as well and then stepped away from the car. "You both have a good night and a great holiday." She walked back down the sidewalk, and Dutton leaned back, closing his eyes. At least the kids were okay. His throat ached as Randy pulled away and they slowly made their way back to Dutton's apartment.

Dutton didn't want to ask Randy to stay again, but Dutton didn't want to be alone. Randy parked the car and got out, then followed Dutton up the stairs. Dutton expected him to say good night the way he had the last time they spent the evening together, but once the door was closed, Randy held him tight. Dutton clung to him, wishing things in his life could have been different.

"Do you want to go to bed?" Randy asked, and Dutton nodded. He felt wrung out with relief that Todd and Cassie had people looking out for them, and sadness because he wished he could be one of them. Randy followed him to the bedroom and closed the door behind them.

They undressed, and Randy climbed into bed. Dutton did the same, and Randy held him tightly. "Did you mean what you said?"

"About what?" Randy asked.

"Tonight being the most Christmassy thing you ever did?"

Randy held him tighter. "Are you kidding? I got to play Santa." He smoothed a patch of hair out of Dutton's eyes. "I think I'll always love you for that."

Dutton swallowed hard. "You love me?"

Randy smiled with just enough light for Dutton to see it. "How could I not? You're the kindest, gentlest, and most caring man I've ever met. Hell, you're those kids' secret Santa." He kissed Dutton hard.

Dutton chuckled. "I love you too," he whispered, almost afraid of the words, but Randy kissed him again, and all doubt slipped away. Maybe Randy was his gift this year. Dutton sure hoped so. He closed his arms around Randy, holding him in the darkness. "And you were the real Santa. After all, you delivered the gifts."

Randy paused. "Then you're the Secret Guncle."

"Just as long as the Secret Guncle gets the Secret Santa."

"Always," Randy whispered before kissing away anything more that Dutton had to say.

Epilogue

UNCLE FOSTER—AS he'd told Dutton to call him—refilled his glass of sparkling wine for the second time. The house smelled amazing, the tree was huge, and happiness seemed to fill every inch of space. Picky and Muffy lay together on the floor, because apparently at Randy's family gatherings, dogs were included.

Randy's aunt worked in the kitchen, occasionally bringing out fresh plates of snacks and treats, looking at the three men like they were supposed to finish them off before the next round. Everything was danged near perfect. He had talked to his dad in California, wishing his family a Merry Christmas, and now it seemed it was time to get down to some serious imbibing of the Christmas cheer.

Randy sat next to him, holding his hand as It's A Wonderful Life played on the television, coming up to the point where the angel gets his wings. "This has been almost perfect."

"I know." Randy squeezed his hand as his phone chimed. Randy pulled it out. "It's from Rachel. She says I'm supposed to show you this."

Dutton leaned over as Randy started the video. His niece and nephew sat on the living room floor.

"Open what Santa brought you," Mary said from off camera. The kids began unwrapping the gifts he and Randy had picked out and wrapped, squealing their delight. Dutton's throat ached as he smiled, watching as the kids held up what they got, Todd doing a little dance when he peered into the bag of Legos. Cassie opened the easel, her hands shaking as she showed it to her mom. "Santa knew, he knew," was all she said.

Dutton sniffed as the video came to an end.

Randy sent him the video and then put his phone away. "It seems that Operation Secret Guncle was a big success. And the kids really seemed to get what they wanted."

Dutton leaned over to kiss Randy. "So did I."

Randy smiled, lightly cupping Dutton's cheek. "Me too." A truly happy Christmas.

ANDREW GREY

Frosty

THE
SCHNAUZER

A MUST L♥VE D🐾GS COMPANION STORY

For Sasha and her Mama Karen and Papa Martin.

Prologue

HE LIED. The breeder man lied to my first family. Lies smell bad, and the breeder man really stunk. Even as a puppy, I could tell. I didn't know what the lie was, but I was happy to get away from him.

I liked my first family. They were nice and gave me good food to eat, and I used to stretch to climb up on the couch. Mom Violet would lift me up and hold me. I used to lick her face, and I was really happy.

Then I grew and got bigger and bigger, and I could get up on the couch all by myself. I used to like to sit on Mom Violet's lap, but then I got too big and heavy, and it was all kind of "no, don't do that," or "bad dog." I hated the last one most of all because it made Dad Charles smell like the stinky breeder man, and his voice got really mean and I wanted to hide.

But still I grew and explored the house we lived in with the small yard full of flowers and places to dig. There were so many flowers and great smells, and I wanted to find them all and keep the house safe, but all I got was more "bad dog" and Mom Violet upset as she put the flowers back.

Then one day I heard them talking, though they were so quiet. Mom Violet was upset, and I did my best to comfort her. I sat next to her chair and rested my chin on her lap. She petted me, and I closed my eyes, wanting her to feel better. I didn't move, not even when there was someone coming up the walk. I knew I had to be good and not bark or anything. After a while, Mom Violet didn't feel better, but she put the leash on me like we were going for a walk. I loved walks and all the smells. It was my favorite time of the day. She opened the door and then took me to the car. I was excited. I loved the car—getting to see things and go places and smell all the new smells, especially the country kinds of smells.

When we stopped and got out, there were lots of other dogs. Some of them barked and yipped to play, and I really wanted to. Mom Violet took me inside a building, and she talked to a man for a while. I did my best to be good, but there were so many other dogs to say hello to, and I was so happy to get to play. Then the man she was talking to took my leash, and he led me back to the other dogs. I was so excited and thought it was going to be fun puppy time.

I was wrong. He put me in a big cage all alone, away from everyone else. I had food and water but no other dogs to sniff and smell, and worst of all, Mom Violet was gone. I lay awake all night, watching the door, waiting for Mom Violet to come and get me. But she never came back.

Chapter 1

"I KNOW. I remember. I'm on my way there right now. Would I disappoint my only niece? And just for the record, it's snowing like hell out here, so remember that the next time I ask you for something." Riley was about to end the call.

"Will that be tomorrow or the day after?" Davis teased.

Riley suppressed the biting retort at the tip of his tongue. "Yeah, look who thinks he's funny," he said instead, borrowing a line from their mother, who had passed away two years ago, leaving each other and Davis's wife and child as their only remaining family. Davis had married just out of college. Less than a year later, he and Stephanie had a daughter, Lilly, now six. Since then they had been trying for a second child, with no luck yet. Though Davis admitted that he was enjoying their efforts. Each time he said it, Stephanie would shrug and then blush big-time. "Seriously, I need to get off the phone so I can pick up Lilly's birthday present and get back there in time."

"Fine. Be safe," Davis said, and the call ended just as the wind blew a wall of white in front of the car.

Riley slowed even further, waiting for it to clear. He was about to turn around when lights shone on the right. He passed a house all lit up with enough twinkle lights to be seen for miles. At the next drive just past it, he turned into a small yard. Riley came to an abrupt halt as a damned lion materialized out of the snow. He thought he had to be seeing things, but no, it was a lion. Riley stared at it through the windshield, and then it turned and went back inside the shelter.

"What the heck?" Riley asked out loud to no one in particular as a man came out of the shelter to greet him. He mustn't have been able to hide his surprise.

"Oh, you met King," he said, chuckling. "Don't worry. He's in an enclosure of his own."

Riley nodded. "Why is he here?"

"I never let an animal suffer for any reason," he said. "I'm Mitchell, and this is my shelter. I'm also a vet, and to answer your question, I got a call a week ago about King here. Someone decided he'd make a good pet, but when he got too big, they just let him go. I had to sedate him to get him here." They both turned toward the now-empty enclosed area. "I have heat lamps inside for him, so he's plenty warm in there."

"But what will you do with him?"

"He's being sent to a zoo just as soon as the weather breaks. I'd love to be able to return him to the wild, but he wasn't raised that way and would never be able to survive." He didn't smile, and his eyes were tinged with sadness. "At least he'll have a good life and will be well cared for." Riley didn't know what to say and stood silently until the wind picked up and Mitchell motioned to the door. "You must be here to pick up Lilly's birthday present."

"Yup." His brother and sister-in-law had picked out just the dog, but she needed to be spayed, and they wanted her to be a surprise.

"Then come on in while I get Princess." Mitchell let him go inside first and closed the door behind them. The old barn was solid and surprisingly warm. The barks and yips of the dogs greeted him excitedly.

While he waited, Riley wandered through, looking at the various enclosures. Some dogs came up to greet him, tails wagging, eyes bright, while others stayed back. One even growled.

"Don't mind him. He's hurting. Whoever had him treated this little guy pretty badly." Mitchell knelt down and spoke softly. "Didn't they? Well, you know I'd never do that, don't you?" He continued speaking softly, and damned if the dog didn't come up to Mitchell, who lifted him gently, stroking his back. "Some of their stories will rip your heart out. I started the shelter as an offshoot of my veterinary practice because people would bring in dogs I could save and ask me to put them to sleep. I couldn't do that, so I started the shelter to give them a place to rest and heal. At least that was my initial thought. Since then I have rescued hundreds of dogs and found them good homes." He held the small dog so gently.

"He really seems to love you," Riley said.

"I know. And one of our dogs passed away a few weeks ago. I'd love to take Ralphy here home, but we have a daughter, and I don't know how well he'd do with her or the other dogs. But I have a lady who is interested in this little guy. She lives alone, and I know they get along.

So I'm giving him a chance to heal a little more before placing him with her." Mitchell gently placed Ralphy back in his enclosure and closed the door.

Riley turned down the aisle across from Ralphy, which held the larger dogs. He approached one cage with a nearly all-black dog. He checked for a name tag. "Frederica." Riley watched as the black beauty sat down, tail whirling she was so excited, and pressed her nose right against the wire. When Riley put his hand close, she licked it and stood. Damn, she was big, but those eyes. He stared into them for a minute.

"She's another hard story. This older couple got her from a breeder out in Lancaster." Mitchell looked like he'd eaten something bad. "The place was a puppy mill, and the owner said that she was a miniature schnauzer puppy. As you can see, she's a full-size mix, and she turned out to be way too much dog for the couple, so they brought her here." The hurt in Mitchell's voice echoed through Riley's head. "She needs a place with plenty of space so she can run and use up her energy."

"I bet you do," Riley said to the dog, receiving more licks through the cage. Riley watched her, biting his lower lip. She was a gorgeous dog and incredibly affectionate. He understood why Davis and Stephanie wanted a small dog for Lilly. It made sense. But growing up, they had always had full-size dogs. Riley remembered their collie, Shawn. That dog would play frisbee until he collapsed. He never gave up and was always so ready to play.

"Anyway, Princess is right over here." Michell led Riley up to the front, where a dog carrier sat near the door. "She's all set to go."

Riley peeked inside and was met with the cutest face, a pink tongue, and big dark eyes that blinked back at him. "Do we need to bring the carrier back?"

"No. That's Princess's. Your brother bought it for when they could bring her home." He handed Riley some forms and asked him to sign that he was taking Princess.

"Thank you for this. Lilly is going to be so thrilled."

"You're welcome. You drive carefully on your way back to town. I only have to go next door." Mitchell leaned down. "And you be a good girl and enjoy your new forever family. I'll see you when they bring you in for checkups." He smiled and straightened up again. "Have a great holiday."

"You too," Riley said, leaving the warmth of the barn and stepping out into the snowy early evening. He hurried to the car and got Princess inside out of the wind. Then he started the engine and got the car warming up. The snow was still falling quickly as he put the car in gear, turned around, and headed back toward Carlisle.

"You okay, girl?" Riley asked after they had gone about half a mile. Princess whined softly and then grew quiet. "I know." He smiled to himself as he remembered Frederica's amazing black eyes and expressive face. He swore he could see Frederica deflate and the joy go out of her when he turned away. That was a dog that deserved a forever home. "Dammit." He pulled to a stop and turned into a partially plowed driveway. He nearly got stuck before he managed to back out again and turn around.

He made his way back to the shelter, pulling into the yard as Mitchell pulled the barn door closed. "Did you forget something?"

Riley smiled. "More like someone." He left the engine running and got out. Mitchell opened the door, and Riley walked right up to Frederica's enclosure.

"I thought I saw that spark between you," Mitchell said as he opened the enclosure door. Frederica came right out and up to him. She bounded around and then sat at his feet for about three seconds before bouncing on her front feet. "In schnauzer, that's 'I'm excited you came back, I love you,' and all those excited, happy doggie feelings."

"She's sweet, but she's so big."

"That's true. She's just over a year old, so she isn't going to get any bigger, and she's wonderful with kids. With some training and attention, she'll be a really good dog, but she hasn't had any up until now. She is housebroken, but that's about all. When she got big, her previous owners gave up on her and tried to make her act like a small dog, which didn't work at all. I will tell you that she gets wound up sometimes, but all she really needs is plenty of exercise and activity."

"That I can do. Most of the year I ride my bike four to five miles a day. Maybe she'd be able to run along with me once she's trained. Exercise isn't an issue. And I have a yard that was fenced by the previous owners for their dog, so she'll have a place to run outside too."

"Okay. If you're serious, I have some paperwork for you to fill out, and there is a small charge to help cover the costs for the shelter." Mitchell seemed excited. "I'm setting aside my usual requirements because of your brother and because I have a really good feeling about you. I also have a really good dog trainer who I've worked with in the past. He's good with both the dogs and the owners, because most of the time when a dog misbehaves, it's the owner's fault." Mitchell continued talking as Riley filled out the form and paid the fee. Then Mitchell gave him a leash and some of the basic dog supplies before walking him out to the car.

Fortunately the wind had died down and the snow had let up, so he was easily able to get Frederica into the back seat. Instantly she tried jumping up front, but Riley was firm and got her to settle in back. He figured he'd set expectations right away—or at least try.

He pulled out of the drive and back on the road as his phone rang. "Where are you?" Davis asked through the Bluetooth connection.

"I'm on my way. It took a little longer at the shelter that I expected, but I should be there in about ten minutes or so. I'll see you then." He hung up and continued driving, the blowing snow becoming less and less prevalent the closer he got to town. By the time he arrived at his brother's, the snow had stopped. He parked out front, and Davis hurried out and opened the back door.

"This isn't Princess, unless someone blew her up," Davis said flatly.

Riley lifted out the carrier and brought it around to his brother. "Here's Lilly's dog. This one is mine." He snapped on the lead and brought Frederica along with him.

"You got a dog?" Davis asked, skepticism dripping off his tongue.

"Yeah, I did." He patted his dog's head, and she leaned against his leg. "Why don't you go inside and take Lilly her birthday present? I don't want to steal your thunder. I'm going to take her for a walk and let her do her business, and I'll be back in a few minutes." He led his dog away and down the sidewalk, where she sniffed at everything and pulled on the leash like it was the devil itself.

"Settle down," Riley said firmly, and she stopped and looked at him with those big doggie eyes before continuing on. They walked to the end of the block and then turned, making it around the entire block before returning to Davis's home. He went inside and was greeted by Lilly with a grin.

"Did you get me a dog too?" she asked.

"No. You have Princess, and I think that's enough for you right now. This is Frederica, and you can play with her when you come to my house."

She made a face. "Fred… who? It's a yucky name." There was no beating around the bush with her. "You need to get her a better name."

Riley took off his coat and brought his dog inside. She settled near the sofa right on the floor. "Then what should we call her?" He wasn't particularly inclined to have a girl named Fred.

"I don't know. Pickles?" she asked.

"I don't think so. I don't like pickles." It was one of his food issues. Pickles and olives—he hated them both.

Lilly put her finger to her mouth. "I know—Frosty."

Riley was floored. "Why Frosty? She's black, and she doesn't have a button nose or two eyes made out of coal."

She shrugged. "Frosty. It's a nice name. And she's nice like Frosty." She hugged the dog, who sat down and soaked in the attention.

"But…."

Lilly looked up at him with that same stare her father had perfected years ago. "Frosty." She hugged the dog once more and then ran out of the room, calling for Frosty, and damn it all if the big black schnauzer didn't follow right behind her like it was exactly what she wanted to be named.

"Great," Riley huffed as Stephanie came into the room and pressed a mug of coffee in his hand.

"You know you are never going to win against her. She is as stubborn as her father and too damned cute to say no to. It's a deadly combination, and I pity your brother when she gets older." She sat down. "What made you decide to get a dog?"

"I guess I looked into her eyes and saw myself reflected back. She's been through a lot and was given up because she got too big." It was like the dog didn't exactly fit the mold and she was rejected for it. Riley knew how that felt… in spades. "What I didn't expect was to end up with Frosty the Schnauzer."

Lilly ran back into the room with Frosty, Princess following right behind. Princess jumped onto the sofa and into Stephanie's arms, and Frosty slid on the rug, thumping the couch to come to a stop before trying to follow the small dog onto Stephanie's already full lap. Riley was definitely going to need to contact that dog trainer—and fast.

Chapter 2

"HAVE YOU had a dog before?" the man with the caramel-smooth voice asked as Riley looked down at Frosty spread out across the kitchen floor. She was finally resting, but he knew that was going to come to an end soon enough and then she would be up, full of energy, and ready to go again.

"Yes. When I was growing up. But I haven't had one this size before, and she's a bundle of energy. Not that she's destructive or mean. She…." He didn't know quite how to put it.

"She needs an outlet for all her energy," the trainer supplied.

"Yes. Exactly. I walk her two times a day and let her run and get some of it out. But then she'll sit next to my chair while I'm working and want constant attention, and I do have to be able to work." He wasn't sure what he was going to do.

"Okay. I think I can help. You said that Mitchell gave you my contact information, so I take it you got your dog from the shelter and that she's still a puppy?" Dang, that voice wrapped around him like a warm blanket on a cold day.

"Yeah. Mitchell thought she was about a year old," Riley supplied. He had had her a week, and Frosty seemed to be settling in. She played with her toys, and Riley got her plenty of things to chew. She hadn't decided to gnaw on the furniture or poop in the house. They had had one accident, but that had been Riley's fault for not letting her out in time, and even then she had looked so ashamed of what she'd done, it had been cute. But when he left the house, Frosty would whimper and cry before he got to the door, and once he left, she barked. That had to stop, or his neighbors were going to complain, and he didn't want that.

"Why don't you come over about six tonight? I have your number and I'll text you the address. We can go over some basic things and get both of you started." Riley's phone dinged with an address. "Don't worry. There isn't anything wrong with your dog. We just need to give her a little structure and let her know that she can rely on you."

"Okay." Riley hoped that was all it was, but he suspected those things were a lot more easily said than done.

WAYNE CHECKED the time and gulped down the last bite of his sandwich before getting up from his tiny table and pulling on his coat. The guy he was supposed to meet would be here soon, and he wanted to be ready. From what Riley had said, Frosty was a big dog, so working with her outside shouldn't be a problem. He went down the stairs and out the front door of his upstairs duplex rental and onto the porch as a small car pulled up out front.

Fortunately the snow that had threatened all day hadn't made an appearance and the clouds overhead were just starting to clear, the setting sun turning them pink and red. A slight man got out and walked around the car before opening the back door. Almost before he could grab the leash, a huge black dog bounded out. He tried to get control of the dog, but she was way too excited and raced over, doing that schnauzer excited bounce with her front paws. "I'm sorry. I took her for a walk, but she's all wound up and…." The dog wound the leash around his legs to the point the guy was about to fall over.

"Sit." Someone must have tried to train her in the past, because that doggie butt went right down, tail swishing like mad. "Okay. Let's get you unwound and then we can go to the backyard," Wayne said gently.

"I'm sorry about this." He got himself untangled and held the leash tightly. "I'm Riley, Riley Whitehall, and this is Frosty." Wayne must have seemed confused, because Riled smiled and went on to explain. "The night I brought her home, I was with my niece, and she named her. Lilly can be a force to be reckoned with."

"So you have a black schnauzer named Frosty."

"Yeah. Her old name was Frederica, which she ignores. But she responds to Frosty, so I'm not going to fight it." Riley had amazing blue eyes, though they seemed tired, and he was frazzled around the edges, which wasn't helping his relationship with his dog.

"That's best." Wayne held out his hand. "I'm Wayne Smith." They shook hands as Frosty's patience ran out and she hurried to him, wanting pets. "Let's get her in the yard and we can start."

"I know she needs a lot of work."

Wayne opened the gate and let both of them through before closing it behind them. "She isn't going to be able to get out, so you can let her loose while we talk a few minutes." It would probably be best if she ran out some of the energy before they started working. "And Frosty is a puppy, and like a lot of rescue dogs, she has a certain amount of separation anxiety. After all, she was given up before. She probably wonders if you're going to do the same thing."

"If you're sure," Riley said, and Wayne nodded. He unclipped the leash, and Frosty took off to check out the yard.

"There isn't anything she can hurt or that will harm her. I work hard to make the yard a safe place." He motioned to two of the chairs, and they sat down. "Tell me about how you got her and why."

Riley turned toward him, pushing his hood away from his face, showing Wayne his eyes and angled jawline for the first time. Wow, he was shy and gorgeous at the same time. "Growing up we always had a dog. My brother and I, that is. But since then neither of us have had one." He sighed softly. "Anyway, my brother Davis and his wife decided to get a dog for Lilly, my niece, and since it was supposed to be a surprise, they asked me to pick it up for them, and well...." He lifted his gaze to where Frosty was sniffing at one of the fence poles.

"And you fell in love," Wayne supplied.

Riley nodded and swallowed hard. "She is so pretty, and she's really sweet, but she thinks she's a lapdog and wants to be held and stuff."

Knowing they were talking about her, Frosty loped over and placed her head in Riley's lap. He petted her gently. It was clear the two of them had bonded already, which was a good thing and told him a lot about Riley.

"How about we get to work. The first thing to know is that it's your fault. If something is wrong, it's often because you aren't listening to what she's telling you. Remember that Frosty is a dog, and they are all about instinct. Their behavior is pretty basic. If they are prowling the kitchen, getting into the trash, then chances are they're either hungry or bored. Make sure that the trash can is empty before you leave her alone. If she's drinking out of the toilet, make sure to close the lid and that her water bowl is full. She's still a puppy and has a ton of energy."

"That I know, and she's really affectionate," Riley said, leaning close with a warm smile that touched Wayne's heart in a way he hadn't expected. "And most of the time she's sweet, but she's also all over the place, and I don't know how to teach her the basic things. Mom did a lot of the training when I was a kid."

"That's what I can help you with," Wayne said and got up. Riley did the same, and they spent a few minutes going over harnesses and collars for Frosty and what was the best kind to use in each situation. Then Wayne got Frosty set up and guided the two of them through some basic lessons.

Frosty was a smart girl and learned the basic commands very quickly. "Sit," Riley said, and Frosty looked at him but did nothing.

"You don't need to yell, but remember that you're the one in control," Wayne prompted, and when Riley was firmer, that doggie butt went right down. "Excellent. Now praise her." Riley's smile was amazing, warm enough to cut through the chill. And when Riley straightened up and adjusted his collar, Wayne noticed the rainbow flag pin and smiled to himself. Unlike most of his friends, Wayne had terrible gaydar. Others described a fluttery feeling in their belly when they met someone they thought might be interested, but Wayne never got that. Maybe he was just oblivious, but knowing that the hunk of cuteness batted for the same team that he did had Wayne's pulse racing a little faster.

"Is this right?" Riley asked, pulling Wayne out of his momentary daydream.

"It's great. She's looking at you like you hung the moon." Wayne smiled as Frosty sat and stayed there for ten whole seconds. "Now get her to lie down." Frosty went down, and Riley praised her big-time. She jumped right up, licking his face. Riley told her to sit, and she did it right away.

"She's doing so well," Wayne said as the lights came on in yard. The sun was fading really fast. "Just keep working with her on those basic commands. You can't do everything all at once. But praise her when she does good, scold in a lower tone of voice when she's bad." Riley continued working with Frosty, and at about seven, Wayne called it for the evening.

"Is that all there is?" Riley asked.

"You have to start somewhere. Once she gets the basics, then we can work with leash training and other behaviors. The biggest thing is to make a start." He smiled, and for a second their gazes met. Riley told Frosty to sit, and she did. "I think you're going to have a really good dog. She wants to please you and doesn't seem stubborn, which can be a really hard trait to work with."

"I want her to be happy. It's just the two of us right now, and she's really good company."

Wayne nodded. "I get that. My Buster is my companion. He's a Boston terrier." He sat back down, and Riley did as well, Frosty sitting right next to her owner. "When my last relationship ended, the only thing we fought about was Buster. Mike tried to say that Buster was half his. It got really messy for a while. But in the end, I'd paid for him and I had the receipt and stuff, but it felt like a betrayal, you know? I don't think of Buster as property. I work for the state and I can work from home three days a week. He keeps me company and makes sure that I don't turn into a hermit. I think of him as a companion. It feels strange to think about owning him that way."

Riley nodded. "Most of the time I think Frosty believes that I belong to her." His smile said that he didn't really mind that, especially when he knelt to give her a good scratch.

Wayne chuckled. "Yeah. Buster is the same way. He didn't like my ex much, which is probably a sign that I should have run for the hills. Dogs are good judges of character." Frosty leaned against Riley's leg, and Riley gently reached down and stroked her head. "Come on inside. It's getting cold out here, and we've been out for a while." He led them up the outside stairs and in through the back door to his toasty kitchen. Being upstairs, this house always seemed warm. In the winter it was great, but in the summer, his air-conditioning bill was something else.

"This is really nice," Riley said, holding Frosty's leash tightly as Buster came up. Wayne watched as the two greeted each other, and then once the sniffing and tail wagging were over, Buster sat on the kitchen floor. "Are you sure it's okay to let her off leash? She can be a little energetic."

"Sure," Wayne said, and Riley released Frosty, who went up to Buster with her usual energy. Buster simply blinked at her and lay down. Frosty blinked back like she was confused and then did the same. "He may be small, but this is his house and he rules the roost."

Riley chuckled as Wayne set about making cocoa. He loved the scent of the stuff. Nothing else said warm and cozy on a cold day the way hot chocolate did. "I see you're ready for Christmas."

Wayne led the way into the living room. "I always put up a tree. Not a really big one. Buster loves the lights and likes to sleep under it sometimes. He never bothers it at all. I think it gives him the feeling of some hunting dogs past. Who knows." He offered Riley a seat. "Maybe I'm trying to put too many human emotions on him."

"I find myself doing the same thing," Riley said softly after sitting down. "I know she doesn't go around wondering about the mysteries of life or worry about ex-boyfriends and stuff. But I know she feels happy, especially at dinnertime and when she bounces. But I also know she gets scared, like the way she won't leave my side when she thinks I'm going to go out without her. I keep hoping that will pass when I keep coming home." He sipped from the mug that his ex, Mike, had given Wayne in his stocking last year. He hadn't thought much about it, but suddenly the whole ugly breakup situation seemed to be rearing its head.

"It most likely will. Just give her a little time." They said that time healed everything, and Wayne sure as hell hoped so, but sometimes he wished that it would hurry up and do its job. He was tired of being lonely and angry. He needed a chance to move on.

"It always comes down to that," Riley said, and Wayne nodded as they both sipped their cocoa.

"Yeah. It sucks." He couldn't believe he said that to someone he barely knew.

"The ex?" Riley asked.

Wayne nodded. "You don't need to hear about all that." God. He never talked about Mike with anyone—not at work, and definitely not with the rest of his family, who had never liked him. And once they found out Mike was gone, they used it as a chance to say I told you so. At least they were in Arizona and he didn't have to endure their lack of support face to face.

The dogs came into the room, with Frosty putting her head in Riley's lap for pets. Buster jumped up into Wayne's lap and settled. Frosty then jumped onto the sofa and tried to climb into Riley's lap. It was so cute. She ended up sprawled out on the sofa with her paws and head in his lap. "Look what you did," Wayne told Buster, who blinked at him.

"I never had much in the way of boyfriends or anything," Riley said. "I didn't feel like I fit in, so I stayed on the sidelines I guess. I always figured there would be time for stuff like that once I got through college." He sipped the cocoa and then petted Frosty, who lay there soaking up the attention. "I didn't count on how hard it would be to meet people after college, you know? I don't go to bars, and I'm not going to use Grindr or one of those other apps." He sat back.

"I get it. I met Mike at a Pride event a couple years ago and we hit it off... or at least I thought we did. Sometimes I wonder if he really cared about me at all or if we were just convenient. Maybe I wasn't picky enough." He closed his eyes, trying to remember those heady days. "But I kept noticing that he was watching me, and eventually he came over. We talked and then went to dinner that night.... It was kind of magical." He shook his head slightly. "I should have been more careful and not discounted certain facts, like how he was busy all the time those last few months."

"Was he seeing someone else?" Riley asked in a gentle tone.

Wayne nodded. "It turned out that he had been almost the entire time we were together and I just hadn't realized it. While I was seeing him, I got Buster, and thankfully I paid all the fees and filled out the paperwork myself. Otherwise...." He hated to think of Buster living with Mike and his form of benign neglect. Mike wasn't mean, he just wasn't the kind of guy who could actively care for anyone or anything other than himself. "Sorry. I asked you up to get warm, not to give you a rundown on my pathetic love life." Sometimes he needed to learn when to be quiet.

What Riley did next surprised him. He leaned forward, and Frosty slid back on the sofa. Then Riley reached over and took his hand. "It's okay. Sometimes we all just need a chance to talk." It wasn't his words that Wayne concentrated on, but the warm touch of his hand and the excitement that raced through him. Part of him said to pull away so he wouldn't have to go through this again, but Riley smiled just as warmly and cheerfully as the twinkle lights on his small tree.

Chapter 3

RILEY USUALLY wasn't this forward, but Wayne seemed to need some sort of care. The two of them sat like that for a few seconds, their gazes locked, and then everything went dark. Riley pulled back, holding Frosty and sitting still. "Maybe the power will come back on."

The lights flashed back on, and Riley relaxed before they were plunged into darkness once more. He waited, but there were no more flashes of light, and the darkness seemed to settle in to stay. Wayne's phone lit his face for a few seconds, and Riley's chimed with a message. He checked it and groaned. It was from the power company telling him that his power was out as well and that they would message with an ETA for restoration. "Great," he said softly. "It looks like it's going to be out for a while."

"I think so." The wind blew outside the windows.

"It's probably best if I get home." He stood and realized he had no idea where anything was.

"Give me a minute," Wayne said and hurried to the kitchen, returning with a battery-operated lantern. Now that he could see, Riley clipped the lead on Frosty, and then Wayne opened the door to the front stairwell. "When do you want to meet again… for dog training?"

"Is next week good? Same day and time?" Riley asked.

"Sure. That works." Riley and Frosty headed down the stairs, but he stopped halfway down. "If you want to get together for dinner or something before then, just message me." He watched as Wayne returned his smile and nodded. Then Riley continued the descent and went out the door. He headed right to the car and got Frosty inside before looking up. The wind was picking up and the sky was clear. It was going to be a cold night without any heat or power.

THE AIR was cold, but Riley was nice and warm with Frosty pressed to him, generating enough heat to warm the Arctic. The power had come back on near midnight, so the room wasn't all that cold, but after a night like that, it was good to have all the heat he could get. He sat up, and the dog scooted into his warm spot. "I hope you know that last night was a special treat because there wasn't any heat, and you're going to sleep in your own bed tonight."

Frosty blinked up at him, and Riley groaned softly as he slipped out of bed.

His phone chimed, and Frosty growled at the sound, probably because it was disturbing her sleep. "Come on. Get up and off the bed." He got her down, and she stretched before leaving the room, probably to see if anything had been added to her food dish. Riley checked his phone. He had a message from Davis about the upcoming plans for Christmas. Riley responded to his message just as another text came in. He smiled when he saw it was from Wayne.

Dinner on Thursday?

Riley smiled. *That sounds great.* He stretched and began getting dressed before going to his office. He signed onto the computer and logged into work in plenty of time, then checked on what he had to do. He left the window open and hurried to let Frosty out and give her food and fresh water.

Do you have power back? Wayne asked.

Yeah. It came back about midnight here. You? He sent the message as he went to the back door to check on Frosty, who bounded through the yard as she played.

Not yet. They say it should be back on by noon. The place is cold, and I'm afraid to use the fireplace because I don't know the last time it was checked. He sent a sad face.

You can come over here if you and Buster need to warm up. He made the offer before he could stop himself. There was no way he was going to let both of them be that cold. The wind still hadn't let up, and without heat, that upper apartment was going to get icy pretty fast. *Just let me know.* He opened the back door for Frosty. It really was starting to feel like Christmas, and he tried to get himself in the holiday spirit.

"Did you go?" he asked as Frosty hurried back inside out of the cold air. She blinked at him before attacking her food dish, and Riley went back upstairs to work.

He liked his job. It was a pretty good one, even if the people he worked with were strict about his work-from-home hours. Riley liked that he didn't have to commute into Harrisburg every day, and he was a stickler for making sure he got his work done. Once his project was well underway, Frosty came into the room with one of her toys and placed it in his lap.

"I can't play with you right now." Riley continued working, but she kept putting the squeaky hedgehog in his lap. He hated to crate her during the day, but he needed to get his job done. He set the toy on the floor and returned to work, and Frosty finally settled down with a sigh. "You know, you're really good company, but I can't play with you now. I have to work." He gently patted her head and returned to what he needed to do.

He continued to work until his phone rang. "Riley?" It was Wayne. "Were you serious? The power is still out, and I got another message that it's going to be hours before they get to us." He sounded miserable.

"Of course. Let me text you my address." He switched to text and typed in the address. "Come on over, and bring whatever Buster is going to need. I have Wi-Fi if you need to work and stuff."

"Thanks." He seemed totally stressed, and that piqued Riley's curiosity. He'd messaged him just a few hours earlier. Was this more than just the power being out?

"I'll see you when you get here." He ended the call and turned to Frosty. "It looks like you're going to have some company. Your friend Buster is going to come over." Her tail thumped the wood floor. "You need to be good and not go all nuts, okay?" He returned to work and got as much done as he could before the bell sounded. Riley hurried to the front door and let Wayne and Buster inside.

Buster hurried right up to Frosty, and the two of them greeted each other before hurrying off toward the kitchen, where Frosty's food and water were.

Wayne shivered. "It's so cold, and the downstairs neighbors are gone on vacation. I hope the pipes don't freeze. The inside of my place was below fifty degrees."

"I can make some tea or coffee to warm you." Riley stowed Wayne's coat and led him through to the kitchen where he put the kettle on the stove. "Can you watch that? I need to go upstairs and make sure I didn't miss anything. My boss can be an ass and messages for no reason just to make sure we aren't goofing off while we're working from home." He returned to his office, checked his computer, responded to an outstanding message, and answered an email that had come in.

"This is really nice," Wayne said from the door.

"You can set yourself up in the chair if you want. Frosty will be in here pretty soon." Sure enough, the dogs came inside, with Frosty settling next to his seat and Buster cozying up next to her. "I'll go get the tea made and bring some in here for you." He hurried to the kitchen, set up a couple of mugs, and poured in the hot water. He only had teabags, but at least it would be warming.

"Thank you for doing this. I called a couple of friends, but they were at work, and it kept getting colder. I thought about staying in bed, but I have work to do too, and the idea of sitting in Panera all day did not appeal. And I wouldn't be able to bring Buster, so he'd end up at home in the freezing house."

"It's okay." Riley handed Wayne his mug. "Don't worry about it. I'm happy to share my warmth." He liked having Wayne here. Since he'd moved in, the place had always felt a little empty. Frosty had helped fill it, but he really liked having Wayne and Buster here too.

"I couldn't help noticing that you don't have any Christmas stuff out. Do you not celebrate?" He sipped the mug, those big eyes watching him. Riley could feel that gaze on him.

"I do. I spend the holidays with my brother, his wife, and my niece, Lilly, so I don't decorate or anything here. There's really no need, because they have every decoration known to man taped to every window and hanging from every light, archway, and door. Lilly is a Christmas fiend, and it doesn't help that her birthday is in December as well."

"So she gets two rounds of gifts," Wayne said with a smile on those luscious lips that Riley found hard to look away from.

"Yeah. This year she got Princess, her first dog. I was the one who was sent to pick her up, and I came home with Frosty as well. Anyway, what do you do for the holiday?" Riley checked his work queue, answered another email, and pulled up the data he needed to get the next item on his list completed.

"My folks are in Arizona, and they don't come back here this time of year. Mom can't stand the cold, and it's a long way to travel for just a few days. They send me presents, and I do the same. Then we call each other on Christmas." He shrugged. Riley couldn't help thinking how lonely that sounded. Christmas at Davis's was always a huge affair, though it often got overwhelming with all the gifts, the people, and walls of sound. Still, it was his family, and he loved them and knew they were there for him. "So I put up my little tree and decorate the apartment just so I have some cheer."

Riley sipped his tea and went back to work. He wanted to sit and talk with Wayne, but he had his job to do, and the work was not going to go away. Wayne got out his computer, and Riley gave him the passcode to his Wi-Fi so he could log on. Then the room grew quiet, broken only by the sound of typing. The dogs were both so good, lying together with Frosty sprawled out on the floor and Buster pressed up against her.

Wayne's phone chimed a few times, each greeted with a soft sigh. Apparently the electric company was messaging to say that they were still working on the issue.

At noon, Riley took a break for lunch and got out sandwich stuff for both of them. The dogs crowded into the kitchen, tails wagging as they watched for anything that might hit the floor. Wayne's phone chimed, and this time he smiled. "It looks like the power is back on at home."

"Finish your lunch and give the heat at your place a chance to catch up," Riley suggested. He liked that Wayne was here and wasn't in a hurry to see him leave. "I have half an hour for lunch and then I have to be back at my computer."

"Do they really watch that closely? It seems kind of dumb. I work from home too, and I always get everything done. The boss isn't such a dick about it."

"Yeah, well. Dewey hates that we have a work-from-home policy. He wants everyone in the office so he can micromanage us to death. If we're here, then he can't see us, so he has his other little annoying tricks." He checked his phone and answered the text from his boss by saying that he would get the answer to him right after lunch. "What I'm hoping is that they'll either realize what a jerk this guy is and get rid of him or he'll move on. As soon as he does, I want to apply for his job. I know I can do it and be better at it than he is." He checked the time and grabbed his plate. "I should get back up to the office or he'll call again."

"God," Wayne breathed. "And I bet you work late to make sure everything is done."

"Nope. All his baby antics mean that no one does. We give nothing extra, and that pisses him off too. See, productivity is down since he came in, and he's pissed about that. But everyone liked Judy, the previous supervisor, and we worked hard and didn't think twice about an hour extra here and there. With Dewey, we all log out at the exact time we can and don't work a minute over."

"I'll let the dogs out," Wayne said and Riley thanked him before carrying his plate up to his office and going back to work.

When Wayne returned with both dogs following, Riley was finishing up what Dewey needed and sent it to him.

"I'm going to head back to my place," Wayne said. "But you and I are still on for dinner?"

"You bet. I've been looking forward to it." He checked that there were no immediate messages and walked Wayne to the door. "I'll see you tomorrow night." He flashed what he hoped was his best smile, and his stomach fluttered as Wayne returned it.

"Thanks for letting us warm up." Wayne left, and Riley blocked Frosty from following him out the door as he watched Wayne go. Then he closed the door and turned to his now-empty house. Frosty lay down on the floor with a soft whine.

"I know, girl. I feel the same way." The place seemed a little less warm and a whole lot less cheerful now that Wayne and Buster were gone. For the first time in years, he thought about digging out some of the decorations he had in the back of the office closet, but instead of pulling them out, he sat at his desk and got back to work before he got in trouble.

Chapter 4

BUSTER FOLLOWED Wayne everywhere he went, including the bathroom to shower and then into the bedroom to dress.

"No. I'm sorry, but you don't get to go tonight," he told Buster as he jumped on the bed, standing at full attention, his tail wagging his entire back end. "And no. You can look at me like that all you want, but it isn't going to change my mind. This is my date, not one that you and Frosty get to crash. Not this time."

He splashed on a small amount of cologne and checked himself in the mirror before leaving the bathroom and slipping into his shoes.

He was just putting on his coat when the bell rang. Buster raced ahead of him to the door and jumped as he tried to get past Wayne to go down the stairs. "You need to wait here." Wayne slipped on his heavy coat and managed to get out the door without letting Buster out. Of course he got a few barks as he descended the stairs.

"Hey," Riley said with a lopsided smile. "Are you ready to go? I thought we could go the Café Belgie for dinner, if that's okay. I always liked that place, and the food is really good."

"Sure." Wayne didn't tend to go out to eat much, so this was a real treat. "I've heard good things about the place." He climbed into the passenger seat of Riley's Corolla, and they headed downtown. "I've always found the town kind of charming this time of year with the garlands on the lampposts and the angels on the light poles at the square, as well as the snowflakes. It's like something from years gone by, and yet it seems modern too."

"I take it you're a scholar of Christmas decorations," Riley said.

"Not really, I just like the way they do this. Some places go way overboard, while others do almost nothing."

"I like it too. I live close enough that I like to walk down here when it's snowing. The town is kind of magical at times like that. The traffic slows down, and the snow clings to the garlands and the branches of the trees. Last year on one of those nights, I came down just to watch the play of light on the falling snow." Riley paused. "When I was a kid, my mom used to bring me down here for the old Christmas parade, and then we'd get to see Santa. Those nights it always seemed to snow, and that made it extra special. Maybe that's why I like those times so much."

"Yeah. I grew up where there wasn't snow ever. Mom can't stand the cold. But after I graduated, it was hard to find a job, so when I got the offer here, I jumped at it." Those had been a couple of tough years, working where he could until he got the chance at a more permanent full-time position as a systems designer. "Mom was disappointed that I didn't stay down there, but I'd have ended up working in the mall longer, and that wasn't what I wanted."

"That had to have been hard."

"It was, but it was time. I couldn't live at home for much longer. It was getting tense, and I wanted to get on with my life. Everyone else I knew was building a future of their own, and I was stuck." God, he had hated that time. He'd felt like a failure, and that hadn't helped his prospects or his relationship with his parents. His mom had been supportive, while his father always looked at him like, *Why are you still here?*

Riley pulled to a stop at the light on the square. The town Christmas tree was lit, flashing its cheery message next to the old courthouse, wisps of snow clinging to its branches. This time of year, they didn't always get snow, and Wayne was happy it was happening this year. It always made the holidays seem more festive. Though if he were honest, he'd be happy if it stopped snowing the day after Christmas and they went right to spring, but fat chance on that one. When the light changed, they passed through the intersection, and Riley parked a little ways from the restaurant.

They walked together down the sidewalk. "It's been a while since I was on a real date," Riley confessed.

"Why? You're super cute, and you must have people interested." Wayne wanted to smack himself.

Riley shrugged. "You think I'm cute? You know that's, like, the kiss of death."

Wayne rolled his eyes. "Stop. You know what I mean, and don't try to change the subject. But I get it. Guys are interested in getting it on and then moving on to the next conquest. Especially people our age. It's like some kind of game or something." He paused outside the restaurant.

"Well, that isn't the kind of thing I'm looking for." Wayne smiled at Riley and got one tinged with heat in return. His belly did a little flip of excitement, and Wayne savored the flutter of returned interest. He opened the door and held it for Riley before following him inside the clean, modern-looking dining room with just enough warmth to feel welcoming. The host directed them to their table once Riley gave his name, and they sat down near the front windows. "What have you had here?"

"We had a work thing here a few months ago, and everything was good. The chef who owns it is amazing. But the last time I was here, I had the pork milanaise. It was delicious."

Wayne scanned down the menu before making his choice. There were so many interesting things that it was hard to choose, and the scents that wafted out of the kitchen had his stomach rumbling in anticipation. He wanted to order a little of everything, but he settled on the trout, while Riley got schnitzel with spaetzle.

"How did you get into training dogs? Was that something your parents did?"

"Growing up, the lady next door was into dogs. She raised them for the Leader Dogs for the Blind program. She'd get puppies, raise and train them to be part of the program, and then those that were accepted went on for more training while those that didn't were adopted. She had as many as ten or twelve dogs at a time, and I used to go over to play with them." Their drinks arrived, and Wayne paused. "So I was around dogs all the time, and they responded really well to me. She taught me how to train them, and at fifteen and sixteen, I trained my first dogs for the program. For a while, Mrs. Fells had more dogs because I could help her. Once I went away to college my junior year, she backed off a little. But I had found something that I was good at."

"You'd think you had bacon in your pocket or something," Riley said.

"Nope. Dogs know they can trust me, and that's all it really takes. And for the record, Frosty adores you. When you're in the room, she watches you and will follow you anywhere."

"That's because I feed her."

Wayne shook his head. "No. It's more like she knows you will be there for her. You rescued her and gave her a forever home. They know and respond to what's in your heart." He sighed. "I should have known that my last boyfriend was a total jerk. The dogs didn't like him."

"So your dating profile, if you had one, would read, 'must love dogs.'" Riley smiled. "I like that." So did Wayne. It was the perfect way to explain the kind of guy he wanted in his life, and it did it in a single sentence. "Or maybe, 'must be loved by dogs.'" He loved Riley's smile with that hint of almost impish wickedness.

"That's a given. Buster loves everyone, but he stayed away from Mike. He didn't growl or anything, but he just avoided him. And Buster was right. Mike was selfish and tended to look out for himself and what he wanted. Thankfully, things didn't last long before I figured it out. My track record isn't the greatest."

Riley lifted his glass. "To a better future," he said softly, and Wayne lifted his own, clinking them together lightly before drinking.

THEY HAD an amazing dinner and talked about everything and nothing. It took about five minutes before Wayne let go of his usual carefulness and opened up. The amazing thing was that Riley seemed to do the same, and they talked like they had known each other for a long time. And that never happened for Wayne. He was usually slow to show his true self, but with Riley, it was so easy to be himself. "I have to ask. How long did it take before Frosty slept in bed with you?"

Riley chuckled. "She tries, believe me. But I learned the night the power was out that she is one huge bed pig. So she sleeps in her own space."

Wayne was surprised. "She didn't wheedle her way into your bed?"

"Nope." Riley seemed pleased. "She's been trying, but she takes up so much room and I have a tendency to toss and turn, so it really isn't going to be good if she sleeps with me. One night was fine, but not afterwards."

"I have to give you credit. You're a better man than I am. Buster has a place at the foot of the bed, and he stays there unless it's really cold. Then he'll settle up near my legs. That night without the heat, he slipped under the covers and slept with his head on the next pillow." Wayne rolled his eyes. "I know, I'm a huge softie."

"Well, Buster isn't eighty pounds." Riley leaned over the table as he finished his coffee. "When I got her, I never considered the consequences of all the decisions I was going to make, and I know I made mistakes, but that isn't one of them. Frosty is happier because she has her own bed, and let me tell you, that girl has doggie dreams and she runs in her sleep." He chuckled. When the server brought the check, he grabbed it and handed him a credit card right away. "You can get the next one," he said gently.

Wayne liked the idea of there being a next date.

Once the check was paid and their coffee gone, they left the restaurant. The snow had stopped and the air was still. "I probably should get Frosty and take her out for a walk."

"Let's stop at your place, get her, and then we can walk Buster at the same time." Wayne didn't want the evening to end. Riley agreed, and they went to his small home. Frosty raced into the back seat and made herself comfortable, and then they were off toward Wayne's upstairs place.

"I'll wait down here with her while you get Buster," Riley offered, and he got Frosty leashed up as Wayne went inside and up the stairs. When he reached the top, he unlocked the door and went inside. Buster didn't greet him the way he usually did.

"Hey, Buster, I'm home," he called, but he didn't come running. Wondering what was wrong, he hurried through the house to make sure he wasn't hurt, heart racing. He found the back door ajar and hurried outside. Was Buster out in the yard, cold and unable to get back inside? He went down the back stairs, his heart aching when he saw the back gate was ajar as well. He hurried through and back out front. "Buster is gone. He got out the back, and the gate was open, and…."

"Okay. We'll find him," Riley said. "Is the house closed up?" Wayne tried to remember and then nodded. "Close the gate, and we'll go find him. He can't have gotten very far."

"I have no idea how long he's been out, or if…." The idea that someone might have taken Buster made his heart cold and his stomach clench.

"Buster is out here, and we're going to find him," Riley said. "Can you find your friend Buster?" he asked Frosty. "Go and find Buster."

Frosty perked up and began pulling on the leash. Wayne wasn't ready to believe that the dog knew anything more than they did, but Riley went in the direction she was pulling.

"That's it. Find your friend Buster."

"You know she doesn't know what you're saying," Wayne said nervously as he scanned the area on both sides of the street. A lot of the neighbors had fenced-in yards, so that would make it impossible for Buster to get to some areas, but as they went down half a block, one house had a completely open yard, with dog prints running across the fresh snow. "I think he went this way."

"Okay. You go through the yard, and I'll take Frosty around and I'll meet you in back." Riley pulled out his phone and made a call. "Hey, Davis, I need your help. A friend's dog has gotten out, and we need to find him. He's on South Street and we're heading down Chapel. Do you think you can help…? Thanks." He hung up. "My brother is on his way. He's a policeman here in town, and he knows the area pretty well." He began walking. "I'll meet you in back." Riley picked up speed as Wayne trudged across the lightly whited lawn and through the backyard.

"Buster!" he called, hoping his dog would hear him. When he reached Chapel—technically an alley, but it had a few homes on it—he looked up and down just as Riley turned the corner, heading toward him with Frosty leading the way. "Buster!" He listened but heard nothing.

"There were no paw prints that way," Riley reported, and they continued down the street.

"Where could he be?" Wayne asked as a car pulled down the street and right up to them, rolling down the window.

"I called into the station, and there have been no reports of a dog being found," the driver said. "By the way, I'm his brother, Davis." He stuck his hand out through the open window, and Wayne shook it. "I'm going to continue on down here and then go down Pomfret Street, but it isn't likely he made it that far. All the yards are fenced and closed off from this direction."

"Thanks," Wayne said, getting more worried by the second. "I just hope we find him."

"We will," Riley said as Davis moved slowly forward and then turned the corner ahead of them. "Maybe he went down the road here and out that way."

They continued west and made the corner. Wayne was torn as to whether they should continue on straight or loop back around. He decided to try finishing off the block before moving farther afield, so they turned left and then got back to South Street. He sighed and was about to continue west.

"Wayne!" someone called, and he turned as one of the neighbors, Evelyn, approached from across the street. She had Buster in her arms, and Wayne swallowed hard before sighing in sheer relief. "I found him across the street behind the houses about fifteen minutes ago. I got him in the car so he could warm up." She got closer, and Wayne took Buster and nuzzled him tight. Damn, it felt so good to have him back again.

"Thank you. I'm not sure how he got out." He held him as Frosty went up on her hind legs to peer at Buster. The two of them greeted one another, and then Frosty sat down right next to Riley like she was happy.

"I'll ask Davis to take a look at the doors just in case." Riley made a call.

"Thank you for finding him. We were out at dinner, and when I came home he was gone. Buster is usually so good."

"I was so surprised when he ran across the street. He seemed kind of frantic, and when I called him, he came right into the car. He was cold, and I got him warm and gave him some water. Then I figured I'd bring him home. I would have called, but the tag with the number must have fallen off." She seemed almost as relieved as Wayne, who checked for the tag and made a note to get another one tomorrow. "I'm just glad that he's going to be okay." She gently stroked Buster's head before saying good night and heading home.

Wayne carried Buster the half block home, with Riley and Frosty walking along with him. Once they were inside, he made sure the doors were properly closed and set Buster down. He immediately attacked his food dish and then drank a bunch of water before settling on his blanket near the sofa with Frosty curled next to him, like she wanted to make sure he was warm enough.

There was a knock, and Riley let his brother inside. Wayne showed him the back door and gate and let him look them over.

"How many times did you go down the stairs?" Davis asked once he came back inside.

"Just once. I went down them to the back gate and then came through to the front to find Riley. Why?"

"Because someone has been up and down those stairs at least once if not more, and if it wasn't you, then someone might have let Buster out. Is there anyone else with a key? Did you give a key to anyone?"

Wayne sat down. "Mike Harper, my ex, had a key, but I got it back from him when we broke up." He felt himself pale as Davis jotted down the name. "Buster was the only thing we fought over." He lifted his gaze. "Do you think he could have done something like this?"

Davis shrugged. "I think the more important question is do *you* think he could have done it? Maybe he was trying to get revenge or to trying to hurt you."

"But…," Wayne began.

"Did you leave the back door unlocked?" Riley asked him.

Wayne shook his head. "I never do."

"Then someone got in here. Has anything been taken?"

Wayne rolled his eyes—there was nothing worth stealing. But the TV was still there, and so were the other electronics. "Not that I can tell."

"And remember, they left the back door and the gate open. It seems to me that they wanted to clear a path for Buster, maybe to make it look like you had been careless."

"I'm never careless where he's concerned," Wayne protested.

Riley came to stand right next to him. "Of course not. You'd go without eating so Buster could. I know that. So that means that someone was here. I mean, all they'd have to do is go up the back, open the door and leave it ajar, then leave and not latch the gate. Buster is always curious, and he loves to try to get outside, and with the gate open, he'd be free to go where he wants." Riley made it sound so easy, and maybe that was all there was to it.

"Can you take prints or something?" Wayne asked.

"I could try, but I don't know how much good it would do. I bet there are plenty of them on the lock, though it's likely that with you opening and closing the door, they'd have been covered up. TV shows always depict fantastic things that they can do, but we don't have those kinds of resources, especially when we don't know if there's been a crime." Davis did look around the door once more and then locked it before rejoining them in the living room. "I wish I had more I could tell you."

"It's okay. Thank you for all your help," Wayne said, shaking Riley's brother's hand.

"I'll walk you out." Riley pulled on his coat and left through the front. Wayne found himself looking out the front window, watching the two brothers, hating that he was scared and didn't want to be alone.

Chapter 5

"SO THAT'S the dog trainer," Davis said as soon as they stepped outside. "No wonder you have the hots for him."

"I do not," Riley countered. "I like Wayne, and he's good-looking and nice, and Frosty adores him."

"But…?" Davis said. "There's always a but when you use that tone."

"I always pick the shittiest guys and they turn out to be so awful. What if I'm doing it again?" He hated that he sounded whiny even to himself.

"I have never had that problem, and all my instincts are telling me that he's a good guy and is what he seems to be. He didn't ping any of my cop instincts at all. You've been alone for a long time. Hell, even when you were dating someone, you were alone. Open yourself up a little and see where this goes."

Riley sighed. "Like you're the most open book in the world."

"Neither of us is. It's one of the things that we share. Mom and Dad were never the most forthright parents. Heck, there were times when I used to wonder if they cared for each other, let alone us."

"But you moved right on and met Stephanie and…."

Davis shook his head. "I was as stupid as you're being. I kept her at arm's length for a long time, and she knew it too. She stayed with me, though." He sighed softly. "Look, we don't talk about this kind of shit, and I'd rather sit on nails than actually have this conversation, but here it is. Stephanie put up with my shit until she was going to dump me. But instead of just leaving, she put it on the line and told me that I was being an ass and that it was time for me to man up and talk about feelings and all that shit." He smiled. "Damn, there is something about that woman when she gets mad… she has this fire that—"

"I really don't need to hear about your wife's fire… or anything else along those lines, okay?"

"But that's just it. I'm proud that she's strong and knows what she wants. Instead of fighting like Mom and Dad did, she and I talk to one another. She's my partner… and I can tell you, that's the best feeling there is. But you're never going to find that if you don't open up and let yourself take a chance. Wayne seems like a really nice guy." He leaned a little closer. "Give him a chance—give *yourself* a chance."

"Jesus Christ, when did you get to be such an expert?"

"Since I figured some of my crap out. I dated the wrong kind of person for a long time, and that's what I think you've been doing. The guys you dated—the ones that didn't work out—all had that bad-boy vibe. Remember Vasquez, with that crappy bike that he used to ride all over town making as much noise as possible? I busted him two weeks ago for drug possession, and he's sitting his ass in jail. And since he was using that bike when I busted him, it's going into the sheriff's sale." He headed to his car. "Just think about what it is that you really want, let go of the load of crap you're carrying, and be honest with yourself about your feelings. It's quite liberating, and for the record… you do have the hots for Wayne." Davis got into his car, and Riley went back inside, wondering what the hell had happened.

Riley found Wayne on the sofa, Buster on his lap, and Frosty with her head on the sofa next to him, both dogs getting pets. "You okay?"

"I don't know," Wayne answered, his eyes wide. "Someone was in here, and if it was Mike, then he has a way to get in."

"He might have given you the key back, but he probably had more than one." Riley nudged Frosty away and sat down next to Wayne, giving Frosty a little attention as he took Wayne's hand. "You really need to get the locks changed. Maybe talk to your landlord about having that done."

"Yeah. I probably should have done that long before now, but it never occurred to me."

Riley could understand that. "Another question. Why now? You have been broken up with him for months. Why come after Buster now?" It didn't make sense.

"I saw Mike on Sunday when I was walking Buster. He seemed to remember him and moved around to my far side. Mike seemed happy to see him, but Buster was having none of it. I tried to talk to Mike, but all he did was try to pet Buster and move on, like he was the aggrieved party and I had somehow turned the dog against him. I wasn't the one who cheated."

"So seeing Buster might have triggered something?" Riley said, mostly to himself.

"I don't know. Mike and I dated for over a year, and Mike… well, I found out that he could nurse a grudge more than anyone I ever met. While he petted Buster, Mike kept scowling up at me like I was the devil himself."

"Okay, so he saw Buster. But why let him out? I mean, if it was him, he could have taken Buster and it would have been hard to find him."

"And where was he going to keep him? If Buster had been taken, I would have known it was Mike and called the police. They'd have searched and found him. No. This is classic Mike. Let Buster out and then try to use it to say I wasn't taking good enough care of him, or some such crap. I left Mike because he was manipulative as hell." Wayne's hand shook, and Riley squeezed it gently.

"I believe you," he said softly. He understood manipulative boyfriends. He'd dealt with one of those. They sucked, and not in a good way. "I really do. What we need to do is make sure that you and Buster are safe. So why don't you pack a few things for you and Buster? You can stay at my house for a few days until we can get to the bottom of this and have the locks changed here." Riley figured Wayne wouldn't be comfortable staying here, and he wanted to give him an easy out.

"Are you sure?" Wayne asked.

"Yeah. It's no problem." He patted Frosty and stood. "Go on and get things for the night. We can figure out the rest in the morning." He got Frosty's leash while Wayne packed a bag and got a few things for Buster. Then they got the dogs into Riley's car and he drove them to his place. He led them all inside.

He let Frosty off her lead, and she went back to the kitchen to her dish, with Buster staying by Wayne as though he knew Wayne needed him. Riley took care of the coats and then got them settled in the living room.

"How about something to drink?"

"Yes, please," Wayne said formally. "It's been quite a day."

"It has." Who knew their date would end with such excitement? It wasn't the kind Riley might have wished for, but at least Buster was safe and back with Wayne. That was what mattered.

"Thank you for this. I know I'd be up all night wondering if Mike or whoever let Buster out was going to return."

"We'll see about getting the locks changed and then we can go from there." Riley brought in some tea and set the mugs on the table. Wayne picked up his, and they settled in the warmth.

"I still can't get over you not having a tree or anything."

Riley stood and went to the office, then pulled down a box from the top of the closet. He returned to the living room. "I don't have much, but this is part of it. Maybe there's something in here that you'll like." He pulled out his phone and put on some Christmas music. If adding some holiday cheer would make Wayne feel better, then he was more than up for it.

Wayne opened the box. "Do you even know what's in here?"

"Not really. I haven't bothered decorating since I've been spending Christmas with Davis and his family." He sat down as Wayne began pulling things out of the box, including an old Santa figure that had been his grandmother's. He smiled when Wayne handed it to him, and Riley placed it on the mantel out of dog reach.

Wayne pulled out more goodies Riley hadn't seen in years and had forgotten all about. Even though there was no tree, the room had taken on a more festive air already with the tables and shelves decked out with holiday memories. "I like it."

"Me too." It was funny how long-past holidays came flooding back when he saw these things. They weren't all that special or valuable, just things from his childhood that had made a reappearance. "I hadn't remembered any of this."

"See, that's the fun of this. For me, Christmas isn't so much about the presents or the eating, but the memories of the magical Christmases as a kid. Like the year I got my first bike. I was six years old, and my dad put it together and it was waiting under the tree for me. And then there was the year that all I wanted was a telescope. Mom saved up and got one for me. I had more fun with that. We used to look at the moon or at the planets. It took some getting used to, but I got pretty good at zeroing in on things. It's all about getting the viewfinder set up correctly."

Riley grinned and jumped up, startling the dogs. Then he hurried to his bedroom and carefully pulled a long box out from under the bed. He carried it to the living room and set it on the floor, both dogs coming over to sniff. "I got this for my fifteenth birthday. I was interested in science, and Mom thought I'd like it. The thing was, we were living outside Chicago at the time, and the lights of the city cast so much glare that there wasn't much to see." He lifted the lid, and Wayne gasped.

"Wow, that's pretty amazing." He slid off the sofa to join him on the floor. "Oh my God. It's beautiful." The telescope was still shiny blue, and Riley had all the lenses and pieces.

"Dad and I took it into the country once. We set it up and he fiddled with it for a while but couldn't seem to get it right. He humphed, put it all back in the box, and drove us home. It's been packed up ever since. Mom said that she thought he and I could have used it together, but typical of Dad, he gave up after an hour, and I had no idea what to do with it. I took it into the backyard a few times, but the one thing my father managed to do was lose the instruction manual, so…."

"This is a Zeiss—like, one of the best. I bet if you went online, you could get a copy of the manual and we could put it back together. On a clear night, we could see what there is to see." Wayne grinned, and Riley found himself smiling. It was like getting the telescope as a Christmas present all over again. "Maybe we could take the dogs out with us too. It gets dark early enough, and we'd only need to go a few miles out of town." Wayne slowly ran his hand down the telescope.

"That would be great."

Wayne checked over the box and then went on his phone, grinning as he worked. Then Riley's phone dinged with a message from him along with an attached PDF. "There it is. All you need to do is print it."

"Thank you," Riley said with a grin, hugging Wayne tightly without thinking. He was about to pull away when Wayne returned the embrace.

Riley pulled back slightly, their eyes locking, and slowly Wayne drew closer. Riley stilled for just a moment before their lips met.

Wayne's lips were soft, and the kiss stayed gentle for a moment. Riley pulled back, his gaze not leaving Wayne's. He got to his knees to get a better angle, and Wayne did as well. Before Riley could stop himself, he cupped Wayne's lightly stubbled cheeks in his hands and drew him close, kissing the hell out of him. It was exciting, especially as Wayne gave as good as he got.

"Riley," Wayne whispered when they finally surfaced for air. "I've wanted to do that since I met you."

Riley giggled and stifled it because he didn't want to sound stupid. "Me too." Then they both began to laugh, but Riley cut it off with another kiss that left him warm and sweating a little. Wayne sure as heck knew how to kiss, and it sent ripples of excitement running down his spine.

Buster barked, and Frosty woofed softly. Riley pulled back to see what was going on and found both dogs looking at them. "It's okay. We're just kissing." He turned to a pair of big eyes. "Neither of us is hurting the other." He smiled, and both dogs spread out on the floor. "They are both real goofs."

Wayne snickered softly. "Buster has always been protective. He tolerated Mike some of the time, but Buster was always my dog."

"Well, I'm not going to hurt you," he said quietly. "So Buster—and, for that matter, Frosty—can stand down." He couldn't help chuckling. "Come on. The room that should be for guests is full of stuff at the moment, so I'll make up the sofa for you." He stood and went to his bedroom, then returned with a sheet and some blankets. He figured it would be best if the two of them took things slow. In the past, it was always too easy to go from a first kiss to jumping into bed. And he didn't want that—not with Wayne. There was the old adage that if you wanted a different result, you needed to act differently. And Riley wanted something more than the messes his previous attempts at relationships had turned out to be. He made up the couch, and Buster jumped right on and made himself comfortable at one end. Then Riley showed Wayne the bathroom so he could clean up and get ready for the night.

"Come on, Frosty, it's time for you to go to bed too. It's getting late, and we've all had plenty of excitement." He leaned down and kissed Wayne good night. "I'll see you in the morning." He turned off most of the lights and then went to his room, where Frosty lay on her bed. Riley got cleaned up and then climbed under the covers. He wasn't sure how well he was going to sleep with his mind replaying those amazing kisses, but that was his problem. This was one time he wasn't going to jump into things.

Riley turned out the lights and stared up at the ceiling. He heard Frosty get up from her bed. Once he rolled over, Riley found himself nose to nose with his dog. "You need to go back to bed." He resisted the urge to let the dog stay in bed with him, and eventually she turned around and went to curl up in her own bed. Damn, he had come so close to giving in. Sleeping alone was really coming to suck, and more than once he thought about checking on Wayne, but he resisted that too and eventually fell into a restless sleep.

Chapter 6

BUSTER HAD crawled upward and was now curled up next to Wayne's legs in a nest between him and the cushions, snoring like hell. Wayne reached for his phone. It was a little after four in the morning, and between his mind running a million miles a minute and his snoring dog, there was no way he was going to get any more sleep. On top of that, it seemed that Riley hadn't closed his door completely, because Frosty was now sleeping on the floor next to the sofa, sprawled out and making her own set of doggie noises.

Wayne slowly extricated himself from the dog and sat up. Buster lifted his head, shifted, and then went right back to sleep, while Frosty didn't even move as Wayne made his way to the chair and pulled out his phone to read for a while.

The floor creaked slightly. "You unable to sleep?" Riley asked after yawning.

"With these two?" Wayne said. "I swear they could wake the dead."

"Come on." Riley took his hand and led him into the bedroom. "I promise to be good." He slipped under the covers, and Wayne did the same. The bedding smelled like Riley, warm and rich, very comforting. The room was chilly, so he burrowed down, and after a few minutes, Riley took his hand, just holding it. There was no other contact between them, no moving in closer, just the single gentle touch, and soon Wayne drifted off to sleep.

When he woke later that morning, the bed was very full. Riley was right next to him, with Buster at the foot of the bed. Fortunately, Frosty had not joined them, but she was in her bed, sitting up, watching. Damn, Buster took up enough room. Wayne was glad Frosty was a lady and hadn't crawled into bed with all of them.

"I take it we have company," Riley muttered. "And here I thought I could have my wicked way with you."

Wayne snickered. "Who says things like that?" It was kind of cute.

"My grandmother. I used to spend weekends with her, and she had her shows. Lord, you did not come between her and her shows. She watched them for the men, and she always said that Tom Selleck could have his wicked way with her any time he wanted. I swear she watched every show with a hot leading man. She also had a thing for nerds and said that she wouldn't kick McGee out of bed for eating crackers. Granny was one of a kind."

"I bet she was."

"Yeah. She passed away at ninety. Drove my mother crazy each and every day. My mom is a bit of a prude when it comes to things like that. Grandma and the other ladies in the retirement community were hell on wheels. It always tickled me to death that she didn't stop until she had to. Passed away in her sleep, and I like to think that for her, Saint Peter looked a lot like Tom Selleck."

Wayne closed his eyes for a few minutes before remembering that it was Friday and he needed to get his butt up and get ready for work, and Riley certainly needed to do the same. As much as he liked lying here, warm, comfortable, and turned on by Riley's closeness, he had things to do. Thankfully it was the end of the week, though.

Slowly, Wayne slipped out of bed.

"Where are you going?"

"I need to get dressed and take Buster home before I go to work, and I'm sure you need to get logged in."

Riley sat up and checked the clock. "Damn. I have to go to the office today." He yawned and covered his mouth with his hand. "Are you going to be okay? Let me get dressed quick and I'll take you and Buster home before I go on to work." Riley jumped to it, pulling on clothes. Buster jumped down off the bed and joined Frosty in hers, the dogs watching them. Wayne returned to the living room, dressed in the clothes he'd brought with him, and packed his dirty things in his bag. Then he used the bathroom after Riley had finished. The last thing Riley did was take Frosty outside and then got her settled in her crate the for the day.

"Do you think your ex will be back?" Riley asked once they had Buster in the back seat and the car doors were closed. He started the engine and pulled away from the curb.

"I don't know. He did this for a reason, and somehow I don't think we've heard the last of him." He was scared that Mike would pull something else like this. Letting Buster out was a nasty thing to do, especially on a cold night. Wayne kept wondering what would have happened to him if his neighbor hadn't found him. He could have been…. He swallowed and tried not to think about it.

After only a few minutes, Riley pulled up in front of Wayne's house. "Who is that?" Riley asked as the garden gate closed from the inside.

"It looked like Mike," Wayne said, getting out as soon as the car stopped.

"Wait. You go in the front and be as quiet as you can. I'll go up the back and we'll trap him between us. We can leave Buster in the car and lock the door so he can't get to him. It won't be for very long." Riley was already out of the car and heading for the back gate. He opened it and slipped into the yard while Wayne went to the front and unlocked the door. Once he was inside, his heart raced as he climbed the stairs as quietly as he could, entering through the door into the living room and making his way toward the back.

The house was quiet, and he didn't get the feeling there was anyone here. As he was about to enter the kitchen, he heard the key in the back door. "What do you think you're doing?" Wayne heard Riley ask from outside.

"I live here," Mike said calmly. "What do you think you're doing?"

Wayne strode through the kitchen and yanked open the door, glaring at Mike. "You do not live here." Mike turned back to where Riley was blocking the stairs. "And you are not welcome here. Riley, call the police." He was getting really tired of Mike's attitude.

"I want my dog!" Mike bellowed as Riley made his call. "You aren't taking care of him properly, and he liked me more than he did you."

Wayne drew closer, locking his gaze on Mike's, putting all his anger and the fear of losing Buster into every bit of attitude he had. "Did you break in here and let Buster out yesterday?" Riley spoke on the phone as he circled behind Mike to stand in the doorway.

"I didn't break in! I…," Mike began and then clammed up, but he had already said too much.

"I knew it was you. Buster could have been hurt or he could have died with how cold it was last night. That was brutal."

Mike curled his upper lip. "I could have just taken him. He was home alone." He crossed his arms over his chest.

"Is that why you're here now? You figured you'd come back and steal him once I was gone for work?" Wayne's schedule had changed, and he now went in an hour later than he had when he and Mike were together. All Wayne could do was shake his head.

"Buster should have been my dog," Mike said with much less strength than before.

"No. He was never your dog. If you cared about him rather than just yourself, you would have left him alone." Wayne smiled as a notion occurred to him. "You did come here to take him yesterday. But Buster ran away from you, and you'd left the gate open, and he got loose." Wayne met Riley's gaze over Mike's shoulder as he spoke to the police. "You never intended for Buster to get out, and when you tried to catch him, Buster ran from you." Now the picture was clear.

"That's not true...." Mike's protests were beginning to sound feeble and ridiculous.

"Yes, it is. That's exactly what happened. Buster ran away from you because he doesn't like you. Never really has. Buster loves me, but he wants nothing to do with you." All Wayne could do was laugh, which was only making Mike angrier, but he couldn't help it.

"Davis is on his way over," Riley told them. "He said he and his partner are only a few minutes away."

Mike turned toward the stairs. "You can't keep me here." He tried to push past Riley, but it didn't work. Mike liked to talk big, but he didn't have enough weight or leverage to get around Riley.

"You were trying to get inside Wayne's home with a key you weren't supposed to have." Riley stood firm as his phone rang. He pulled it from his pocket. "Davis, we're around back." He shoved the phone in his pocket as the police came through the gate. Only then did Riley step aside and come around to where Wayne stood, putting an arm around him. "It's going to be okay now."

"I need to go get Buster," Wayne said softly, and Riley held him tighter.

"I know. But he's going to be okay, and once the police get done with Mike, I doubt he's going to be paying you another visit." The police escorted Mike down the stairs and then spoke to him in the backyard.

"Go on through the house and get Buster. I need to get to work or else I'm going to be late. But I'll stop by on my way home." He opened the door, and Wayne went inside. As soon as the door closed, Riley hugged him again, kissing him firmly. "I'll see you tonight."

Wayne followed him, and once he had Buster and his things out of the car, Riley hurried away, and Wayne took Buster inside.

WAYNE HAD hated leaving Buster at home, so he decided to take him in to the office with him. He had never done it before, but others in his office had brought in their pets from time to time, and this was a special circumstance. Buster was the hit of the office, with plenty of people stopping by to give him pets and say hello. Buster was well behaved, for the most part, and spent much of the day sleeping under Wayne's desk.

When it was time to leave, Wayne packed up his things and headed home, half expecting to find another mess of some sort, but he was alone and no one had been there. Wayne made sure the gate was closed and then let Buster run in the yard. After a while, he and Buster went inside, and Buster attacked his food dish, gobbling up what was left from earlier. Then he went to the front door and sat there as though waiting for something.

"I know. You want your friend to come over," Wayne said. Buster simply turned to look at him and then went back to watching the door. "Do you hear something?" Wayne opened the door to see Riley climbing the front stairs with Frosty leading the way. As soon as they came inside, he let her loose, and the two dogs hurried toward the kitchen.

"Hey," Wayne said softly.

"Hey," Riley returned. "How was your day? Well, after the mess with Mike."

Wayne shrugged, his gaze falling on Riley's lips. He drew closer and then kissed him, the heat between them building almost instantly. He'd had enough of work and ex-boyfriends trying to steal his dog. "Better now."

"Me too. And it's Friday." He smiled. "Oh, and I wanted to ask you something. Davis always does Christmas big, especially with Lilly, and I wanted to ask you to join us for the holiday."

"Won't I be… I don't know… a third wheel of some sort? It's your family holiday, and I don't want to intrude." Besides, if this was some sort of pity thing because he usually spent the holiday alone, then….

"You won't be. There will be my family and some old friends. It's a great gathering, and Stephanie is one heck of a cook. She's always asking me to bring someone for the holiday, and I never have because there was never anyone I wanted to bring… until you. So will you and Buster come?"

Wayne paused. "You want me to bring him too? Isn't that going to be too much? I mean, I can come, but…."

"Davis has a huge backyard that's fenced. I have strict instructions from my niece to bring Frosty, so yeah, bring Buster. And I have to warn you, don't be surprised if there are presents under the tree for him. My sister-in-law has already informed me that apparently dogs get Christmas gifts too." Riley smiled, and Wayne let go of some of his apprehension. If they wanted him to bring the dog, then they were his kind of people.

"Okay. Buster and I will spend Christmas with you. I haven't had a family holiday in a number of years." Wayne sat down, and Riley settled next to him. The dogs came running, with Frosty resting her head on Riley's lap and Buster climbing into Wayne's. Riley leaned against him with a soft sigh, and Wayne really relaxed.

"I like the thought of that, a real family Christmas, with you, me, and the dogs. It doesn't get much better than that."

Epilogue

I LOVED the holiday. There were lights and lots of people who slipped me treats while they ate. Papa Riley even gave me some of the turkey, and it was yummy. Princess, Buster, and me all played out back for a long time with Lilly and a bunch of new toys that squeaked. I love squeaky things. We chased each other all over the yard. Now I'm tired, and it's time to be warm and rest, and the rug in front of the fire is perfect.

Papa Riley is sitting on the sofa, next to Buster's papa Wayne. I want to go over to them, but they are happy, and the rug is nice and warm. Besides, they are holding paws and keep giving each other people kisses, and while those are nice, I like dog kisses better.

The rest of the people are talking and stuff, but I think I'm going to stay right here for now. It's comfy, and there are good smells, and the house is filled with lots of love. I know what that smells like, and it's even better than dog treats—but not bacon, because nothing is better than bacon. I think the people are getting ready to eat again, but I'm really full and happy.

I really like Papa Riley. He takes good care of me and he doesn't yell at me or say that I'm bad. He gives me a nice place to sleep, and he even brought me my doggie friend Buster. Last night Papa Riley said that maybe my friend Buster and his people friend Wayne could eventually make a family. I don't know how that kind of stuff works. Maybe they need to fill out a form like they did at the shelter. When Papa Riley brought me home, he filled out forms. They called them 'doption or something. Maybe Papa Riley and Wayne need to fill out a family form.

They're people kissing again and looking at each other with big eyes like they just saw a really juicy bone. They are happy, and me and Buster are happy. I hope they fill out that form soon, because I want all of us to be a family. What Papa Riley doesn't know yet is that we already are. I know it in my doggie heart, and dogs know that kind of stuff. Now the people just need to figure it out.

ANDREW GREY
THE GIFT OF THE
Maltipoo
A MUST LOVE DOGS COMPANION STORY

To Peter, Lisa, and the real Daisy.

Prologue

DAISY STOOD wagging her tail as hope and excitement rose once more. A man and a woman walked through the shelter, looking into the cages. They petted some dogs and had Andrew, the man who fed them sometimes, take one out and then put them back. Daisy wagged her tail harder as they got closer to her cage. She wanted to be good and look cute so they would give her a forever home.

She'd thought she already had one of those. Since she was a puppy, Karla had looked after her and loved her. Mom Karla had given her the best treats, and she slept at the foot of Mom Karla's bed. On cold nights, she even slept under the covers. Mom Karla was very special, and Daisy had loved her with her whole heart and soul and even her teeth. There was no part of her that didn't love Mom Karla.

They were in the car when the love came to an end. Mom Karla was taking Daisy to the park when there was a bang, boom, *scrunch* and then a smell that made Daisy want to hide. It was a bad smell, one Daisy never wanted to scent again. It was the end. Daisy tried to get to Mom Karla, but the doggie seat belt stopped her. She wanted to kiss her and make her better, but she couldn't. So Daisy waited with Mom Karla as the angels came and took the love part away. Daisy watched her go, and then a man got her out of the car and held her. He was so gentle, but Daisy was heartbroken. So she lay down and wished with all her might that the angels would bring Mom Karla back.

After that, everything was confusing, but she'd ended up at the shelter when there was no one else to love her. So now Daisy put on her best front. She wagged her tail and circled in the cage, excited to find a love like she had with Mom Karla. Daisy knew she was special and that she had lots and lots of love just waiting to burst out.

"This one is so cute," the woman said, and when the cage opened, Daisy hurried forward. When the woman picked her up, Daisy kissed her hand and nestled up next to her just like Mom Karla liked. "She is so sweet. Reggie, I want this one." She turned to the man, and Daisy did the same, giving her happy face.

"No. Too much of a mop dog, and her leg is bunged." Still, he lightly petted Daisy, and he wasn't rough or mean. "I need a dog I can take running with me. I don't think this little one will be able to keep up with me for very long." He lifted Daisy out of the woman's arms. "She's really sweet, though."

Daisy gave her best smile and, when she was close enough, kissed his nose.

"You are a real cutie. But I run in the mornings." He handed Daisy back, and Andrew returned her to the cage and closed the door.

Daisy watched as they moved on down the way. The woman kept turning around, and Daisy kept hoping, until they opened Lenny's cage. Both of them seemed to like him, and then they put a leash on Lenny and led him away. Daisy tried not to be disappointed, but it was hard. She lay down on the blanket and put her head on her front paws and sighed. Maybe she was never supposed to have the love she had before. Maybe Daisy only got that once. She closed her eyes and tried to rest, because happiness was exhausting, especially since she still loved Mom Karla.

"There you are," Mitchell said from outside her doggie dream. She opened her eyes as he opened the cage and lifted Daisy out. He was so gentle, and even though he had given Daisy a shot when she first arrived, he was so caring that Daisy forgave him. "Let's take a look at your back leg."

The accident that had taken Mom Karla had hurt her back leg, and it sometimes didn't work right. His hands were gentle as he felt along, and she was good, breathing quickly, but she didn't bite even when she yipped from the pain. "I know, sweetheart, but it's healing well, and soon you'll be all better. I promise. The leg will always be stiff, but the pain will go away." He set her back in the cage and gave Daisy a treat from his pocket.

"I know. You wish you could keep her," Andrew said.

"That's the trouble with having a dog rescue. I want to keep them all. But this little girl, she's a sweetheart. Her leg was broken when I brought her in, but it's getting a lot better now, and soon she'll be a hundred percent, just in time for Christmas."

"A couple was just in looking at her, but they chose another dog. Should I not show her yet?"

Mitchell looked through the wire. "Yes, you can show her. She's healing well. The best thing for this little girl is to find someone who will love her." His eyes were big and pretty and filled with love. Daisy licked his nose, and Mitchell laughed. "You're such a flirt. But I will get in trouble if I bring home another dog, so Andrew and I will just have to find you a special home where you'll be loved."

Mitchell closed the door, and Daisy lay down on the blanket in the back.

It was warm in the shelter, and that made Daisy sleepy. She closed her eyes and dreamed of chasing rabbits and lots of yummy treats. Mostly she dreamed of Mom Karla, because that was home. She wondered if anyplace would ever feel or smell that way again. Mitchell said he would find her a forever home, and Daisy hoped with her whole doggie heart that he was right.

Chapter 1

"Mom, I don't think a dog is a real good idea. How are you going to take care of it?" Tyler Lemieux was worried that his mother was going to get in over her head. "You're in the middle of chemo at the moment, and I can't be here every day. You know that. A dog is going to need to be walked multiple times a day, and sometimes you can barely get out of bed." He worried about her constantly.

Tyler picked up the glass of water from the side table and helped her drink before setting it back in place. His mother's cancer had been aggressive, and so had the treatment. The doctors were hopeful that with the tumor now gone, this would be the last of it once this round of chemo was over.

"But I get so lonely. Couldn't you find me a small dog?" she asked.

"Even small ones need to be walked. So how about this? Once the chemo is over, I will get you the dog of your choice. You can go with me to pick out the one you want. That way we can be sure of a great fit." He took her hand, and she half smiled.

"Okay. That's a deal." She closed her eyes, and Tyler left the room, closing the door. Knowing she would sleep for a while, he took a few minutes to clean up the kitchen and get the dishwasher running. He also did a load of laundry and wiped down the sinks and counters in the bathroom. His mother had always been a fastidious housekeeper, so the counters would have driven her crazy. Maybe they still did, but she just didn't have the energy to do anything about it.

Through the last six months, she had her good days and her bad days. Unfortunately, the bad days had been coming more often, but with only two more treatments left, he hoped that she would soon get some of her energy back and actually start to feel better.

He made a quick lunch for her and went into the bedroom. His mom was awake and ate a few bites before handing him the plate. "Everything tastes like sawdust."

"Then how about one of your shakes?" he asked and handed her one. She drank half of it before setting it aside. That was an improvement over the past few days, so he was pleased.

"I'll be fine. You need to get home, and I need to sleep for a while." She took his hand. "Tyler, I'm going to be fine. I know you're worried, but the doctor said that everything is looking good so far. Two more treatments and then this part of my life will be over and I can go back to living. And you know I'll make sure that you keep your promise." She smiled and for a second looked like the mother who had chased after him on the playground and read him bedtime stories.

"Okay. I'm going to go home for a while, but I'll stop in tomorrow if I can. There's some soup in the refrigerator." His friend Lily had made it and sent some for Mom knowing she loved it. "It's the chicken noodle you like so much. There's also some more crackers and the meal shakes."

She patted his hand. "I'll be fine. Don't worry. I'm going to rest for a while and then watch television. You go and have some fun. Stop worrying about me. This is almost over, and I'm going to kick cancer's ass or die trying." She grinned at her little joke, and Tyler did the same. "Carolyn is taking me for my next treatment at the end of the week so you can have a little time off." He'd gone with her to each one and sat with her as the damned machine pumped chemicals into her body. Tyler had hated seeing it, but he kept that to himself. There was no way in hell his mom was going to go through this on her own. It was bad enough that his father had taken off two years ago to start a new life with a woman two years older than Tyler, leaving his mom alone. He wasn't going to have her abandoned again.

"You call me if you need anything," he told her before leaving the room. He pulled on his winter coat and left the house. Snow was just beginning, so he started for home, hoping it was just a few flurries and not the start of something worse.

Tyler got into his truck and slowly backed out of his mom's driveway before heading to his home on the edge of Carlisle.

The way was very familiar. He had driven this route so many times, and he knew he each bump and every turn. Tyler was still thinking about his mother's request for a dog as he approached the dog rescue that he passed each and every day. Usually he just went by, but today his mom had gotten him thinking, so he pulled into the lighted yard and came to a stop near the well-kept barn.

He got out, thankful the snow had stopped, and went inside. The barn was warm and smelled clean. He hadn't known what to expect, except maybe the overwhelming scent of dog.

"Can I help you?" a man in his mid-thirties asked.

"My mom has cancer, and she keeps asking me to get her a dog. She had a pug named Bowser for years, and he passed away just after she was diagnosed. She asked me today about getting her another dog."

The man bit his lower lip. "I'm sorry, but we usually don't allow dog adoptions as gifts. A dog is a real responsibility, and…." He trailed off.

"I understand, and I wasn't in favor of just picking one out for her." He looked around. "Gosh, Mom would love this place. I remember when I was nine…." He leaned slightly on the counter. "Mom and I were on our way home from Grandma's, and we got a flat tire. While we were changing it, she found two puppies on the roadside. They had to be six weeks old, and it looked like they'd just been dumped there. Mom brought them home and fed them, and we had Frick and Frack until I graduated from high school. They were beautiful German shepherds. After they died, Mom got Bowser…."

"Charline? Is that your mom?" he asked, and Tyler nodded. "She got Bowser here. He was an older dog, and your mom fell in love with him. I knew your mom was perfect for him and would give him a good life."

"She really did. Those two were inseparable, and after Bowser passed, she wasn't sure that she wanted another dog, and now she's asking for one. And as much as I'd like to get her one, I know there is no way she can take care of it. Maybe in a month or so."

The man held out his hand. "I'm Mitchell. I own and operate the shelter in addition to the veterinary practice just up the road."

"I'm Tyler, part-time caregiver, full-time computer geek, and all-around good son. At least I try to be." He was so tired.

"Even though I know your mom, I can't let you pick out a dog for her. Too much can go wrong. But if you want to look around, you are more than welcome. Who knows? You might find a furry friend of your very own."

Tyler laughed softly. "My mom is the dog lover in the family. We always had one growing up, but they always bonded with everyone but me. There was Trooper, a beagle mix we got when I was nine. He was supposed to be my dog. I fed him and walked him… and he loved my mother best of all. That dog would follow her around the house all day, and then he'd sleep on the floor next to her bed. He could have slept on my bed and I would have loved it if he had been my best friend, but it didn't turn out like that. After that, I figured that I wasn't meant to be a dog person."

Mitchell shrugged. "If you want to take a look around, go ahead. We have some wonderful animals. There are a few that are not ready to be adopted. They're in the back. We found them last month, running wild in the woods to the west of town. They'd been there awhile, so we're trying to get them accustomed to people once more. But the rest are available." He seemed so nice that Tyler wandered through the shelter, looking at the various dogs.

At first he was just making a show of it, but after a while, he found himself really looking. What if he did get a dog? Or better yet, what if he got a dog and kept it at his house until his mom was feeling better? He could bring the dog over to her house to visit and keep her company while she was feeling badly. This was a good idea. He'd have a dog, and his mom would have company a day or so a week. A dog would be the perfect Christmas gift for her, and this way there was no pressure. He started looking more in earnest.

There was a small terrier with bright eyes and a tail that wagged like crazy. He stood on all fours, as excited as anything. He might have been too high energy, though he was cute. There was a small collie mix who sat right near the door. As soon as he put his hand near the door, the dog leaned against it, then turned and licked his fingers.

"He's a real good dog. His owner passed away, and his daughter is allergic, so they brought him here," Mitchell said. "Though he needs a yard and space to run. He's about three and still has a lot of energy." He opened the cage and let Ralphy out. He sat next to Tyler's feet and leaned against his legs.

"He's really nice." Tyler knelt down and ran his hands down Ralphy's back, gently petting him. He was beautiful, but way too much animal for his mother—or him, for that matter. Mitchell put Ralphy back in the cage, and Tyler continued on. "Who is this?"

Mitchell opened the cage and gently lifted out a white dog with the cutest face. "This is Daisy. Her owner was killed in a car accident. The police brought her into the practice. She had hurt her leg, and we've gotten her fixed up and on the mend. She is really sweet, and her leg is healing as well as we can expect. She is always going to be a little stiff because of the injury, but she is super sweet." Mitchell gently put Daisy into his arms, and she settled right down. After a few seconds, she looked up at him and that tongue licked his chin.

"Well, aren't you a sweetheart," Tyler crooned softly. She gave him another kiss, and he smiled. "She's got a real tongue on her, doesn't she?"

"Yes. Daisy is a Maltese mix, probably part poodle. I've had a number of people look at her, but because of her leg, they always move on. She is just as sweet as can be. But everyone wants a perfect dog. She's going to have trouble getting up on a bed herself, but I knew her owner. I've looked after Daisy since she was a puppy."

Tyler looked into her big eyes and could feel himself falling in love. "Do you want to come home with me?" Tyler asked, and Daisy licked his chin and nose. Then she settled down into his arms and rested her head against his chest. "Okay. I'm going to take that as a yes." He held her gently. "I know you're excited, but I have to set you down so I can fill out all the forms that Mitchell needs." The truth was, Daisy felt so good in his arms that he didn't want to release her.

"Okay." Mitchell led him to the desk area, and Tyler set Daisy on a blanket on one of the chairs. Then he filled out the forms and made a donation to the shelter for the care of the other dogs. Mitchell made sure he had the basic supplies, and Tyler took them to the car before returning for Daisy. He placed everything into the cab of his truck and set off to take her home.

"I hope you like the house. It's nice enough, but I'm going to have to move some things around so its doggie-proofed." He kept talking to her as he drove through the snow before pulling into the driveway of his home.

The first thing he did was get Daisy inside, and then he brought in her things. He set up a bowl with food and one with water in the kitchen, then placed her down on the floor.

She walked slowly to the dishes and ate a little before drinking some water. When Tyler started working in the kitchen, she made her way back to where he was pulling some things out of the refrigerator for dinner. Daisy sat near the open refrigerator door watching him, and then, once he had warmed up his dinner, sat next to him at the table. She didn't beg or make a fuss, just settled at his feet as he ate.

"You really are a good dog," Tyler told her.

As he was finishing, the doorbell rang. Daisy barked and hurried over, limping a little as she moved more quickly. She barked once more and slid back as Tyler opened the door.

"Who is this?" his neighbor, Anthony, asked, kneeling down.

"This is Daisy," Tyler said. "I got her today at a dog rescue. I thought she could keep Mom company sometimes. She's really sweet." Tyler watched as Anthony gave Daisy some attention. Part of him was a little jealous because he had been trying to get Anthony to notice him for a few months now. Anthony had dark hair and eyes, and Tyler wished he could say something to him, maybe ask him out or something, but he never got up the courage.

"She's a real sweetheart," Anthony said. "But it looks like she has a hurt leg." He kept stroking her, and Daisy soaked it up.

"Yeah. She was in an accident. The vet said to make sure she takes it easy and not to let her jump up and down from the furniture by herself. He said she should get better but that she might always have a slight limp."

Anthony stood back up, and Daisy came over to Tyler, looking up expectantly. He lifted her into his arms. "Would you like a beer or something?" He wasn't sure what had brought Anthony over, but he hoped he would stay awhile. During the summer, Tyler had noticed on more than one occasion that Anthony tended to mow his lawn shirtless, and that was quite a sight.

"Sure."

Tyler went to get two beers and handed one to Anthony before taking a seat. He placed Daisy on the sofa, and she settled right next to him. "Is there something you need?"

"Yeah, I guess," Anthony said. "Ummm… I'm not sure how to ask, but I was hoping… see, I have a work thing, and my boss is being a real dick about it. He's made a big deal about everyone bringing someone to the office party. My law firm isn't that big, and I'm hoping to make partner in the next few years." He took a big swig from the beer. "Anyway, I don't have anyone to go with, and I was hoping you might want to go with me."

Tyler was shocked. He and Anthony had waved and said hello through the summer and fall, but they hadn't talked much. Maybe that was because Anthony was just really busy. "When is the party?"

"On the eighteenth, and I'd understand if you'd rather not go with me. I mean, we say hello and stuff, but I've been so busy that we never really get a chance to talk. But you were always nice, and you helped me out when that tree fell across my driveway and I needed to get to work." Anthony seemed a little tightly wound.

"Sure. I'd like to go." He had forgotten all about the tree incident. "I'm free that day. What sort of dress is it?"

Anthony sighed. "Black tie. I should have said that earlier. I can pay for a rental for you if—"

"I have a tux. A few years ago I had three cousins get married in the same year, so I bought a tux and wore it to all the weddings rather than renting one. It also saved me from having to rent one of those godawful gray things with a purple shirt. So yeah, I'd like to go. Do you want to pick me up?"

"Yeah. That would be great." Anthony leaned back in the chair, more relaxed. Daisy snuggled closer, and Tyler gently stroked down her back, wondering how he'd gotten a dog and a date on the same day. Though this was probably just him helping a neighbor with a work thing. Tyler needed to remind himself not to get too ahead of things. He was going with Anthony to a work event. It wasn't like he had been invited to a romantic evening at a fancy restaurant or anything. It was just dinner. And yet, every time he looked at Anthony, he couldn't help but hope that it meant just a little more.

Chapter 2

ANTHONY CARTER fussed with his damned tie. He wore one every day, but this morning he couldn't seem to get the front longer than the tail, and it was driving him crazy. He undid it and started again, finally getting it so the damned thing looked right. Some mornings it didn't pay to get out of bed. He adjusted his collar before heading to the kitchen for a cup of coffee. Then he pulled on his overcoat and went to his car to head into the office.

It was still dark when Anthony arrived, and he turned on a few lights as he went. He entered his office and left the door open before sitting down at his desk. He started by answering his email and forwarded others to his paralegal for him to handle. Then he reviewed the brief he'd finished after having a beer with Tyler. He'd probably stayed too late at his house, but Tyler was nice, and it wasn't like Anthony had much time to socialize or that he was generally very good at it.

"Morning," someone said from outside the door, and he responded automatically, barely looking up from his computer. He had a lot to do, and this appeal brief needed to be right. His client had been convicted of robbery and assault during a liquor store holdup, except that the court-appointed attorney had made so many errors during the trial that it was hard to keep track of them. The client's sister had hired Anthony to do the appeal. He checked his notes, reviewing all his points and making sure they were in the brief, including the suppression of evidence that his client was actually somewhere else at the time of the robbery. In his opinion, Judge Marshall had been sloppy, but he couldn't say that in the brief. Happy with his work, he saved the file and sent a note to Jasper to see him.

"Tony," a gruff voice said from the doorway.

Anthony took a deep breath and held it. He hated being called Tony. He was not a Tony and he never would be. But the senior partner, Richard Langley, insisted on using that nickname, and he needed to keep the old jackass happy.

"Morning," he said.

"Is the Johnson brief done?" he asked.

"Yes. Ready to be filed this morning," he answered. Richard always treated him like he was a fool and like he was going to be late for everything. The brief was complete and ready to be electronically filed today. He had also drafted the brief for the Phillips case, but that would need another day or two.

His phone rang. "Is there something you needed? This is a client I've been talking to." He waited for Richard, who seemed to be debating.

"Take the call and then come to my office." He turned away, and Anthony answered the call just before his voicemail kicked in.

"Anthony Carter, good morning," he said, and what he got was silence.

"I wish it was. The police charged Hansen this morning, and I've decided to engage you for his defense." Connor Jacobs was the patriarch of one of the oldest families in Carlisle. "How soon can you meet with us so we can review everything?"

Anthony checked his calendar. "Is he out on bail? Do you need me to help arrange it?"

Connor cleared his throat. "His previous attorney, who I just fired, didn't botch that, at least. So yes, he has bail."

Anthony pulled up his calendar. "Then can you all come in on Thursday at one?" He was already reserving a secure conference room.

"Yes. That will be fine," Connor said firmly, but his voice broke suddenly, and that told Anthony a lot. This might be a high-powered parent, but he loved his son a great deal.

Anthony finalized the conference room and brought up their standard engagement form and fee structure. "Okay. I have the email address you gave me after our last call. I'm going to email you an engagement letter as well as a fee agreement. I believe that clients should be clearly informed up front what they are paying for. You'll have those within the hour. Please sign both and return them to us. As soon as I have them, I'll begin work."

"Fair enough. Can I reach you at this number?" Connor asked.

"Yes. But if I'm engaged, you can also call my paralegal, Jasper." He gave Connor the number. "Is there anything else you need at the moment?"

"You need to know that I'm an impatient and demanding man. I expect excellence."

"Then that's what you'll get. But I caution you, patience is something you are going to need. The gears of the legal process sometimes grind slowly, and quite often patience is rewarded. Just remember that. This isn't a sprint but a marathon, and we need to be ready for that."

"Fair enough," Connor said. "Get those forms over and we'll get this moving forward." He ended the call. Anthony got to work customizing the letters to the client and called Helen, Richard's assistant.

"Is he available?"

"Not at the moment," Helen said. "I'll call you when he's off the phone."

"You're a gem," he told her, and she chuckled as she hung up.

Anthony finished the letters and sent them to Connor just as Helen called. Anthony grabbed his iPad and headed to Richard's corner office.

Helen ushered him right in and closed the door after him.

"I'll get right to the point. Rumor has it that Connor Jacobs is looking for new representation for his son." Anthony was about to give Richard the good news, but he plowed on. "We are going to chase that particular whale, and Harry Phillips will be leading the effort. I'd like you to assist him on this one." Anthony and Harry had both been bucking for partner for the last couple of years. "We think that he'll be a better fit to take the lead on this case."

That was a load of bullshit. Harry was a schmoozer. He always talked a great game. It bowled Anthony over that Richard and some of the other partners didn't see that he was all hot air. A message came across the screen of his iPad, and he opened it and quickly brought up the documents already signed by Connor. "I'm sorry, but that isn't possible." He left the agreement up and set the iPad on Richard's desk. "Connor Jacobs engaged us—and me—just before I came in here."

Richard glanced down at the signed agreement and blinked like he didn't believe it. "You landed Connor Jacobs?" He sat forward in his chair.

"I have a signed engagement letter, and he reviewed and acknowledged our fee structure."

A smile graced Richard's lips. "Send me a copy of it. I want to put together the best team that the firm has for this." He was practically salivating.

"Umm. I think you need to read the letter more closely. He specified that I was to be his attorney, and that is how I wrote the engagement letter." Richard snatched up the iPad and read through what Connor had signed. "You can see he even underlined that part of the agreement." Anthony didn't know if Richard was going to be angry, but he just smiled.

"Damn, you have some brass nuts on you, that's for sure. Okay. If that's what the client wants...."

"I have a meeting with him at one on Thursday. Part of that meeting is to discuss how much of a defense team he is willing to commit to." Anthony knew Richard was eager to throw everything the firm had at this case, but Connor had to be willing to pay for it, and Richard knew that.

"Good. If we win this case, then it's likely Connor will send more of his legal work our way, and that would be beneficial to the firm—and could facilitate the advancement of the lawyer who makes it happen." Richard just couldn't help dangling that carrot.

"I understand."

"Also, the Christmas party would be a good chance for you to interact and impress the partners in a social setting." Of course Richard had to bring that up. "I hope you aren't planning to show up alone... again." The near derision was hard to miss. "You remember that every year we collect donations to support a local charity, and this year my wife convinced the partners that we should support a dog rescue."

Anthony couldn't figure out why it mattered so damned much what was happening in his personal life, but he had been told that he wasn't being singled out; Richard was like this with everyone. Gene, one of the other partners, had once told him that in a past life, Richard had probably been a professional matchmaker. Still, Anthony did his job and was damned good at it. His billable hours were at the very top of the firm on a regular basis. He smiled and nodded. "Was there something else you wished to speak about?"

"Not at this time," Richard said and Anthony left the office, stopping by Jasper's desk on his way to his own.

"We need to talk right away," he told him, and Jasper followed him in and closed the door. Anthony sat at his desk and motioned for Jasper to take one of his chairs. "I just landed the defense for Hansen Jacobs. His father engaged us on his behalf after firing his previous attorney. Now, of course we're acting as defense, but you know how I like to do things."

"You want me to find out the facts?" Jasper asked.

"Yes. I want to build a case for the defense, and get me a copy of the police reports and any witness statements. Let's see what we're dealing with. Also, I sent you the Johnson brief. Get that filed with the court this morning."

"I saw it and filed it electronically along with all our exhibits while you were in your meeting. I got a confirmation of receipt and added it to our files and emailed you a copy."

"Great. We have a meeting at one on Thursday. I want you to be there, and make sure Brenda is there as well." She was his intern, and he wanted her there to listen and learn. Brenda was smart and showed real promise.

"What about anyone else?" Jasper asked.

"Part of that meeting is to figure out what resources Jacobs wants us to put on the case, so for now, this meeting will be the three of us. From there, we'll bring in others as needed and authorized." He sighed. "Now I just have to deal with the office Christmas party."

Jasper glanced at the door. "Richard has been a real jackass to a couple of the new associates about dates and family and shit. They may be inexperienced, but it is not going to look good if they quit and charge the firm with harassment. Especially since he's doing it to multiple people. I know he likes this to be a couples type of thing, but he's skirting close to the line."

Anthony was well aware. "Tell them to ignore it and to come and have a good time. I have come alone for the last three years. It's just Richard's way of playing matchmaker." He smiled. "And apparently we're supporting a dog rescue this year." He couldn't help snickering. "I wonder what Richard would say if one of us actually brought a dog to the party?" Instantly his mind went to Tyler and Daisy. Damn, he was willing to bet Tyler looked danged good in a tux. And just like that, an event he'd been dreading became something he was looking forward to.

"Are you seeing someone?" Jasper said with a wicked grin. Sometimes he was too observant for his own good.

"Why ask that?"

"Because you went all gooey-eyed. The last time you did that was last year when you were seeing that painter guy. Every time someone mentioned anything to do with art, you got all gooey, and then you stopped when he turned out to be a shit. Is he your date this year?"

"I'm coming with a friend. He's my neighbor, and I do not get gooey-eyed, so let's not mention that again."

Jasper gaped at him. "So you're bringing your neighbor to the party. Is it a date? Because if it is, you do not want your work party to be a first date. That is way too tacky for words. You need to ask him out properly and take him to dinner or something. I mean, what sort of nice evening out is a dinner of rubber chicken, cheap alcohol, and small talk with your boss? Then follow it all up with the damned chicken dance, because you know he's going to play that song." Jasper cringed. "And he makes everyone get out on the floor."

"Good God," Anthony groaned.

"Yeah. So ask your neighbor out, and I'll make a reservation at a nice place. At least you'll find out if you'll get along or if the work party will be even more tedious and tension filled than normal." He smiled, and Anthony knew he was right. In most parts of his life, he was confident and self-assured. In the courtroom, he knew his opponents' next moves long before they did. He was steps ahead of everyone, including the judge. But his personal life was a disaster. Hell, he spent the previous summer and fall watching his neighbor and wondering about him, but he never did a damned thing. Granted, his dating life was a real mess. He seemed to attract losers and cheaters. And it seemed like he was destined to spend another holiday season alone.

"Okay. I will. He agreed to come with me to the party yesterday, so I can ask him to dinner to thank him in advance."

Jasper rolled his eyes. "Jesus, just tell the guy that you like him and ask him to dinner. You don't need to beat around the bush like you're fourteen years old. The worst he can say is that he wants to be friends, and that isn't so bad." He got up from his seat. "And with that bit of relationship advice, I'm going to get a start on the things you need, and you can get yourself back to work. We want to be as prepared as we possibly can before this meeting." He left the office, and Anthony checked on the status of each of his cases before digging into as much information as he could get on Hansen Jacobs.

FORTUNATELY IT wasn't snowing and the sidewalks in the subdivision were clear, the sun having done its work. Anthony got out of his BMW and was heading inside when Tyler came down the walk with Daisy on a leash. They walked slowly, and she limped slightly as they moved.

"How was work?" Tyler asked as they approached. Daisy hurried over to Anthony, and he gave her pets.

"You're a sweet girl," he said to her. "Work was fine. I landed what could be an important client today. The case is reasonably high-profile."

"What sort of law do you practice?" Tyler asked.

"Mostly I'm a defense lawyer. In a lot of my cases, I either try to instill reasonable doubt in the jury or, on rare occasions, I'm trying to prove innocence. That doesn't happen very often, but I have had cases where I was able to fully prove that my client couldn't have done it. But I've never had a Perry Mason moment where the real guilty party confesses on the stand." He grinned. "I also do appeals. I'm very successful with the ones I take on. What sort of work do you do?"

"I'm a games designer. I'm currently working on *Zombie Apocalypse 3*. The first two have done really well, so I decided to try to come up with an interesting concept for the third one."

"No way," Anthony said. "I played the first one when I was in law school. I must have killed thousands of zombies. It was the one thing that I could do to relax. There's so much pressure, and I got little downtime, but when I did, I played with friends for a few hours every Sunday afternoon. We were all in the pressure cooker. You created that game?"

Tyler grinned. "Yeah. That was my first really big hit. I'd come up with a few concepts before that, but they never got picked up. Up until that point, I worked on other people's games. But that one was all mine, and it paid for my house. The second one is almost as popular, and once I finish this one, we're going to bring out updated versions of the first two." He was really excited, and Daisy sort of danced around his legs. Tyler picked her up, and she curled up against him.

"I think she's getting cold."

"Yeah, she probably is." Tyler unzipped his coat and placed her nearer to his warmth.

"I was wondering if you would like to have dinner with me Friday night? We could go to Café Belgie or something." God, why was he so nervous?

"You mean like a date?" Tyler bit his lower lip, and Anthony realized he was just as nervous.

"Yes. Like a date. I can pick you up at seven and we can go to dinner." He tried to sound confident.

"Okay. That would be nice." Daisy licked Tyler's chin as though she approved of the plan. "I'll see you Friday at seven." He smiled and then turned and headed back home. Anthony walked slowly and didn't go inside until Tyler was out of sight.

Chapter 3

"YOU'RE LOOKING better," Tyler said when he found his mom sitting in her living room, a mug of tea in front of her along with the remains of her lunch. He closed the door and let Daisy explore the room.

"I'm hungry, which is a good sign." She leaned forward. "And who is this sweet girl?"

"Daisy," Tyler said. "I got her at the dog rescue on my way home after our last visit. Your request got me thinking, so I stopped in for the heck of it." He smiled as Daisy came over to him and looked up with those big eyes. He lifted her onto the sofa next to Mom, and Daisy accepted pets from her like the little princess she was.

"She's a sweetheart." Mom looked her over. "She's hurt."

"Yeah, but her leg is getting better. She isn't supposed to jump down yet, so don't let her." He gathered up the dishes and took them to the kitchen before getting his mom one of her shakes. Tyler opened it for her, and she drank half, which was an even better sign. She must be feeling better. She hadn't eaten that much in a long time. "When is your next appointment?"

"I had a treatment two days ago, and my last one is next week. Then I'm done. While I was there, they ran some more scans, and the doctor called an hour ago to say that everything is looking good, so I'll be done and through this mess before Christmas." She smiled and slowly petted Daisy, who watched Tyler like a hawk.

He sat on the far end of the sofa, and Daisy came over to him and settled on his lap with a sigh. "She's really taken with you."

"I guess so." He scratched her ears and watched her. The little one was really worming her way into his heart. "I had thought to get her and then, when you were feeling better, she could live with you. But…."

Mom chuckled. "No. She's your dog. This little girl has bonded with you, and she's happy. I bet there's a story locked behind those big puppy eyes."

"She was in a car accident that her owner didn't survive. Mitchell told me that, and he said that was how she hurt her leg. Apparently her owner adored her. Mitchell was Daisy's vet for most of her life, so he knew her pretty well." He leaned down, and Daisy got him with that Gene Simmons-length tongue. "Sometimes I swear she's mostly tongue."

"She likes you." Mom sighed and leaned back. Soon she nodded off. Tyler hadn't gotten a chance to tell her all his news, but there was no need to worry about it. He gently set Daisy aside and got a blanket, covering Mom with it before helping Daisy down to the floor. Then he quietly left the house to let Mom rest.

DAISY LAY on the bed, watching as Tyler stood in front of his closet, trying to figure out what to wear. "I know a suit is too much, and I'm not wearing jeans, so what else is there?"

He turned to Daisy, who blinked at him and put her head on her paws.

"You know, you're not helping."

Her tail thumped the bed a few times, and then she closed her eyes like she'd lost interest. Tyler continued looking and found a pair of dress pants. He set them on the bed and found a shirt that he hoped went with them.

Then he dressed and checked himself in the mirror. Daisy stood up on the bed, tail going a mile a minute. She seemed to approve, but that only proved that dogs were color-blind, because he looked terrible. The shirt was all wrong. He took it off and found a white one. At least it went with everything, even if it would be a challenge to keep from spilling on it.

"Is that better?" he asked.

Daisy huffed and lay down. Clearly the previous shirt looked better to a dog.

Tyler checked the time and slipped on his shoes before lifting Daisy into his arms and taking her downstairs. "You know that once your leg is better you're going to have to do this yourself." He set her down, and she ambled off to check her dish. Then he got his coat and set it near the door. "You need to be good while I'm gone." He settled Daisy on the blanket on the sofa where she could see out if she wanted to. Then, when Anthony knocked, his heart skipped a beat, and he hurried to answer it.

"Are you ready?" Anthony asked.

"I just need to put on my coat." He got it and shrugged it on as Anthony said hello to Daisy. Thankfully she stayed where she was and didn't try to jump down. Still, she was about to, so he set her on the floor, and they left for the evening.

"Apparently her leg is feeling better," Anthony said. Daisy looked out the front window, giving them sad eyes.

"It is, which is good, but I keep worrying she'll reinjure it." He got into the car, and Anthony closed the door before hurrying to the driver's side. He slid into the warm car and started the engine, pulled out, and they were off toward town.

Café Belgie was full, and they were shown right to their table. "I haven't been here before."

"Really?" Anthony said. "I often call ahead and get something to go after I've had a long day at work. It's always really good." He smiled, and Tyler looked over the menu, his stomach growling. Apparently he had worked head-down through lunch and completely forgotten to eat since breakfast. "How was your day?"

"Really good. I made a lot of progress on the game and even went back and added a few hidden traps as well as a few Easter eggs and a wormhole or two just for fun. I've got the first nine levels completed, and the next eleven are designed. The basics of the game are set, and so is the overall goal, so now it's just getting all the details filled in." He loved this stage of game development. "And since it's Christmas, I already added two levels that will only appear during December." He leaned over the table. "And I'm not telling anyone. The game is supposed to release in August, so by doing this, I can get the die-hard fans to play again, just to experience these two levels where I make Santa a zombie fighter and the elves get turned into zombies with special powers. The player actually has to make Santa decide if he wants to kill the zombie, and if he doesn't, then you must or you both die. But if they can find the 'cure,' then they can change the elves back and save Christmas."

Anthony laughed as Tyler continued, "Except the evil elf Rachel, because she's the one that turned the elves into zombies in the first place."

Anthony's eyes widened. "I love that. Zombie elves. But what about Mrs. Claus and the reindeer?" he added.

Tyler gasped. "I could make the second level harder by making the reindeer zombies too, and they are after Mrs. Claus. The player and

Santa have to protect her, and to save all of Christmas, they have to find the reindeer cure as well. It can be a game within a game, and the option will only be available in December." Tyler pulled out his phone and sent himself a reminder note. "That's awesome." This was so exciting.

"But what happens if they save Christmas? What do they get?" Anthony asked. "I mean, these games often give a reward like a special item, but what if they got a real-world gift?"

Tyler gasped. "I'd need to check with my producer, but we could make up Christmas action figures, and if they finish the Christmas levels, they get a unique code that they can use to get the special action figure. We've already put out limited-edition ones to go with the games, so we could make one specially for this, and the only way to get it is through the code. The fans will love it." He made another note to run all this by his agent and Xavier at the game company to see what they thought. "How are things going for you with this big case?"

"I can't go into any details, but it's going well. I had my first meeting with my new client, and he told me his version of the events. Apparently he wasn't even there at the time. The prosecution is saying that he's an accessory, and believes he was still in the car." He grinned. "What I think the South Middleton police are really angry about is that when they came calling, he refused to answer any of their questions and said he would only speak through his attorney. This is mostly good for us, but it puts him smack in the middle of an issue, because he potentially knew of a crime to be committed and simply went home."

"But he didn't know they were going to do actually do it. Knowledge is one thing, and he could be a witness, but extricating himself from a situation he wasn't comfortable with or happy about is a good thing. It showed he wasn't going to be pressured into doing wrong."

"Yes. But if it's a gray area for us, it is for them too, and I can exploit it." They paused their conversation and ordered drinks.

"You really seem happy." Anthony really did have an amazing smile.

Anthony chuckled, and Tyler loved that happy sound. "I love to win, I really do. Losing in court sucks, especially when you believe in your client. I don't always. Being a defense attorney means that you sometimes have to take on people you know are guilty and still do your best for them. Anyway, that's enough of that sort of talk. I've got some news on the office party."

"Did they cancel or something?" Tyler asked. He'd been looking forward to it.

"Oh, no. But there is always a charity involved, and this year it's a dog rescue. I'm not sure which one, but it could be where you got Daisy. Anyway, I wanted to extend to her an invitation as well. She is a rescue, after all, and if that's what we're supporting, then she should be able to come."

"Really? You want Daisy to come? You know she'll want to see everyone."

"That's okay. We can get her a Christmas collar with a pretty bow, and she can be as festive as everyone else. Besides, it will give us an excuse to sit out the chicken dance."

"Oh my God... no." Tyler leaned over the table. "You have to be kidding me."

"Nope. Richard insists on playing that song every year, and he waits until everyone is well lubricated before doing it."

"Fine, we'll stay with Daisy, and I can take video so we'll have a record of this. Can you imagine the blackmail potential?" He put his hand over his mouth and giggled like a kid. "Oh my God. You could use that alone to make partner." He was kidding, and thankfully Anthony got it.

"I really hate that sort of childish stuff. It's like he does it just to show that he can strong-arm people into it. The associates feel intimidated, and... it's just wrong."

"Then we'll sit it out this year, and I'll even let you hold Daisy so you have a visible excuse." Tyler was more than willing to have Anthony's back.

"It's this sort of thing that makes our profession seem stupid. It's like it's a frat house all over again, and everyone is trying to make the grade. You'd think we'd all have grown up a lot by now, but nope." Their server arrived and took their orders. "What do you do for fun?"

"Not much at the moment. I've been very busy. My mom was diagnosed with liver cancer six months ago. They operated and removed the cancerous tumor, and she's been undergoing chemo. They believe that they got it early enough that she is going to make it through, but the chemo has been really tough, so I spend a lot of my spare time at her place. There's a lot she can't do right now, so I'm pitching in. She has just one more treatment to go, and we're hoping that's the end of it and she'll start to get stronger."

"I'm sorry to hear that. What about your dad?"

"Oh… he's in Hawaii with his much younger wife, desperately trying to turn back the clock. He's a surgeon, so he used some of his connections to have himself youngified for his nubile wife. They just had their second baby. So my dad has children who are young enough to be his grandchildren. He and my mother don't speak much, and he's too busy with his new life to get involved." The only bright spot was that the court had ruled that since his mom had supported him through college and medical school, he had to pay her a portion of his income for the rest of her life. "What about your folks? I bet they're really proud of you."

"They are." Anthony smiled. "They live in the mountains of North Carolina. They wanted a place that wouldn't get too cold in the winter or too hot in the summer. They found a really nice, relatively small community there, and they love it. I go to visit them a couple times a year. They're right outside Cherokee."

"Sounds nice. What are they like?"

"Well, Mom was a kindergarten teacher, and my dad started out teaching third grade. In his forties he was made a principal, and in his fifties he became superintendent of schools in the Little Spring School District. They retired a few years ago and got out of town. I think that after all those years of raising me and staying in this area, they wanted something different. I just want them to be happy and live a good life. They deserve it."

Tyler found himself nodding. "Mom deserves it too."

THE FOOD was amazing and the conversation lively and fun. They stayed away from serious topics for the rest of dinner. Tyler found out that Anthony had a great sense of humor and that once he came out of his shell, he could laugh at a joke and even at himself, which was a rare trait.

Their dessert was gorgeous, a mint and chocolate mousse in a dark chocolate shell. They shared one, and Tyler almost wished he could have another. But he was full and happy. Best date he'd had in a very long time. The two of them left together and got into Anthony's car before slowly riding through town.

"When I was a kid, Mom and Dad used to pile us in the car so we could go look at the lights. Let me show you something." Anthony headed east out of town and turned past the Giant. As they neared the freeway, they entered a fairyland of lights and motion. "These homes always go all out."

"How did I not know this was here?" Tyler asked. Six houses were fully decked out with thousands of lights, inflatables, and even dancing lights set to music. It was amazing. They watched the display for a while before turning around and heading back through town and out to their development.

"I think I need to put up some lights of my own," Tyler said. "I never have, but after seeing those, I think we need a little more festiveness around here. I know I have lights around somewhere, and the tree on the side of the front yard would look good with lights on it."

"Yeah, it would. The previous owners left the brackets on the house, so I can light the eaves." Anthony sounded as excited as Tyler felt. "You want to see what we have and put things up tomorrow?"

"Sounds like a plan," Tyler said as Anthony pulled into his drive and up to the garage. "Would you like to come in for a drink?"

"That would be nice, but I haven't left Daisy alone for very long since I got her. So if you don't mind, we could go to my place. I have beer and the mixings for some basic cocktails."

"Then cocktails it is." Anthony got out, and they walked through the yard to Tyler's door. Daisy barked on the other side as he unlocked it, and then she stood there wagging her tail. As soon as Tyler got inside, she bounded around until he picked her up. She wriggled and gave him kisses before settling in his arms. She definitely was his dog.

"Come on." He set Daisy on her blanket on the chair and took off his coat. "What sort of cocktail do you like?"

"A dry gin martini would be perfect."

"Right up my alley." He got out the pitcher and began mixing them before chilling the glasses with ice and finding a couple of olives. Then he handed Anthony his drink and sat next to him on the sofa.

"I love these," Anthony said, humming softly as he sipped. "This is good." He sipped again and then set the glass on the coffee table. Tyler did the same. He turned to Anthony to ask a question and locked gazes with him. Anthony leaned closer, and Tyler held his breath. Then

Anthony stopped, his eyes filling with doubt. Tyler gently slid his hand over Anthony's cheek and drew him closer until their lips touched.

Daisy yipped from the chair. Anthony deepened the kiss, and Daisy yipped once more. "I think she's jealous," Tyler said.

"I'd say she had a right to be," Anthony whispered before the intensity of the connection blocked out everything else.

Chapter 4

ANTHONY WAS on solid ground for probably the first time that day as he strode into the conference room for an initial meeting with the prosecutor's office regarding the Jacobs case. He had read the arrest report as well as everything else Jasper had been able to help him dig up, so he felt prepared, but he also knew that these things could be unpredictable.

Jasper and Brenda joined him, and they walked into the room and made introductions around the table. Casey Brannigan was the assistant district attorney in charge. Anthony had worked with him in the past. He was a good prosecutor and could be a bit of a bulldog,

"Look, I'm going to start by saying that we have a solid case against your client," Casey began. "We can place your client at the scene of the robbery, and he was part of the conversations regarding what they intended. We have a witness statement from one of the others in the car."

"I see. And did you make some sort of deal with this person? Because if you did, then I suggest you terminate it, because they're lying to you." Anthony opened the folder in front of him. "As you know, I'm not required to provide you anything during discovery, but I'm going to do you a huge favor. See, the police in South Middleton missed something." He pulled out a still photograph and passed it across the table. "Check out the time."

Casey took the image and looked at it. "That's the same time as the robbery."

"Yes, it is. According to my client, he heard their talk and got out of the car because he wanted nothing to do with what they were planning. And he walked home. I'm sure you read that in his statement." Anthony tapped the image. "That proves that what he says is true. That is from the ATM camera on Carlisle Pike, at least a mile away from the robbery, at the exact same time. Now, I can't provide you with a copy of the entire video, but I'm sure you can get your own with a warrant. But if I were you, I'd abandon this prosecution now and save yourself embarrassment and time." He pushed the image across the table.

"And how did you get this recording?" Casey asked as he leaned over the table.

Anthony turned to Jasper, who answered. "It's my bank. I simply went in, told them what happened, and asked for a look at the camera feed. The manager was kind enough to let me look, and when I told him that it could prove someone's innocence, he contacted his supervisor and they let me have a copy with the stipulation that I not distribute it. However, I do have permission to use it in court. But you can get your own copy. Just ask nicely."

Casey swallowed hard. "Can I view the entire video?"

"Of course. Jasper...?" Anthony motioned to him, and Jasper turned his computer and played the one-minute-long clip.

"This is the raw clip, and you can see our client in the background. If we zoom in a little, he becomes even more discernable." Jasper zoomed in on what was clearly Hansen Jacobs, who even turned toward the camera at one point, expression miserable.

Casey sat back in his chair with a sigh. "How did you find this?"

Anthony shrugged. "We listened to our client and believed him. The police didn't check everything that they should have. The police report clearly documents that Hansen said he left the car, but they only chose to believe the statement of the people who actually robbed the store. All we had to do was trace his route home and we found a camera that could prove where he was." Now was the time to press his advantage. "I have a press conference scheduled for first thing in the morning, so you have until tonight to drop all of the charges against my client, or we will go public with everything." He handed Casey the photograph. "Look, I'm doing you a favor. You need to concentrate on the people who actually performed the robbery. Hansen is more than willing to cooperate regarding what was said in the car and why he got out, but not until all charges are dropped. Then he will give a statement and cooperate with your case. Once all charges are dismissed, then and only then will he help you, and you are to treat him as a witness—period." Anthony stood, and Casey did as well. He held out his hand, and Casey shook it with a sigh.

"You shouldn't have had to do the police's work for them, but I agree. The video is solid proof that he wasn't in the area at all." Casey slipped the photo into his briefcase. "Would your client have called the police if they hadn't picked him up?"

Anthony rolled his eyes. "Would you have called the police on your friends when you were nineteen? He's a kid, but hopefully one who will be much smarter and more careful about choosing who his friends are." That was all he was going to give Casey. If he needed more, he was going to have to do his own legwork. "I'll wait to hear from you in the next few hours." He left the repercussions hanging in the air and gestured toward the door.

Casey clearly wasn't happy. "You really enjoyed this, didn't you?"

"I'm a defense attorney. This is what I do, though I have to admit that the police usually don't give me an opening like this. If you want my opinion, I'd have a real come-to-Jesus talk with the department in South Middleton. They really screwed the pooch. I know it's not your fault. But I'm sure I'll be seeing you around."

Casey smirked. "Look forward to it." He left the conference room, and Anthony smiled as soon as the door closed.

"It was Brenda's idea to check the camera," Jasper said. "I got the video, but she noticed the ATM."

"That was good work, both of you," he said, grinning. "You saved a client from a lengthy process, and you saved our client a great deal of money, which I intend to remind him of." He gathered his papers. "Now, the two of you take off for the night. The office party is in a few hours."

Jasper gathered his things and held the door for Brenda. Then Anthony sighed and sat back down, taking a moment to savor his victory before he had to go on to the other cases that were waiting for him.

ANTHONY CHANGED in his office bathroom, his phone on the sink in case he got a call. Then he put on his overcoat and pulled it tightly around him before walking through the half-empty office. Most people were packing up in preparation for the party. Originally Anthony had planned to pick Tyler up at his house, but Tyler had said that he would meet him at the restaurant, so Anthony left the building and walked a block to the square and then down to Café Belgie, which Richard had bought out for the evening. The venue had been a bit of a surprise, and a welcome one. At least they wouldn't be eating rubber chicken for dinner.

Tyler approached him with Daisy on a red leash and collar with a plaid Christmas bow. She did her little dance, and Anthony knelt to greet her. Then he stood back up and kissed Tyler lightly. "Are you sure it's okay to bring Daisy?"

"Yes." He opened the door, and Tyler lifted Daisy into his arms and went inside. Anthony looked around the restaurant, which had been turned into a Christmas wonderland.

"Anthony," Richard said as he approached with Anita next to him.

"This is Richard, our managing partner, and his wife, Anita," Anthony said as an introduction. Richard shook hands with both of them, and Anita air-kissed their cheeks.

"Who is this?" Anita asked as Richard scowled.

"This is Daisy. When Richard told me that we were supporting a dog rescue, I asked Tyler to bring her along. He got her from the same rescue we're supporting tonight."

She petted her gently. "Isn't she a sweetheart?" she said to Richard. "I have two dogs myself. One I got from Mitchell as well. He does such good work. Last year he took the animals of a hoarder and ended up with a tiger. Mitchell doesn't turn any animal away. And that's why I convinced Richard to have the firm support his work." She gave Daisy another gentle pet, and then they moved on to find a table.

Servers with appetizers mingled through the room. Anthony got them each a glass of champagne, and they sat at a table with pâté on crackers and lamb lollipops. Anthony snuck Daisy a bit of cracker.

"Does your firm usually go all out at the holidays?"

"No, not like this. Last year it was dinner at one of the conference rooms at the Comfort Inn. That food was okay, but this is amazing." He caught Tyler's gaze, and for a few seconds everything and everyone in the room seemed to slip away.

"I see you're off to the side," Gene said as he took one of the empty seats at the table. "You should be out there talking to everyone." He tilted his head toward where Harry stood telling two of the other partners a story.

Anthony shrugged. "Harry can tell a good story and make it seem like he's the hero, but…." As far as he was concerned, Harry was all talk and little substance. Anthony's phone vibrated, and he excused himself. "This is Anthony." Thankfully, as he answered the phone, Gene and Tyler were introducing themselves to each other.

"Casey Brannigan. I wanted to let you know that all charges have been dropped against Hansen Jacobs. We would like to speak to him as a witness, and we assume he'll cooperate."

"You let me know what you need and I'll make sure my client is available to you. Thanks for letting me know." Anthony was grinning from ear to ear by the time he hung up. Then he dialed Connor Jacobs.

"Do you have news?" Connor asked right away.

"Is Hansen with you?" Anthony asked and heard the phone shift to speaker. "Hansen?"

"Yes. I'm here with Dad."

"Good. Merry Christmas. We found video of you walking home, proving your story. I showed it to the prosecutor, and all charges have been dropped. They had no case." He heard whoops go up in the background. "They are going to ask you to testify as a witness, which is what they should have done in the first place. I'll be there with you. So don't worry, and have a great holiday, you and your whole family."

The phone shifted, and the background sounds cut off. "Thank you for helping and for believing Hansen."

"You're welcome."

"Call me after the holidays. I need a smart person like you to be the lead on my company's new legal team at Langley and Kraus. We'll finalize details in the New Year. Thank you again." He ended the call, and Anthony could barely feel his feet touching the floor as he returned to the party. Tyler was still speaking with Gene, who had Daisy on his lap, the little sweetheart looking like the princess she was.

"Something good happened," Tyler said. "I can tell."

"Yes." He glanced at Gene knowing he could keep his mouth shut. "I got the charges against Hansen Jacobs dropped, and Connor Jacobs asked me to call him after the first of the year. He wants to bring on our firm for his company, and he wants me to be the lead attorney." Anthony couldn't help grinning.

Gene motioned to one of the servers with drinks and grabbed a glass. "Then congratulations," he said with a bright smile. The three of them clinked glasses. "To your new client and deflating some of the hot air in Harry's sails." He shared a smile with Tyler, and Daisy yipped happily, like she wanted to join in the celebration. They each sipped, and Gene excused himself, handing Daisy over to Tyler. "Don't worry. I'm not going to steal your thunder. If you tell Richard at the right time, he may even forget about that damned chicken dance." He patted Anthony on the shoulder as he moved off into the gathering as more people arrived.

"I'm sorry if everyone is talking a lot of business," Anthony told Tyler.

"It's fine. Gene was nice. He and I were talking about golf. He asked me to contact him in the spring so we can play a few rounds. His handicap and mine are pretty close."

Anthony was a little surprised. "You play golf? I never would have figured that, for some reason. Gene and I play sometimes, though last summer and fall it just seemed like I was too busy."

"I love it. My very first game was a golf simulator. It really sucked. But I managed to learn some things from it, including how to take more subtle movements and translate them to the screen. I never went anywhere with my golf game, and there were others who came out with really good ones, so I let it go and started work on other things."

Jasper and Brenda found their table and joined them, with Anthony making introductions. "Who is this little cutie?" Brenda asked, and Daisy sat on Tyler's knees, showing off her cuteness to the max.

"Daisy. Anthony invited me for the evening, and since I just got her, I didn't want to leave her alone for too long." Tyler slowly petted her as others came up to say hello, including Harry.

"Why the dog?" Harry asked.

"Because this is the face of what we're trying to do this evening," Anita said and then clapped her hands for silence. "As most of you are aware, our charity this year is a dog rescue, and this little girl here is the face of the dogs we're trying to help." *Take that, Harry, you jerkface.* "So please remember that some pets need a home, especially at the holidays and through the winter." She smiled and gently lifted Daisy into her arms and got plenty of kisses for her efforts. "Richard should be so affectionate," she quipped, and everyone laughed. Then she placed Daisy back on Tyler's lap.

She moved away into the room, and servers began bringing the entrees. Salads, bread, and wine were already on the tables. "This is really something," Brenda commented.

"Yes. Everyone works hard, and this is the firm's way of saying that it's appreciated."

Harry sat in the last open chair, and Anthony tensed, but he refused to let it show. "I understand you landed Connor Jacobs. Good luck with that. You know everyone is going to be watching, especially Richard." He slipped his napkin into his lap as Anthony met the gaze of everyone at the table in an effort to make sure they stayed quiet.

"I know what I'm doing. Some people talk a good game, but I play one." He took a bite of the steak with béarnaise and stifled a groan of ecstasy, because damn.

"Is yours good?" he asked Tyler, who had the same dish, and he got a nod. Brenda was vegetarian, so hers was different, and Harry had some sort of chicken, which looked amazing. Tyler got out a small baggie of kibble from his jacket pocket, took his saucer, and put the kibble on it before placing it on the floor for Daisy, who ate from where she sat between their chairs. He also set down a small dish of water for her, but picked it up again so it didn't spill once Daisy was done.

"I didn't know they let dogs in here," Harry said. The man clearly didn't know when to keep his mouth shut. "Aren't there rules with the health department?" he added as he chewed like a cow.

"Therapy dogs and service dogs are allowed almost everywhere," Jasper told him. "And there is nothing inherently dirty or unsanitary about a well-trained dog."

"Yeah, and her table manners are better than some people I know," Brenda added. She and Tyler shared a grin. It was clearly open season on Harry, and he was completely oblivious.

"Is everyone enjoying dinner?" Richard asked as he stopped at their table while making the rounds.

"It's excellent," Tyler told him. "I appreciate being included."

"Yes, it's great." Anthony said. "Oh, before I forget. I got a call an hour ago. The DA dropped the charges against Hansen Jacobs. Their case fell apart after we found evidence of his innocence. Brenda and Jasper did a great job." He was determined to recognize them. "And Connor asked me to call him after the New Year. He wants me to head his legal team." Harry just about choked on his chicken, and Brenda patted his back as he coughed. "We can talk more about it on Monday." He grinned and refused to look at Harry through the rest of the meal because he knew he was not going to be able to resist the urge to gloat.

ONCE THE food was done, the music began. Tables had been removed from one section of the floor, so Anthony asked Tyler to dance.

"I'll watch Daisy," Brenda volunteered, and Anthony led Tyler to the floor and took him in his arms as other couples joined them.

"I wasn't sure you'd do this here," Tyler said softly.

Anthony shrugged. "They all know I'm gay, and I'm here with you. So yes, we're going to dance." He spun Tyler on the floor, and he chuckled. "So let's show the straight couples how it's done." It seemed Tyler could dance as well, and they had a marvelous time. Where he led, Tyler followed, and they seamlessly glided over the small dance area. Anthony looked deep into Tyler's eyes, and the world narrowed to just the two of them. He forgot about senior partners, lawsuits, and even one-upping his nemesis. All that mattered was Tyler as they slowly moved across the floor.

As soon as the music stopped, Anthony stood still, but he didn't move away. He liked holding Tyler in his arms and didn't want the moment to end. He could sense others moving around his periphery, though, so he stepped away and let the rest of the world come crashing back for only a few moments until a song began again and they started to move once more.

Anthony honestly lost track of how long they danced. But it was wonderful, and maybe that was the point. He was happy. If his Christmas present this year was a few minutes on the dance floor with Tyler, then it was an amazing gift. But finally the music ended and they stepped back. Anthony blinked and led Tyler back to the table. Daisy was waiting for him, and he lifted her and held her as Anita took over the mic, encouraging a little holiday giving. "And if we raise a thousand dollars, then my dear husband will not request the chicken dance."

Everyone laughed, but twenties and fifties made an appearance as the hat went around the room. Richard then got up and gave a version of his usual Christmas talk before thanking everyone and wishing them an amazing holiday season and announcing that the office would be closed the day after Christmas as well so that everyone could enjoy some extra time with their families. That got a happy round of applause. Then the dancing began again. This time Brenda and Jasper headed to the floor.

"Do you think those two…?" Tyler started.

Anthony scoffed. "No way. They're friends, but nothing more. Besides, while Jasper is very much into women, so is Brenda. I think that's part of what they have in common. They go out sometimes and they're each other's wing person. It's really funny." He looked down at

Daisy, who had sprawled out as much as she could on Tyler's lap and had closed her eyes. "Are you ready to go?"

"If you are."

The way he said those simple words lit a fire in Anthony's belly. He stood and waited as Tyler gently lifted Daisy before setting her on the floor. Then he attached her leash, and Anthony made the rounds saying good night before pulling on his coat.

They had come in separate vehicles, so Anthony kissed Tyler and patted Daisy and then saw them off before going to his car and heading home through the cold, clear night.

He pulled into his drive, and Tyler met him with Daisy still on her leash. Tyler took his hand and led him across the drives to his front door and unlocked it. Daisy went inside, and Tyler held Anthony's gaze before leading him into his house. He closed the door, and Tyler kissed him, hard and with enough passion to turn winter into spring, at least for a little while. Anthony responded, cupping Tyler's cheeks in his hands and taking possession of lips that tasted like passion personified.

"Do you want another drink or something?" Tyler whispered.

Anthony shook his head. "Right now, all I want is you." His breathing was difficult, in the best way possible, and Anthony was warm. He took off his coat as Tyler did the same, and then Tyler led the way upstairs.

Daisy followed, and Anthony wondered how this was going to work. Tyler settled Daisy in her bed in the corner of the room and then took Anthony's hand and led him to the bed. "Is this what you had in mind?" Tyler asked.

"Yes, and so much more," Anthony said before kissing away any more words that Tyler might have had. Anthony made his living with words, but he knew there were times when they weren't necessary. It was best if he let his hands and lips do the talking—and it was sweet, passionate, and as intense as anything Anthony could ever remember, certainly more so than even the liveliest day in court. Tyler was warm and as responsive as anyone he had ever met. He seemed to feel each touch as special, and that only built the fire between them. The taste of Tyler's lips, the way he quivered when Anthony worried the spot at the base of his neck, or how his hands shook when Anthony plucked one of his pert nipples—all of it only drove Anthony to give him more. And the more he gave, the more he got, a perfect circle of desire that never seemed to end, and one that Anthony hoped would go on until the sun came up the next morning.

"Don't stop," Tyler whispered when Anthony pulled back for a second.

"What was that?"

Tyler cupped his cheeks and guided Anthony to his lips. "That, sweetheart, was Daisy going somewhere else because we're too loud for her." He drew Anthony down into a kiss that curled his toes, and he forgot all about everything else but Tyler.

Chapter 5

TYLER WOKE to getting his face licked. As soon as he opened his eyes, he found Daisy with her paws on his chest, looking down at him. "I take it you want some attention."

"What I think she wants is to go out, and then she needs to eat," Anthony said softly and then yawned. "Morning, gorgeous."

He pushed the covers back and then pulled them up again. "It's cold out there."

"Yeah."

He got out of bed anyway and pulled on sweatpants and a shirt before lifting Daisy off the bed and setting her down. She followed him down the stairs and through the house to the back door. He let her out and then got her some food and fresh water before letting her back in. Daisy attacked her dish, cleaning it quickly, and then drank before trotting through the house and up the stairs. She still had a few issues with her leg, but fortunately she had her mobility back, which was good. Nothing much stopped her now.

By the time he got back to the bedroom, Daisy was on the bed and had settled on his side. "Come on, princess. You have your own bed. This is mine." He carried her to her bed and then climbed in with Anthony, who was warm and still half sleepy. "I figured you'd be keyed up."

Anthony groaned. "I'm sorry. I have been working insane hours for months, and I finally get to relax. I have the whole weekend with nothing to do. I don't even have to go into the office, and I get to sleep in a little." He yawned and tugged Tyler to him. "You're warm and comfy."

"Yeah. Ummm." He whispered something, and Daisy joined them on the bed. She tramped around until she found a place she liked near their feet.

"The princess doesn't want to get left out," Anthony whispered. "What do you have to do today?"

"I need to visit my mom. She had her last chemo treatment earlier this week. I stopped in to check on her Wednesday, and she was resting.

I've talked to her a few times, but I have to go see her and see how she's doing." He settled down because it was warm and cozy in bed with Anthony.

"Do you need to see her now?"

"No. I can go visit her later this morning," Tyler said.

"Good." Anthony pulled up the covers and snuggled against him. "Give me an hour and I'll be all ready to go." He sighed. "You wore me out last night. I have to have a little time to recover before I meet your mother."

GETTING READY to go took more time than Tyler figured. First they had to shower. You'd think showering together would save water, but nope. It took until the hot water ran out for them to get out and dress. Anthony ran home to get fresh clothes because he didn't think he needed to meet Tyler's mother in his rumpled tux, and Tyler picked him up ten minutes later.

He drove to his mother's in town, and once inside, he set Daisy down. She immediately began exploring, sniffing around the furniture and into each corner. "What is she looking for?" his mother asked as he gave her a hug.

"Who knows? She'll be over to say hello in a minute." He sat down and introduced Anthony.

"You're the lawyer," she said and sat back against her pillows. "How did the party go last night?" She seemed with it, and her eyes were bright.

"It was nice. And the senior partner's wife used her influence to stop her husband from requesting the chicken dance, so that was a real win." He smiled, and Tyler took the chair near his.

"Anthony just won a big case." Tyler seemed proud, and Anthony liked that. Tyler took his hand.

"How are you feeling, Mrs. Lemieux? Tyler said that you had your last treatment this week."

She nodded. "I know it's too soon, and maybe it's just anticipation, but I feel better than I have in a while. It will take a while longer before my energy begins to come back, but every day I feel better. It won't be long until my hair grows back, and I have some real plans. A bunch of my friends go to the Y every day for exercise class, and I'm going to join them and keep moving. That's going to be my new life."

"Well, Mom." Tyler looked over at Daisy. "You asked me to get you a dog, and I originally thought that—"

She put up her hand. "No, honey. I was out of my mind on pain meds and chemotherapy drugs. You know that." She called Daisy, who came over, got pets, and then hurried over to Tyler and put her paws on his knees to tell him to pick her up. "Besides, she's your dog. Daisy is all about you, and that's so good. The more I think about it, the more I want to travel and see as much of the world as I can in the next few years."

"Okay." He cuddled her closer. "That's really good, because I was going to tell you that I was going to find something else for you for Christmas, because this little one is too precious to me." Daisy licked his chin.

Mom smiled. "I know who's important to you. You could never keep that sort of thing a secret. Remember Lance Crawford in the tenth grade? You had such a crush on him. He never knew; no one else did but me. And you don't need to worry about that sort of thing. I want you to be happy, and Daisy—and Anthony—make you happy." She turned to Anthony. "He told me about you last summer. You were the hot neighbor who mowed his lawn without a shirt."

Anthony laughed, while Tyler wished the floor would open up and swallow him whole. "I talk to people all day and I can be a tiger in the courtroom, but when it comes to my personal life, I'm a mess. So I would mow my lawn on hot days, without a shirt, to try to get the attention of my cute neighbor, and I was sort of hoping that he might come over and say hello or something. But he never did. And I got too busy and wound up in my own crapulence until a few weeks ago, when I needed a date for my work party and I thought I'd ask my cute neighbor."

"Awww," Mom said softly. "You two are so cute… and so stupid."

"Mom," Tyler protested.

She waved her hand at him. "Just like most men, you are so oblivious to everything around you. And you need to get hit on the head before you realize what is right in front of you." She rolled her eyes. "I thank your boss for having his party. Otherwise my son would never have figured anything out."

"Geez, Mom. You know I've been busy too."

"Yes. Taking care of your old mother rather than keeping your eyes open to someone who might love you. I am going to be fine, and you need to find yourself a life—something more than killing zombies." She sighed. "I wish you would make a less death-like game."

"The good guys kill the zombies," Tyler explained. "And when they win the game, they kill the alpha zombie, the one who started it all and infected them. So when they kill him, they rid the world of zombies and everything is good."

"Have you played one of his games?" Anthony asked.

Tyler's mother scoffed and pointed to the cabinet under the television. "I have one of those video game players. Tyler bought it for me some time ago. I play all his games, and I'm very good. I haven't played in a while. But I will when the next one comes out."

"I had no idea," Tyler said.

"You're my son. Of course I look at your work. It's very good. But after cancer and all these months of surgery and treatment, I want something less—"

"Bloody?" Anthony asked.

"I want something playful and funny. I don't have any ideas, but that's what I really want."

Tyler took his mom's hand. "I know you do. But it's these kinds of games that really sell. I could try to come up with something different next time, but I'm not sure what it would be. *Save Grandma*? Maybe a game where you battle disease and in the end cure cancer."

She shook her head. "Or maybe a game with ducks, geese, and turkeys where you try to keep them from becoming dinner. I can just imagine. The ducks drop eggs and bomb the hunters who are trying to shoot them. Or maybe they just poop on them."

"Mom, I am not going to make a feces video game. Can you imagine what that would look like? It's gross, and what happens if the hunters get the birds? If they shoot them, then do they instantly turn into duck dinner? No, sorry. I'm going to stick with zombies. They pay the bills."

His mother rolled her eyes. "Fine. But I'm going to think of more ideas. I'd like something I can play with the ladies when they come over."

Anthony giggled like a teenager. "You could develop a whole new video game segment. Games for old people."

"They already have those. It's called solitaire," Tyler grumped. "Can we please change the subject? I brought Anthony over to meet you, and you both gang up on me." He held Daisy like a security blanket. "Do you really not want a dog of your own?"

"Nope. Not right now. Though if you need someone to babysit my grandpuppy, I'm more than happy to do that." She yawned and leaned back. Soon she was asleep, and when Tyler gently set Daisy on the sofa, she curled up near Mom. Tyler got a blanket and put it over her before leaving the room.

"Old lady video games," Anthony said. "I really think there's a market."

"Seriously?" Tyler questioned.

"Yeah. It doesn't have to be a first-person shooter game, but something where an older person as opposed to a marine or an army guy is the hero. Think about it. Your mom probably played on the first Atari system all those years ago. Or maybe she had one of those Texas Instrument game systems. She started playing when she was a kid, and most older people did. So give them something they can play together or with their grandkids. Could you imagine a *Grandma Got Run Over by a Reindeer* video game? Or *Nursing Home Breakout*? They could be funny and geared to older people."

"You're serious?" Tyler asked, and Anthony shrugged. "I suppose it isn't going to hurt to run it by the company and see what they think. But I find it hard to believe that it's going to be something they would be interested in." It seemed to him like his mother and his boyfriend had drunk the Kool-Aid or something.

"I don't think this going to be a blockbuster or anything…."

"And that's the problem. It takes a lot of time and effort to develop, distribute, and market a game, so they have to hope with each one they make that it is a mega hit. You can't go through all that for middle-of-the-road returns. It just doesn't really work." It was hard for others to understand, but the stores wanted games that would fly off the shelves, otherwise they weren't going to put their time and shelf space behind it. "Can we talk about something else?" He really needed a change of subject. "Anything."

"Sorry. I was just teasing you."

"I know. But I have people giving me game ideas all the time. The thing is that if I don't feel it, I can't do it. My job is creative, and it's not something that I can do on command. Most people, including my mother, don't understand that. It's not something I can turn on and off at will." It was a major source of tension for him.

"I get it, and thank you for telling me." He quirked his eyebrows. "So no games for little old ladies?"

"Not from me."

"Awww," Anthony said. "So I suppose a game about lawyers isn't going to happen either."

Tyler grinned. "Oh, that I can do. But it will be underwater, because first we drown all the lawyers." He grinned, and Anthony groaned.

"I give up," Anthony told him, and Tyler put his arms around his neck.

"Good. Because I like to win too." He kissed Anthony as Daisy yipped. He pulled away and peered from the kitchen through the dining room to where Mom sat. Daisy was on her lap, licking her face, and Mom was laughing. He couldn't help turning away. "Dammit," he said as he wiped his eyes.

"Is something wrong?"

"No." He swallowed hard. "It's just been a long time since I saw her smile like that." His mother was on the mend, and some of her vibrancy seemed to be starting to show again. That was wonderful to see, and something he had almost begun to think was gone forever.

"You are such a sweet grandpuppy," Mom said, getting her to calm down and settle back on the sofa. Then she reached for the remote and turned on the television. But instead of a show, there was music— Christmas music.

"It really is beginning to feel a lot like Christmas." He almost gasped as a thought sprang into his head. "What plans do you have for this year?"

"Nothing. I usually either visit my parents or use it as a day to sleep. This year my parents are taking a cruise through the Panama Canal. They asked me if it was okay months ago, and I told them to go. I sort of wish…." He shook his head. "I'm not going to say that I should have told them not to go, but I guess I wish things had been different."

"Then you can spend the day with us. You'll have to endure my cooking, because Mom isn't going to be up to her usual culinary masterpieces, so the turkey will probably be a little dry and the beans may be a little crunchy…."

Anthony held him tighter as Daisy slid down off the sofa and bounded into the kitchen, doing this little dance around their legs. Obviously someone was getting attention and it wasn't her, and that wasn't going to do. "You need to be careful of your leg, sweetheart," Tyler chided as he picked her up.

Daisy kissed both of them and then settled into his arms like she belonged there. "I think she's happy."

"Of course she is," Mom said from the living room. "Now unless you came over here to hide in the kitchen and talk to each other, come in here so we can have a visit. My nap is over." She sat up, and Tyler snickered.

"I guess we got told," Anthony said and headed for the living room, but then stopped. "If I'm going to join you for Christmas, I need to pick up a few gifts. Maybe you can give me a few ideas?"

Tyler grinned, and Daily kissed his chin. "I know, sweetheart," Tyler said softly, and then he lifted his gaze to look into Anthony's eyes. "I already got the best gift."

"What? Daisy?" Anthony asked, his eyes shining.

"No. Both of you," he told him and brought their lips together in a kiss as Daisy yipped, because, after all, she was the princess.

Epilogue

TYLER WOKE warm and toasty. It had snowed during the night, judging by the white outside on the windowsill. He rolled over, and Anthony pulled him closer. "Do we have to get up?"

"It's Christmas," Tyler said, and Daisy jumped up onto the bed. Thankfully she had taken to sleeping in her own bed, but joined them in the morning as soon as she heard them talking.

"When do we need to be at your mother's?" Anthony asked as he stretched.

"She isn't going to expect us until about eleven. Mom is going to want to rest and sleep in. Some of her energy is coming back. I think she thought it would return more quickly now that she's done with treatment, but at least she's feeling better. Give her a few weeks or a month and she'll be a force to be reckoned with once more." He chuckled as his phone vibrated on the nightstand. "Speak of the devil…." He answered it.

"Aren't you up yet?" Mom asked. "Geez, are you old men? It's Christmas. So get up and get yourselves over here. I'm starting breakfast in five minutes."

"What is with you? Did they change your meds and put you on speed or something?"

She laughed. "Just get up and come on over." She hung up, and Tyler closed his eyes.

"I take it that was your mom," Anthony said. "And here I was hoping for a little Christmas-morning nookie."

"Yeah, that was her. Apparently she's starting breakfast and we're summoned. But it's okay." He ran his hands down Anthony's firm chest. "After dinner, we can come back here and carry on our own private celebrating well into the night. I promise." Tyler kissed him and then bounded out of bed. "Besides, I want to see what I got for Christmas."

"You're like a little kid," Anthony said with a chuckle.

"You say that like it's a bad thing," Tyler countered, already pulling on his underwear. "She's just going to call again in fifteen minutes, so we may as well get going."

Anthony got out of bed, and Tyler couldn't help watching him as he hurried to the bathroom. Once the door closed, he finished getting dressed and got Daisy into her Christmas collar with the cute bow. "We're going to see Grandma." He set her on the bed. Daisy lay down, her head on her paws, and closed her eyes, like she had no idea what all the fuss was about.

When Anthony returned, he dressed, and they all went downstairs. Tyler had planned for a gift opening between him and Anthony before going to Mom's, but he didn't want to hold everyone up, so he found large shopping bags and put all the gifts in them. Then he made sure Daisy was ready before they put on their coats and got into his car, bags of presents filling the trunk.

The snow from the night before was just enough to make the roads slick, so he drove slowly as Anthony texted Mom using his phone to tell her they were on their way. Once they arrived, he parked and they carried everything inside.

Mom had turned the living room into a Christmas wonderland, just like she always had when he was a kid. There was a small tree, the mantel was filled with greens, and lights twinkled on the windowsills. "When did you do all this?"

"A little bit at a time over the past few days. I wanted this to be a celebration," she said before hugging first him and then Anthony. "Now put your presents under the tree and come in for breakfast. I made pancakes, bacon, and eggs."

"You didn't have to do all this," Tyler said.

"You can stop treating me like an invalid and sit down to breakfast. I'm feeling more like myself."

"Well, let me get the food," Tyler said and got his mom to sit down. Then he dished up everything and brought it to the table. There was nothing like his mother's cooking. She just knew how to make things tasty. Once everything was set, he joined them, and they all had an amazing Christmas breakfast before moving to the living room.

Tyler sat in the chair nearest the tree and began handing out gifts. There were some for everyone, including Daisy, who tore into her present to get the chew bone. She settled and worked on it while Tyler handed his mother his gift.

"You didn't need to get me anything," Mom said as she opened the small box.

"I didn't know your size, but there's a gift card to your favorite boutique for new clothes, and you have an appointment on the twenty-seventh for a facial, manicure, and massage at the Downtown Spa. I thought it was time you started looking and feeling more like yourself." He smiled, and she lightly kissed his cheek.

"Thank you," Mom said and handed him a package. "I know you don't need much." He opened the box and grinned when he pulled out a new game console and controllers. "But I always know you wear these out."

"Thanks, Mom. It's perfect." He hugged her and then passed Anthony his gift, only to get one in return. They had agreed to small gifts, so he was surprised when he opened the box. "Oh my God… how did you get these?" It was two tickets to a sci-fi convention. "I tried to get them, but they were sold out in minutes."

"A client got them months ago and couldn't use them. I sort of figured I'd go to check it out. But…." Anthony shrugged as though this was no big deal. Tyler stared at the tickets, unable to believe his luck. "I figured you and I could go and make a weekend of it."

"And all I got you were a couple of ties for work," Tyler said as Anthony opened his gift and grinned. They had dogs that looked like Daisy on them.

"Now I can take her to work with me," he said as he gently petted Daisy, who barely looked up from her chew bone. "Thank you."

Tyler was still looking at the tickets, and then he leapt at Anthony and hugged him tightly. "These are perfect."

"I'm glad you like them." He hugged him, and they sat together as Mom went to the kitchen to make coffee. "Did you enjoy your Christmas, sweetheart?" Anthony had called him that before, though Tyler smiled at the endearment just the same. It was too early for huge declarations, but he knew he was growing to care, and Anthony showed his feelings every day.

Tyler nodded as Daisy hurried over to join them. He lifted her, and the three of them sat together. "I did." Then Daisy kissed him, and Anthony laughed before nosing her out of the way.

"He's mine, girl." Anthony kissed him hard enough to curl his toes. A boyfriend who liked and understood him for who he was, a dog who loved them both, and Mom on the mend. Best Christmas ever.

Keep reading for a preview of
Rescue Me
Must Love Dogs Book 1
by Andrew Grey

Chapter 1

"OKAY, GUYS, I'm coming," Mitchell called as he opened the door to what had once been the low barn of the family farm. Few things made him happier than the barks and cries that started when he slid the door open first thing in the morning. "Everyone is going to get brekkie and no one will be left out, I promise," he said to calm the rabble, but it had no effect. He slid the door closed, smiled, and opened two of the cages so the dogs could run around his legs as he went to start preparing the food. They jumped around him, tails wagging. *Come play with us.* Mitchell scratched their heads and got to work, the dogs occupying themselves until he set down the bowls. They both attacked their food, eating and drinking, happy dogs. And Mitchell loved all fifteen of them.

Once Bowser and Bruno were fed, he let the two young labs out into a play yard and went about feeding the others. Those he could, he put with the labs so they could run and play. The newer arrivals he kept isolated in case of disease. And there were a few, like Jasper, who didn't get along well with other dogs. He fed him separately but paid him just as much attention as he did the others. These boys and girls were like his family.

"Knock, knock," a deep voice said from the doorway.

"Careful," Mitchell called back to the stranger. "Don't let any of them out." He believed in letting the dogs run and play as much as possible. He scooped up Randi before she could make a break for it. She was a little Chihuahua mix, lightning fast, and loved to try to make a run for it. He soothed her with pets as the door opened slowly and a man of about forty, in tan pants and a blue shirt and carrying a clipboard, stepped inside. He closed the door behind him.

"Well...," he said as he looked around. "What have we here?"

"I need to finish feeding," Mitchell said. He put a bowl out for the final dog and then put the old St. Bernard into one of the runs so he could either get some exercise or, more likely, take a nap. "What can I help you with?"

The man sighed. "There's been a complaint about the barking."

"I see. Let me guess—from the people who moved in over there." He pointed toward the now butter-yellow house on the other side of his. "They moved in two months ago and have called me three times because of the dogs. I've been running this shelter here for four years now. I was here first and I'm not going to stop." He put his hands on his hips.

"They apparently have a baby and—"

"Then they should have thought of that before buying the place," Mitchell interrupted. "I have fifteen dogs—" He stopped. "Maybe you should start by telling me who you are?"

"Clark Fenner. I'm with codes compliance at Carlisle Borough. We received a complaint about barking, and they claimed that the dogs were left unattended for long hours, that they weren't being fed properly, and that you had fighting dogs."

"Mitchell Brannigan, and my dogs are all well cared for. They're fed and well exercised. And I have a few *former* fighting dogs." He took Clark over to one of the runs. "This is Bosco. He was rescued a few weeks ago from a place in Lancaster. Bosco was injured badly in a dog fight. The police over there raided the place, and one of them called me. I picked him up and brought him here. Bosco is a good dog when people are around, but he's aggressive with other dogs. I keep him isolated from the others and am working with him. He may never be comfortable around other dogs, but I'm hoping to help him to behave better so he can be adopted out. Right now I'm near the cap of what I can handle, but I have three dogs being adopted out today and two more couples coming in tomorrow."

Clark narrowed his gaze. "How do you make money at this?" he asked.

"I don't. This is a nonprofit." Mitchell continued petting Randi; she calmed him down. He had considered adopting her himself. But then, he wanted to do that with all the dogs, and he'd long ago told himself that he needed to keep a distance or else his house would be as full as the shelter. "I'm also a veterinarian, and my practice is a mile up the road. I have regular office hours, and during those times, the dogs are in their cages. I know they bark sometimes, but it's a fact of life. These dogs are good dogs, and they are cared for. All have their shots, and I would never allow any of my dogs to be abused in any way, least of all used for fighting."

Clark's expression softened. "I see." He looked around once more. "I wasn't informed of that." He peered into some of the cages and then looked out into the yard at the runs where the dogs were playing. "Dang, that one's a beauty." He stopped in the doorway.

"Rex... yeah, he is. His family got him as a pup and thought they could handle taking care of him. He's a giant schnauzer and weighs about seventy-five pounds." Mitchell opened the door to the run. "Come here, Rex," he said gently, and the large black dog approached and nuzzled right in for pets. "He was too much once they had a baby, so I took him." Clark stroked him. "He's wonderful and incredibly affectionate. Rex has been with me for almost six months now."

"How long do you keep them?" Clark asked.

Mitchell stared, tensing. "Until they're adopted. I don't put dogs down here for any reason other than illness. There is no such thing as a bad dog, just bad pet parents. Rex will be with me until he finds a home. They all will."

Rex approached Clark, and soon he sat right next to him as Clark petted and talked to him softly.

"I have a fenced-in backyard in town, and my wife spends a lot of time alone during the day while I'm working. Would it be okay if I brought her over later to meet Rex here?" He knelt down, and Rex practically put his head on Clark's shoulder, soaking in the attention.

Mitchell knew that look, and he turned away, smiling, because he knew Rex had likely found a home. That spark when a dog and person clicked was definitely there.

"That would be great. Please take some pictures of your yard, and I'll have some paperwork for you to fill out when you come back, and I can explain the adoption fees. I want to make sure you understand how to care for him. Of course he's had all his shots, and I have his records. If you adopt one of my dogs, then I give a discount on all vet care for the rest of the dog's life." He was going to be sad to see Rex go, but if it was to a good home, then that was the best thing.

Clark smiled brightly. "Thank you." He continued petting Rex, and Mitchell had a pretty good idea that he was falling in love. That sort of thing was a lot easier with dogs than it was with people. Dogs gave love no matter what, and they did it without regard to looks or taste or whether you happened to snore. And dogs certainly had a sense about people... something Mitchell sorely wished he could borrow. His history of relationships left a lot to be desired, and he much preferred the company of animals to that of people. At least he understood their motives.

"I'll be back with my wife. I'm sure she's going to be as taken with him as I am." Clark took a few pictures and sent them off, and his phone chimed a few seconds later. Clark rolled his eyes and messaged back. "She says she's wanted a dog for years and was waiting for me to come around. So I guess if you'll hold him for us, we'll come around later and get him."

"Wonderful," Mitchell said. He went to the office and pulled out the papers he required, along with a list of supplies he recommended for a dog like Rex. "Here is the information I need filled out. Also a list of supplies and the kind of food he's on. When you come back, I'll talk to both of you about his care." This was a banner day as far as he was concerned. "I take it there's no problem with the shelter."

"None. I'll address the complaint at the borough and close it as baseless. I would suggest you might want to see if you can talk to your neighbor. Try to get to know them a little. Maybe if they understand what you're doing, you can patch things up."

What Clark said made sense. Mitchell needed to figure out how to smooth things over with his neighbor.

MITCHELL CLOSED the clinic and then stopped at the shelter to feed all of the dogs and get them in for the night. As usual, he was greeted with yips, barks, and wagging tails. He started the process for evening feeding as a car pulled into the drive, followed by another, and then a third. Mitchell greeted his visitors and reviewed the care of their new pets with each of them before waving goodbye as three of his dogs found new homes. Once the shelter was quiet again, he finished feeding and brushed Rex so he looked good when Clark and his wife stopped by. He was truly sad to see him go, but the way Rex perked up when he heard Clark's voice, and then the excitement when his wife saw him, sent a jolt of joy racing through his heart.

"He's beautiful."

"Isn't he?" Mitchell said as he led Rex out on a leash. He went right up to her and nuzzled in, and she began petting him like Rex was a long-lost friend.

"We'll take him, of course," she said. "Clark has all the paperwork done, and we have the supplies in the trunk. And because he's so big, we got him a raised water and food bowl as well as a bunch of toys." She took the leash, and Rex practically pranced as she walked him around the yard outside the shelter. "Is there anything else we need to do?" she asked brightly.

"I don't think so. Not right now. Just make sure he has a bed or he'll want to sleep on yours, and Rex will take up most of the space." He smiled, and they nodded. They both shook his hand before they left the shelter. Mitchell watched them go and went back inside, closed up the shelter for the night, and headed out to the house.

Mitchell figured he could eat once he got back, so he packed up the cookies that one of his patients had brought to the clinic, checked himself in the mirror, and then headed up the street to the neighbors' for a visit.

He wasn't quite sure what to expect. He knew someone was home. He'd seen a man out in the yard a few times, but mostly the place seemed buttoned up and quiet. Still, he strolled along the road and then up the drive and the walk, to the front door, where he knocked softly. He heard movement inside and was about to ring the bell when the door opened and a haggard man in his midthirties, the same as Mitchell, stared at him. A baby wailed on his shoulder. "I'm sorry, did I wake the baby?"

The man shook his head. His hair was all askew and his brown eyes half-lidded, lips drawn into a line, and his skin a little sallow, like he was too tired to move. Still, he was handsome under all the dishevelment, with a granite jaw and high cheekbones. "No. She's been fussy all night." Mitchell held up the plate of cookies, and the man pushed open the door. "Come on in. I hope she'll wear herself out soon." He patted her back, and the little thing fussed and sniffled.

"Is she sick?"

"I don't know. She doesn't have a fever, but she keeps pulling up her legs and cries like crazy. The doctor says she's losing weight, so I feed her whenever she's hungry, but the little thing doesn't have an appetite." He was clearly worried sick and at his wits' end. "I'm Beau, by the way. Beau Pfister."

"Mitchell Brannigan. I have the farm next to you." He wasn't going to hide who he was. That wasn't the way to start things off with a neighbor.

"The one with the dogs? How many do you have over there, anyway? I just get her down to sleep and they bark, and she wakes… it's…."

"At the moment, twelve. I adopted out three today. I run a shelter out of the old barn. I insulated it and made a good home for them in there. Basically, I rescue the dogs that no one else seems to want and find them good homes. I'm also the vet with the office up the road."

The little girl took the opportunity to wail once again and then farted, except she did more than that.

"Excuse me, I need to change her." Beau made a stink face. "I'll be right back. Have a seat if you like." He raced away.

Mitchell set the cookies on the table and automatically folded the blankets strewn over one end of the sofa. Then he sat down to wait. At least the baby had stopped fussing.

"Sorry," Beau said when he came back, a quiet baby in his arms.

"No need. I understand. The hard part is that she can't tell you what's wrong." Mitchell understood that. His professional life would be so much easier if he were Dr. Doolittle. "Can I ask what she's eating?"

"Formula. Her mother, Amy, is… *was* my best friend, and she named me Jessica's guardian in case something happened." He leaned forward, holding his head in his hands. "How was I supposed to know some drunk driver would hit her on her way home from work?"

"I'm sorry. How long have you had Jessica?"

"Just over three weeks, I guess."

Mitchell sighed. "Why don't you show me what you're feeding her. Was she being breastfed prior to that?"

Beau hefted himself out of the chair. "No. Amy couldn't, so Jessica was always on formula, and I got the same kind." He brought back two containers. One was empty and the other half full. "I kept this one so I'd know what to get."

Mitchell saw the issue almost immediately. "This is what she was eating before?" he asked, just to be sure, and Beau nodded. "Then it's the formula. Get this exact same kind in the orange container. This is lactose-free. I bet little Jessica has a milk sensitivity and the lactose is upsetting her tummy. Does she always have explosive diapers?"

Beau nodded.

"That would explain it. Change her formula. I bet her appetite will come back when her tummy doesn't hurt, and her diaper changes won't be as messy."

"Are you sure?" Beau asked.

Mitchell shrugged. "I'm not a doctor, I'm a vet. But a lot of what goes into various creatures and people makes a huge difference in their lives and health." He showed Beau the label. "This is lactose-free, and what you're using isn't."

Beau sighed. "To tell you the truth, I'd give just about anything for her to sleep for a few hours. Maybe then I could do the dishes or just take a nap." He yawned and sat back in the chair. Mitchell was afraid Beau was going to drop off to sleep any second.

"Maybe I should go and let you rest. I just wanted to stop by and say hello." He didn't go into defusing the situation about the dogs. He didn't want to bring that up.

"I'm glad you stopped. It's been nice to talk to someone who can talk back." Beau half smiled. "And thank you for the cookies. It's been so long since I ate anything that didn't come out of the freezer and the microwave, I think I've forgotten what real food tastes like." He opened the door, and Mitchell got set to leave.

"Then why don't you and Jessica come over for dinner sometime? My cooking isn't gourmet, but most people find it edible, and a lot of what I cook I learned from my mother. If you want home cooking, I can manage that." He smiled.

"Are you sure?" Beau asked. "A lot of the time, Jessica gets fussy and I need to take care of her. I used to have a lot of friends, but most of them don't know what to make of me with her, so they call and stuff, but the nights we used to get together have turned into story time, diaper changes, and bottles. Even the ones who had kids, theirs are older now and they have their own lives." He shrugged. "But if you're serious, I'd be happy to come to dinner."

Mitchell stepped out into the late evening air. The last of the summer light was just fading as he turned toward home. "Stop by tomorrow. I usually get home about six, and I have to feed the dogs. So about seven will work."

"I'll see you then," Beau said and closed the door.

Mitchell headed for home, wondering what he was going to make for dinner tomorrow. At least he seemed to have patched things up with his handsome neighbor.

Scan the QR Code below to order

ANDREW GREY is the author of more than one hundred works of Contemporary Gay Romantic fiction. After twenty-seven years in corporate America, he has now settled down in Central Pennsylvania with his husband of more than twenty-five years, Dominic, and his laptop. An interesting ménage. Andrew grew up in western Michigan with a father who loved to tell stories and a mother who loved to read them. Since then he has lived throughout the country and traveled throughout the world. He is a recipient of the RWA Centennial Award, has a master's degree from the University of Wisconsin–Milwaukee, and now writes full-time. Andrew's hobbies include collecting antiques, gardening, and leaving his dirty dishes anywhere but in the sink (particularly when writing). He considers himself blessed with an accepting family, fantastic friends, and the world's most supportive and loving partner. Andrew currently lives in beautiful, historic Carlisle, Pennsylvania.

Email: andrewgrey@comcast.net
Website: www.andrewgreybooks.com

Follow me on BookBub

ANDREW GREY

Rescue Us

MUST L♥VE
D🐾GS

Must Love Dogs: Book Two

Everyone needs to be rescued sometimes.

As a vet tech, Daniel is usually first in line to come to animals' aid. When he and his boss get a call about an animal hoarding situation, they expect the handful of badly treated dogs… but the tiger comes as a surprise.

Wes recently left his job to care for his sick mother. Now that she's on the mend, he needs work, and he finds it at a bustling shelter. But the animals aren't the only ones in need. His kind, chatty coworker Daniel is dealing with an abusive boyfriend—something Wes, whose father was an alcoholic, has experience handling. Wes steps up to help Daniel kick his boyfriend to the curb, but in the process, he finds himself falling for Daniel himself.

Navigating a new relationship when they both have traumatic pasts is one thing. But when a shady group starts targeting the tiger they are trying to find a zoo placement for, the stakes are raised even higher. Can Wes and Daniel come together to rescue the animals—and each other?

Scan the QR Code below to order

ChrisMyths

Regret Me Not

Late for Christmas

Sweet Anticipation

Stardust

Rudolph the Rescue Jack Russell

Fall in love this holiday season with Holiday Cheer, a delightful collection of romantic Christmas tales from bestselling authors Amy Lane and Andrew Grey. From snow-filled streets to cozy fireside moments, these charming romcoms bring warmth, laughter, and love to the most wonderful time of the year.

Whether it's a chance meeting under the mistletoe, the magic of an unexpected holiday getaway, or a second chance at true love, these heartfelt stories capture the joy of the season. With plenty of festive cheer, witty banter, and swoon-worthy moments, Holiday Cheer is the perfect holiday treat for anyone who believes in the power of love and a Christmas miracle.

Grab a cup of cocoa, cuddle up, and let the romance of the holidays begin!

Scan the QR Code below to order

HELLO
GOODBYE
Amore

ANDREW GREY

In college, Chase Anderson and his twin sister, Elaine, met Antonello Glorioso and became best friends. Chase fell in love with him—but so did Elaine, so he kept quiet. Then heartbreak happened: they graduated, Antonello returned to Italy, and Elaine died, leaving Chase to raise her son as his own.

Returning to Florence to run the family business had felt like Antonello's only option. He did his duty to his legacy, but he's been second-guessing that decision since he got on the plane. Still, he doesn't know what he could've had until it shows up on his doorstep.

Chase never wants to see Antonello again. His departure tanked the business the three of them had planned to start and hurt his sister deeply. But his engineering project needs specialized metals, and the Glorioso firm is the best supplier. Reluctantly, Chase agrees to head to Italy for a few months to oversee production, hoping he'll be able to keep a low profile… only to run into Antonello the first day.

As Chase and Antonello spend time together, old hurts fade, replaced by renewed friendship and the possibility for a love they've only fantasized about. But duty, family, history, and big secrets could topple any possibility of a future.

Scan the QR Code below to order

HUNKS
OF THE
MONTH

ANDREW GREY

Former fashion photographer Sterling Vaughn reached the pinnacle of his profession only to have his life and heart come crashing down around him. Now he's attempting to rebuild his life as a portrait photographer in the town where he grew up.

Connor Hillyard is proud of his Scottish ancestry and dresses accordingly. The civic-minded college history professor has spent more of his life collecting degrees than experience. His only family is his sometimes matchmaking great-aunt Lucille, who thinks nothing of pulling him into her community gardening projects.

When Lucille needs a photographer for a calendar project to save her failing garden club, she recruits Sterling, who ropes Connor in as a model. Their eye-opening hunky gay calendar pulls the two men closer together. But just as things get interesting between them, the calendar polarizes the town, threatening to pull Sterling back into the high-profile world of fashion and away from the man who brought his heart back to life.

Scan the QR Code below to order

STEAL MY
Heart

ANDREW GREY

In college, Chase Anderson and his twin sister, Elaine, met Antonello Glorioso and became best friends. Chase fell in love with him—but so did Elaine, so he kept quiet. Then heartbreak happened: they graduated, Antonello returned to Italy, and Elaine died, leaving Chase to raise her son as his own.

Returning to Florence to run the family business had felt like Antonello's only option. He did his duty to his legacy, but he's been second-guessing that decision since he got on the plane. Still, he doesn't know what he could've had until it shows up on his doorstep.

Chase never wants to see Antonello again. His departure tanked the business the three of them had planned to start and hurt his sister deeply. But his engineering project needs specialized metals, and the Glorioso firm is the best supplier. Reluctantly, Chase agrees to head to Italy for a few months to oversee production, hoping he'll be able to keep a low profile… only to run into Antonello the first day.

As Chase and Antonello spend time together, old hurts fade, replaced by renewed friendship and the possibility for a love they've only fantasized about. But duty, family, history, and big secrets could topple any possibility of a future.

Scan the QR Code below to order